Murder of a
Smart Cookie

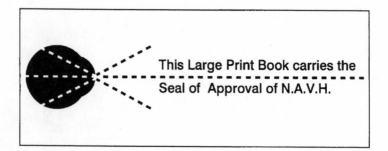

This Large Print Book carries the
Seal of Approval of N.A.V.H.

Murder of a Smart Cookie

A Scumble River Mystery

Denise Swanson

Thorndike Press • Waterville, Maine

This is a work of fiction. Names, characters, places, and incidents either are the product of the author's imagination or are used fictitiously, and any resemblance to actual persons, living or dead, business establishments, events, or locales is entirely coincidental.

Published in 2005 by arrangement with NAL Signet, a division of Penguin Group (USA) Inc.

Thorndike Press® Large Print Mystery.

The tree indicium is a trademark of Thorndike Press.

The text of this Large Print edition is unabridged.
Other aspects of the book may vary from the original edition.

Set in 16 pt. Plantin by Christina S. Huff.

Printed in the United States on permanent paper.

Library of Congress Cataloging-in-Publication Data

Swanson, Denise.
    Murder of a smart cookie : a Scumble River mystery /
by Denise Swanson.
       p. cm. — (Thorndike Press large print mystery)
    ISBN 0-7862-7765-3 (lg. print : hc : alk. paper)
    1. Denison, Skye (Fictitious character) — Fiction.
2. School psychologists — Fiction.   3. Women psychologists
— Fiction.   4. Large type books.   I. Title.   II. Thorndike
Press large print mystery series.
PS3619.W36M875 2005
  813'.6—dc22   2005008988

To my dear friends
Joyce and John Favero
Monika and Joe Bradley
Nancy and Robert Chidel
Andrea Pantaleone,
Wes Dodd, Kay Lynn Shoemaker,
Laurie Bianchetta,
Sandy Kral, Donna Sears,
Monica Granger, and Anne Hiller

As the Founder/CEO of NAVH, the only national health agency solely devoted to those who, although not totally blind, have an eye disease which could lead to serious visual impairment, I am pleased to recognize Thorndike Press★ as one of the leading publishers in the large print field.

Founded in 1954 in San Francisco to prepare large print textbooks for partially seeing children, NAVH became the pioneer and standard setting agency in the preparation of large type.

Today, those publishers who meet our standards carry the prestigious "Seal of Approval" indicating high quality large print. We are delighted that Thorndike Press is one of the publishers whose titles meet these standards. We are also pleased to recognize the significant contribution Thorndike Press is making in this important and growing field.

Lorraine H. Marchi, L.H.D.
Founder/CEO
NAVH

★ Thorndike Press encompasses the following imprints: Thorndike, Wheeler, Walker and Large Print Press.

Acknowledgments

Thanks to Dave Stybr for Dante's Route 66 speech, and George Stybr for Monty Lapp's great one-liner.

As always, I couldn't have written this book without the continuing support of my husband, mother, relatives, and friends.

Special hugs to my fellow Deadly Divas, the Windy City Chapter of RWA, and the TeaBuds.

Also, to Mark Dosier, welcome to the family.

Although there is a vase named *Curtain of the Night*, *Curtain of the Dawn* exists only in my imagination.

Scumble River is not a real town. The characters and events portrayed in these pages are entirely fictional, and any resemblance to living persons is pure coincidence.

Chapter 1
To Tell the Truth

Cookie Caldwell died the third Sunday in August, and the Scumble River First Annual Route 66 Yard Sale almost died with her. She had lived in town only a few years, and no one seemed to really know her. This isolation would suggest that no one would have a reason to murder her, but obviously that supposition would be incorrect.

Cookie's death raised a lot of questions. Two of the most puzzling ones were what was she doing at the Denison/Leofanti booth in the middle of the night, and how did a piece of jewelry manage to kill her?

For the next week, until the crime was solved, these questions were asked over and over again on the TV news, while a picture of Cookie stuffed into Grandma Denison's old Art Deco liquor cabinet, one hand thrust out as if she had tried to claw her way to freedom, flickered on the screen.

Heartland TV had been on location taping a program about the Route 66 Yard Sale and thus were able to get exclusive footage of the postdiscovery activities. While the other news stations managed to get a shot of Cookie's body, Heartland's film clip included a group of locals who were ignoring the dead woman and arguing amongst themselves. It was not an attractive depiction of the citizens of Scumble River, Illinois. It was an especially unflattering portrayal of its mayor, Dante Leofanti.

Leofanti's niece, Skye Denison, didn't look much better. Playing tug-of-war with her uncle over Cookie's purse was not the image she aspired to project as the town's school psychologist.

Even though her profession had nothing to do with her involvement in the mess being broadcasted via HTV into homes across the Midwest, the reporters tended to play up her occupation in their stories. That, and the fact that she had solved several of Scumble River's previous murder cases.

If the journalists had dug a little deeper, they would have discovered that it wasn't Skye's full-time job but how she spent her summer vacation that had gotten her into the purse-wrestling predicament. However, the media tended to focus on the here and now, even though the real story had started nearly eight weeks before, after Skye had already lost two summer jobs and been forced to accept a third.

The first loss of employment occurred because of geese with loose bowels and poor toilet habits, and the second because she couldn't keep her mouth shut. Too bad that the only job she could hang onto came with a dead body attached to it.

Skye stood next to her new boss, Cookie Caldwell, as the proprietor of Cookie's Collectibles carefully examined a ceramic vase. When Cookie turned it over, Skye leaned down to see the words inscribed on the bottom: "Curtain of the Dawn."

Alma Griggs, the elderly woman on the other side of the counter, twisted the cracked handles of her white patent leather handbag while she anxiously watched Cookie inspect every inch of the vase's surface, then repeat the process with the interior. Finally the old lady offered, "Mr. Griggs bought that for me in Texas on our honeymoon in 1932."

Skye did a quick calculation — even if Mrs. Griggs was married at eighteen that would make her eighty-nine years old. Skye snuck a peek at the woman. There was no sign of frailty. Mrs. Griggs was nearly the same height as Skye, about five-seven, and even at thirty pounds lighter, she was a solidly built woman. Her white hair was worn in a braided crown on top of her head, and her jewelry consisted of a necklace of red plastic raspberries with matching earrings and bracelet.

Cookie interrupted Skye's inspection of Mrs. Griggs by placing the vase on the counter and saying, "I'll give you five hundred dollars for it. It is in good shape for its age, but unfortunately there's not a lot of call for this style around here."

"Only five hundred?" The older woman's shoulders slumped under the calico print of her cotton dress. "But Mr. Griggs always told me it was very valuable, and I need at least three thousand to pay the taxes on my house this year."

Skye impulsively reached out and patted her blue-veined hand. "Maybe he meant sentimental value."

Cookie nodded approvingly at Skye and ran a fingertip caressingly around the vase's metal rim. "I'm sorry, Mrs. Griggs, but the market isn't very strong right now, and I'll probably have to hold on to the vase for quite a while before I find a buyer."

"I need to think about it." Mrs. Griggs

packed the vase back into its box. "I'll let you know tomorrow."

"I won't be here tomorrow, but I'll leave a check with my assistant." Cookie walked the older lady to the door and watched it shut behind her before returning to where Skye stood. "If she doesn't come back by closing tomorrow, I want you to call her and persuade her to sell that vase to me."

"Me? Why? I've only worked here for two weeks," Skye stammered. "You didn't seem all that interested."

"Oh, I'm interested, alright." Cookie smiled thinly and smoothed her ash blond chignon. "I just don't want her to know that I'm interested."

Skye frowned. "You've offered Mrs. Griggs a fair price, haven't you?"

Cookie shrugged. " 'Fair' is such a relative word." She toyed with the sapphire ring on her left hand. "Anyway, that's not your concern."

"But why do you want me to call? Wouldn't it be better for you to talk to her? I'm not sure what to say."

"You are a psychologist, aren't you?" The store owner narrowed her cool blue eyes. "I'm sure you'll think of something soothing to tell our Mrs. Griggs. I don't care if you have to hypnotize her. Just get that vase."

Skye cringed. Too many folks seemed to think her degree in school psychology gave her magic powers. If that were the case, would she still be working for the Scumble River School District? And would she have to take a summer job as a shop assistant to make ends meet?

Before Skye could explain the limits of a school psychologist's abilities, Cookie glanced at her watch and said, "It's nearly noon." She made an impatient face. "I have to attend that luncheon for local business owners at city hall. I'll be back in a couple of hours."

Last winter the new mayor, Skye's uncle Dante Leofanti, had come up with a scheme to get people off the highway and onto the state roads, thus bringing tourists — and their dollars — through Scumble River rather than allowing them to bypass the town while zooming by on Interstate 55. He had convinced the officials of other Illinois communities also situated along the famous Route 66 to co-sponsor a hundred-mile-long yard sale. The sale was now less than eight weeks away, and the purpose of the business lunch Cookie would attend was to bring the movers and shakers up to speed on the current status of plans for the event.

After her boss left, Skye stood behind the counter of the empty store and looked around. Unlike many antique or collectible shops in the area, this one was beautifully arranged, with the merchandise grouped into inviting tableaux. There was plenty of room to walk around, and everything was bright and clean.

Growing bored with the inside of the store, Skye turned her attention to the front window. The early-June sun glinted off the windshields of cars parked along Basin Street, Scumble River's main drag. Other than the empty road, there wasn't much to see. Her view was limited to Ye Olde Junque Emporium, on the opposite corner from Cookie's Collectibles, which didn't seem to be doing much business either. Or maybe it wasn't open. Much of downtown had taken to closing on Mondays due to the lack of customers.

Skye was glad her boss hadn't decided to follow that trend. Not that she enjoyed standing around, bored out of her mind, but she needed the money, especially now that the owners of her rental cottage had decided to sell it. Skye had to either come up with an offer to buy or move out.

All in all, this was not turning out to be a good summer. Skye had lost her usual summer job because of goose poop. The Scumble River Recreation Club, where she had worked the past few years as a lifeguard, had been forced to shut down its beach when an invasion of geese polluted the swimming area. Who knew that bird shit could be so toxic?

As she stood idle, Skye's thoughts returned to Alma Griggs. She had felt an immediate kinship with the older woman, almost a sense of déjà vu, as if they'd had a relationship in another life. That connection, and something about Cookie's desire for Mrs. Griggs's vase, nagged at her. Skye wondered how much it was really worth. She checked her watch. It was only twelve-thirty; her boss wouldn't be back for at least another ninety minutes, maybe more.

Skye moved closer to the window and looked both ways down the sidewalk. The coast was clear. She spun around and headed toward Cookie's office. It was small but exquisitely decorated in a style that reminded Skye of a Victorian lady's parlor. An ornately carved walnut settee, upholstered in moss green velvet, faced a delicate porcelain-inlaid writing table that served as a desk.

A bookcase full of reference books stood against the far wall. Skye moved a gilt chair out of her way and scanned the shelves. She selected a couple of volumes on ceramics and quickly returned to the sales counter.

Half an hour later, Skye was still trying to find an example of Mrs. Griggs's vase. Since she didn't know what to look under, the index was useless, and she was forced to go through the book page by page.

She finally found the vase in the section on art pottery. It was one of a series made by Frank Klepper, a Dallas-based artist who worked in ceramics during the early 1930s. A similar vase, *Curtain of the Night*, had been sold at auction a couple of years ago for eight thousand dollars.

Before Skye could assimilate the fact that her boss was about to cheat a little old lady out of thousands of dollars, the bell above the front door tinkled and a high, thin voice called out, "I'm back."

Skye's heart stopped for a quarter second, until she recognized the returnee as Mrs. Griggs, not Cookie. Then her pulse started to pound at double speed when she realized she had to decide immediately whether or not to tell the woman about Cookie's deception.

Mrs. Griggs came up to the counter and asked, "Could I see Miss Caldwell, please?"

"I'm sorry, she's stepped out for a while."

Skye pasted a smile on her face, her thoughts racing. "Can I help you?"

"Well, I went home and thought about it and decided that if my vase is only worth five hundred dollars, I'd better figure out some other way to raise the money to pay my taxes, so I wondered if Miss Caldwell would be willing to come out to my house and see if there's anything else she'd be interested in buying." The older woman's voice broke, but she swallowed and went on. "Mr. Griggs and I used to be fairly well off, and we traveled a great deal. There has to be something I can sell to save my house."

Once again Skye felt a weird sense of connection with the older woman and she made an abrupt decision. She couldn't let her invite Cookie into her house to cheat her over and over again. Skye took a deep breath. "Mrs. Griggs, that may not be such a good idea."

"Why ever not?"

Should she sugarcoat it or tell it to her straight? Skye struggled to make the right choice. "Well, uh, I think Miss Caldwell may have made an error earlier when she appraised your vase."

"What do you mean?" Faded blue eyes narrowed suspiciously at Skye.

Skye flipped open the book she had been

consulting, pushed it toward Mrs. Griggs, and pointed to the relevant section. "Look here."

The elderly woman clicked open the gold tone clasp of her pocketbook and drew out a pair of glasses. After adjusting them on her nose, she peered at the part of the page Skye had indicated. The minutes ticked by as she read and reread the passage. Finally she picked up the volume and held it close to her face, examining the small picture. Her chest strained the fabric of her dress as she took a deep breath and slammed the book closed. "That bitch! She was going to rip me off!"

Skye jumped slightly. She couldn't have been more surprised by Mrs. Griggs's reaction if she'd started to speak Klingon. "Um, maybe it was a genuine mistake."

"When pigs fly." The older woman thumped her purse down on the counter. "When is she coming back?"

Skye looked at her watch. It was nearly two. Cookie would be back anytime now, and then the goose poop would surely hit the fan.

Chapter 2
Truth or Consequences

A few minutes later the bell over the front door tinkled, and Skye cringed behind the sales counter as she watched her boss stroll into the store. Cookie's powder blue silk sheath and matching high-heeled sandals looked as if she had just put them on, though she'd been wearing them since eight that morning. Skye had noticed that clothes didn't dare crease or stain on Cookie, nor did wrinkles have the courage to mar her smooth, golden-tanned face. If Cookie had not mentioned the year she'd graduated from high school, Skye would never have guessed that the shop owner was in her late forties.

Before Skye could think how to avert the impending disaster, Cookie spotted the woman standing near the counter. "Mrs. Griggs. What brings you back here so soon?"

"I had decided to sell you my vase at your price, but lucky for me there're still some honest people around."

"What do you mean?" Cookie's expectant smile flickered.

"You're not from Scumble River originally, are you, dear?" Mrs. Griggs moved closer to the store owner.

"No." Cookie took a step back. "I moved here from Chicago a couple of years ago."

"Well, maybe they do things different in the city," Mrs. Griggs said, continuing to advance, "but around here we don't lie and cheat our neighbors."

"I don't know what you're talking about." Cookie had retreated until she was pressed against the front window.

"Skye, here, showed me a picture of my vase in the pricing guide. Seems it's worth about sixteen times what you offered me."

Cookie threw a venomous glare at Skye before turning to Mrs. Griggs. "Pricing guides are only a suggestion. There's no guarantee that your vase would bring anywhere near the amount they list."

"You know, if it were a couple of hundred dollars either way I'd believe you, but more than seven thousand — I'm not senile yet."

"I've got to make a living," Cookie cajoled. "Think of my overhead."

Mrs. Griggs moved in front of the store owner and ordered in a cold, clear voice, "Don't say another word."

Cookie ignored the woman's command. "But —"

Mrs. Griggs didn't hesitate; she drew back her hand and slapped Cookie full in the face. Before Cookie could react, Mrs. Griggs leaned forward until their noses were nearly touching. "I'm leaving now, and when I get home, I'm getting on the phone and telling everyone I know what you tried to do to me. You might as well close your doors right now, because not a single soul in Scumble River will ever do business with you again."

Cookie stood frozen, her hand cradling her cheek, until Mrs. Griggs left. The sound of the slamming door seemed to rouse her, and she whirled on Skye. "What have you done to me?"

"Nothing!" Skye was trapped behind the counter, her furious boss blocking her only exit. She had never noticed the muscles in Cookie's arms before, but now she remembered a conversation they'd had about Cookie's obsession with playing tennis. Suddenly Skye was afraid the enraged woman would physically assault her. What could she use to defend herself?

"Nothing?" Cookie screeched. "You ignorant hick. You've ruined me. Why would you tell that woman the true value of her merchandise?"

"Because it's not right to cheat people?" Skye said the first thing that came to her mind as she reached for a pair of scissors on a shelf to her left.

"It's called business, you hayseed." Cookie shot forward and grabbed Skye's arm, pulling her out from behind the counter before she could grasp the shears. "Caveat emptor. Ever heard of that?"

"But isn't that 'let the buyer beware'? Mrs. Griggs was the seller." As soon as the words left Skye's mouth she regretted them. When would she learn to shut up?

"Get out! Get out right now!" Cookie went ballistic, shoving Skye toward the door. "You're fired!"

Skye started toward the back room to get her purse.

"Where do you think you're going? I told you to get out of here." Cookie plucked a sword with an elaborate hilt from a box with SOLD written across the side in red Magic Marker.

A hollow elephant's foot full of walking sticks was to her right. Skye tried to grab a cane to protect herself, but Cookie slashed the sword downward between Skye and the umbrella stand, nearly slicing off Skye's hand.

Cookie thrust her weapon at Skye's chest. "Don't ever come back into my store."

Skye abandoned the idea of retrieving her purse, turned, and pushed frantically on the bar that opened the door. Suddenly, just as the heavy door began to swing outward, she felt a painful smack across her derrière. She twisted around just in time to see Cookie pulling the sword back for another wallop.

Skye yelped and ran outside. As she cleared the threshold, she heard Cookie muttering, "Enough is enough. I've done my time in Scumble River. I'm moving back to civilization. I don't care who finds out."

Chapter 3
All in the Family

Skye sat in her car trying to regain control of her breathing and figure out what to do next. How had she managed to get fired from yet another job? First her school psychologist job in New Orleans three years ago, then the lifeguard position earlier this summer, and now this. But none of the dismissals had been her fault, had they? Well, she definitely hadn't had anything to do with the geese pooping in the lake. And no way could she have ignored the teen in Louisiana being molested by the girl's own father. But maybe she should have kept her mouth shut about the vase.

She rocked from cheek to cheek. Cookie was obviously a terrific tennis player with a great backhand. That whack from the sword still stung.

Skye twisted a chestnut curl around her finger until it formed a dreadlock. Now what should she do? Without a summer job, how could she earn the extra money she needed for the down payment on her cottage? She couldn't even make an offer until she was sure she'd have the cash.

Suddenly a wave of exhaustion hit her and she slumped over the steering wheel. Just when things started going well in her life, there was always a bump in the road. Maybe that was why her dad and godfather had restored such a sizeable vehicle for her. They must have known that nothing less substantial than a 1957 Chevy Bel Air convertible could take the jolts. Although why the car had to be bright aqua she would never know.

Sighing, she straightened up. Self-pity wouldn't get her anywhere. She had to think. Where would she find another job in this economy? She had already checked around to see if there was any contractual work for psychological testing in the neighboring school districts, but school budgets were too tight for any extras.

Was she allowed to do private counseling? She'd have to check with the Illinois School Psychologists Association to see what the rules were about that. Should she go home and try to call someone right now? It had been such a salmon day — she felt as if she'd spent the entire twenty-four hours swimming upstream, only to get screwed and die in the end — maybe it would be better to wait.

As she was pondering her next move, a white Oldsmobile pulled up behind the Bel Air. Skye paled as she watched a short woman wearing a dark blue police dispatcher's uniform and an angry scowl on her face jump out of the car and scurry toward her. Skye felt her eyelid twitch; things were about to get worse.

As the passenger door was wrenched open, Skye's mother, May, exploded, "That man will drive me to my grave."

Skye looked at her mom's red face and, half afraid of the answer, asked, "What did Dad do now?" May had never quite forgiven her husband for his failure to tell her when he discovered the dead bodies of the town's perfect couple, Barbie and Ken Addison, last Thanksgiving. Because she held that grudge, anything else Jed did was twice as annoying to her.

"I've been asking him to fix the toilet in the big bathroom since Christmas and he's always too busy."

"Well . . ." Skye struggled to defend her father. "Farming takes a lot of time, and he is the only mechanic in the family, so he has to keep everyone else's tractors running, too. Plus he cuts both your lawn and Grandma's."

"I understand that." Emerald green eyes that matched Skye's own blazed. "What I don't understand is, if he is so dang-blasted busy, how did he find the time to work on that old clunker Bunny Reid just bought?"

Oh, oh. No wonder May was blowing a gasket. Skye's mother had taken an instant dislike to Bunny when she had moved to town last November. Knowing Jed was spending time with that woman, even innocently, would drive May wild.

Skye had been silent too long. May huffed, "I suppose you think that's perfectly all right. That he should help her get that car running. Don't you?"

To complicate matters, Bunny was the mother of Skye's boyfriend, Simon Reid, the town coroner and owner of the local funeral home, which placed Skye squarely in the middle of the situation. Although she opened her mouth several times, nothing brilliant sprang into her mind to say.

After a few seconds May demanded, "So, whose side are you on? Mine or your father's?"

Skye knew she should refuse to answer on the grounds she might infuriate her mother even more, but she felt compelled to try and smooth the waters between her parents. "Well, uh, I understand how frustrated you must be with the toilet running all the time, but it is usable, right?"

May nodded grudgingly.

"And Bunny really has no transportation until Dad gets her car running, so —"

"So, nothing. He's *my* husband, and I don't want him hanging around with that hussy. She only bought that wreck so she could get Jed over to her place and into her clutches."

"I'm sure that's not true, Mom." Skye tried to pat May's hand, but her mother snatched it away. "Bunny knows Dad is happily married."

"Oh, really?" May sputtered. "Then why did I catch her with her arms around your father's neck when I stopped over there a few minutes ago?"

Shit! Skye's eyes widened and her mind raced trying to come up with an innocent reason for the embrace.

Finally she settled for saying, "I'm sure there's a good explanation."

May snorted, crossed her arms, and tucked her chin into her chest. "Your father went over to that woman's place right after lunch. Since I hadn't seen him all afternoon and wanted to tell him something before I started my shift at the police department, I decided to stop by on my way to work and talk to him. You know he doesn't answer the phone when I'm gone, right?"

"Right." Skye was well aware of her father's aversion to the telephone. It had made communicating with him difficult when she had lived away from Scumble River. "Then what happened?"

"At first I wasn't sure where he'd be. I knew Bunny lived above the bowling alley, but I didn't know where she'd keep her car, so I called Simon. He said there was a garage in back that was part of the property and her car was there. By the way, he wasn't at all happy to hear that she had roped Jed into helping her either."

"So you went to the garage?" Skye prodded, ignoring the side issue of Simon's displeasure.

"Right. And when I walked in, that floozy was wrapped around your father like hair around a curler, and she wasn't wearing nothing but chiffon and feathers."

Skye blew out a puff of air. This was worse than she'd thought. Bunny had been a Las Vegas showgirl for twenty years before moving back to Scumble River, and her taste in clothing reflected her past career. "Mom, I'm positive that Bunny was just thanking Dad. He would never look at another woman. And despite what you think of Bunny, she's all flirt and no fu . . . uh . . . fulfillment."

May brooded in silence for a while, then said, "I don't want to talk about it anymore."

"But what are you going to do?"

"Nothing, for the moment. I've got to think about it some." May took a deep breath. "And I said I don't want to talk about it anymore."

Skye knew that when her mother put up that emotional shield even a photon torpedo couldn't break through it. She just hoped her parents could patch things up and she wouldn't have to get involved.

Without warning, May demanded, "Why were you sitting in the car rather than inside working?"

For a split second Skye considered lying, but what would be the use? The whole story would be all over town by supper that night. "I was fired."

"Why?" The expression on May's face was hard to read.

Skye explained the day's events, leaving out the part where she was whacked on the rear end with a sword and concluding with, "Maybe I shouldn't have said anything to

Mrs. Griggs. Maybe I should have just closed my eyes to what Cookie was doing and minded my own business for once."

"Right." May's lips twisted skeptically. "I can almost picture you doing that. That would be the same day you got your nose pierced and a tattoo of a snake on your butt." She shook her head. "Cookie Caldwell is a fool for trying to cheat someone like that in a small town."

"I'm sure she thought no one would ever find out."

"She was wrong." May punctuated her statement by pulling down the visor and smoothing her hair away from her face. The short salt-and-pepper waves immediately sprang back. She scowled at her reflection. "Vince isn't cutting my hair short enough again." Vince was Skye's older brother and the owner of Great Expectations Hair Salon.

Skye shook her head. "Never mind your hair, Mom." It was hard to keep her mother's attention on any one issue. "Do you know of any other job openings in the area?"

May paused in reapplying her lipstick. "Sure. I have just the thing for you. And you'd be doing the town and the family a favor."

"No." Skye felt a bubble of panic in her throat. "Tell me it's not what I think it is."

"I'm sure I can't read your mind, Missy." May's false huffiness cinched Skye's hunch.

"I can't work for Uncle Dante. He doesn't like me. He blames me for exposing his fiddling with the Leofanti trust." A couple of years ago May's older brother had had his hand slapped by the rest of the family when Skye discovered he'd been using some creative accounting to buy his personal vehicles and farm equipment.

"He's in a real bind. Dante'd hire the devil himself, if he thought Satan could help him out of his predicament."

Skye wished she didn't, but she knew what her mother was talking about. "What happened to the last one?"

"Phyllis quit Friday."

"Why? He didn't make a pass at her, did he?"

"Of course not. He's a married man," May protested, then muttered under her breath, "Besides, she was older than I am." May was fifty-nine.

"So's Uncle Dante."

May arched a brow at Skye, who shrugged. Everyone knew, although no one would say it out loud, that Dante liked 'em young. He considered Skye at thirty-three to be over the hill.

Skye persisted. "So why did Phyllis quit?"

May suddenly found the aqua and white leather seat fascinating, staring at it as if she had never seen it before. "She said she wasn't being paid enough to be yelled at and humiliated."

"Uncle Dante lost his temper."

May nodded.

"And threw a tantrum."

May nodded again.

"Did he break anything?"

"His middle finger." The corner of May's mouth lifted, but she swiftly suppressed the smile.

"I won't ask how he managed that."

"Something to do with a file drawer and a statue of Napoleon."

"Sounds creative," Skye commented. "Let me get this straight. Uncle Dante's big moneymaking scheme for the town, the Route 66 Yard Sale, is less than eight weeks away and the project coordinator has quit?"

"Yep."

"So, he has no one to attend to the thousand and one problems that will pop up between now and opening day?"

"Yep."

"How many coordinators has he run through?" Skye asked.

"Phyllis was the fifth one."

Skye thought it over. It would be hell

working for her uncle, and she wasn't even sure she could do the job. The Route 66 Yard Sale was a much bigger undertaking than the Greek Olympics Fund-raiser she had organized for her sorority, Alpha Sigma Alpha, back in college, and that had nearly killed her.

"Dante's already spent more than half of the money Gabriel Scumble gave us," May explained. "The townspeople will lynch him if the Route 66 Yard Sale is a failure." The previous fall Gabriel Scumble, the last living descendant of the town's founder, Pierre Scumble, had given the community a check for one hundred thousand dollars in order to make up for his ancestor's having cheated the people of Scumble River two hundred years ago.

"Is Uncle Charlie still against the yard sale?" Skye's godfather, Charlie Patukas, owned the Up A Lazy River Motor Court, was president of the school board, and was one of the town's most influential citizens. He had made it clear that he thought Dante, and Dante's idea, were both idiotic.

"Yesterday Charlie said the only difference between a yard sale and a trash pickup is how close to the road you put your junk."

Skye snickered. "So, I take it he hasn't changed his mind?"

May's expression was unhappy. "He doesn't think it's a wise use of the money. However, since the yard sale is going to happen, with or without his approval, he's agreed to stay in the background and not do anything to ruin it. But he won't help, either."

Great. If Skye took the job, she'd end up in the middle of Charlie and Dante's feud. "You know I have no experience or training to coordinate an event as huge as the yard sale."

May ignored Skye's statement. "Our family will never live down the humiliation if Dante blows the town's money."

"Are you even sure he'll hire me?" Skye asked. "How about his son or daughter-in-law?"

"Oh, he'll hire you, all right. Your aunt Minnie and I will see to that." May opened the car door. "Hugo has said he's busy with the used-car lot, and even Dante knows Victoria's too much of a twit to handle the job."

Skye nodded, agreeing with her mother's assessment of her cousin's wife.

"Besides, where else can you get a job that pays anything like this one?" May got out of the Bel Air and stood leaning into the open doorway. "Dante will give you ten thousand dollars for nine weeks' work."

Skye sucked in her breath. More than a thousand dollars a week! She could feel her resistance slipping.

"Plus he's offered a bonus of five thousand if the yard sale is successful," May coaxed.

Wow! With that kind of money, Skye would have enough for a down payment on the cottage. She knew she would be sorry, but greed won out and she nodded. "Okay. Tell Uncle Dante I'll start tomorrow." She paused, then asked meekly, "One other thing. Could you run in and get my purse from Cookie? I don't think it's a good idea for me to go back in there right now."

Skye figured May was more than a match for the shop owner, even if Cookie was still armed.

Chapter 4
Beat the Clock

"No. I'm sorry. It's impossible." Skye cradled the receiver between her ear and shoulder while she frantically flipped through a pile of papers. "Look, there's no room at the inn. I couldn't find a vacancy for Mary and Joseph at this late date. Even the manger has been rented."

She slammed the handset down, blew the hair from her eyes, and went back to searching for the entertainment folder. Who in their right mind thought they could call two days before an event and get a place to stay? The answer was simple — no one who was sane. They were all crazy.

Just as she found the elusive file, she heard a bellow, a thump, and a string of curses. Great. Uncle Dante was back from lunch. No doubt he had discovered the boxes of Charmin stacked in the middle of his office.

"Skye!"

She sighed and got up. Edging between the maze of cartons that took up all the floor space between her desk and the door, she made it to the hall just as Dante roared out her name again.

Seven and a half weeks had passed since she had reluctantly taken the job as the Route 66 Yard Sale coordinator, and she had regretted her decision every hour of every day.

Dante wasn't a bad mayor, but he was a lousy boss. And who knew that a simple yard sale would result in so many details that had to be sorted out? Well, okay, it wasn't a simple yard sale — it covered a hundred miles and would last nine days — but still, who would have thought Skye would need a master's degree in public safety to make it all happen?

The list had been endless. They needed everything from liquid soap for the Port-A-Potties to wooden pallets that kept food items at least six inches off the ground. Not to mention the logistics of running water, trash collection, and traffic. It was almost as if Skye had been put in charge of establishing a miniature city within the town.

Now, two days before the sale started, she could almost see the light at the end of the tunnel; she just hoped it wasn't a train about to run her over.

As she stepped into the mayor's office, Skye said, "Yes, Uncle Dante?"

"Get these goddamned boxes out of here!" Dante was less than five-six, and he carried all of his considerable weight in the chest and stomach regions. With his thick gray hair slicked back, red nose, and black suit, he looked like a penguin, only not as cute.

"Where shall I put them?"

"How should I know? Move them to the storage closet or the garage or your office. I don't give a flying fart. Just get them out of here."

Skye shook her head. "The closet's been full for the past two weeks, Wally has said if I put another thing in the police garage he'll arrest me, and I already can't move in my office."

Dante narrowed his eyes. "Tell Wally that as chief of police he works for me and I said we are commandeering the garage until further notice."

"Okay, but he won't like it."

"Who gives a shit what he likes? Just do it. Then have the custodian get these boxes out of here."

"He's in the hospital. Gallstones. Remember, you signed the card for the flowers I sent?"

Dante's face turned maroon and he started to wave his arms around, shouting, "They're all against me." He took a step backward. "But once they see how successful the Route 66 Yard Sale is, they'll be singing a different tune."

He took another step backward and Skye watched in horrified fascination as his foot hit the bottom corner of the precariously stacked brown cartons.

Just as he yelled, "Then they'll all realize how great I am," the first box came tumbling down on his head, followed by the rest of the tower. The cartons burst open and the contents went flying.

Skye's first instinct was to go to his assistance, but the crazed look in his eyes convinced her that self-preservation was more important than politeness. It was clear from the sheer volume of his voice and the energetic flapping of his arms that he wasn't hurt.

Her last view of her uncle as she hurried away was of the mayor sitting in the middle of the floor covered with sheets of toilet paper. He looked like a tree that had been TP'ed on Halloween night. His cussing followed her down the hall, and she could still faintly hear him even after shutting her door. She had to admit he had a real talent for coming up with new and inventive swear words.

Giggling, she went back to work. Her amusement was cut short when she answered the next telephone call. It was Faith Easton, the star of *Faith's Finds*, a popular TV show on the Heartland cable channel. In every episode Faith went to flea markets and garage sales to discover the hidden treasures buried amid the junk.

The Route 66 Yard Sale had drawn her attention like a hog to mud, and she had been calling Skye with outrageous requests ever since she decided to film a *Faith's Finds Special* that would cover the entire nine-day event.

Today's call was a repeat of the last thirty calls, and Skye forced herself to answer in an even tone. "No, Miss Easton, I'm afraid it still isn't possible to let you have a 'little peek' before the public is allowed into the sale." She listened to the honey-coated voice on the other end. "Yes, I understand it's for TV, but it wouldn't be fair to the others to let you have first crack at the goodies." Skye put her feet up on the desk and counted the ceiling tiles as Faith droned on. "No, I still can't get you more than one cabin at the Up A Lazy River Motor Court, either. The others are all reserved. No, I'm sorry, but no other motels have been built since we talked yesterday." Skye resumed her perusal of the ceiling as the star ranted. Suddenly she straightened, nearly falling off her chair. "Could you repeat that, please?"

Faith's self-satisfied voice with its slight British accent oozed from the receiver. "I said, if that's the case, then I shall take the mayor up on his suggestion and lease your cottage from you. He told me I could have it all nine nights for five thousand. I'll be arriving tomorrow afternoon. My assistant will call you for directions and to arrange a time for you to meet us there."

Skye yelped, "Wait!" but Faith had already hung up. Skye slammed down the handset and marched into her uncle's office.

He had extricated himself from the toilet paper, but the mess remained in the middle of the floor, looking a little like a deflated wedding cake.

As she entered, Dante glanced up, his expression sour. "Why haven't these boxes been removed?"

"Why did you tell Faith Easton she could rent my cottage?"

"You need money to buy the place. I checked your lease and you have the right to sublet. Between what I'm paying you — provided you get the bonus — and the amount of rent Miss Easton is willing to shell out, you'll have enough for the down payment and all the fees and points that go along with a mortgage." Dante sat back in his chair and laced his fingers over his stomach. "You don't have to thank me."

Skye bit her lip. She hadn't thought of the extra costs of getting a mortgage. Dante was right. She needed the money that renting the cottage would bring. "So, uh, I guess that means I'll stay in the cabin at the motor court?"

Her uncle shook his head. "No, Miss Easton is keeping that, too. She said she needed it for her producer/director. She made a big deal about him not being able to stay in the cabin with her because they're 'secretly engaged.' And since the Heartland Channel is a Christian-owned network, she can't afford the suggestion of impropriety." Dante scratched his head. "I guess the cameraman, writer, and Miss Easton's assistant don't count, since they'll be sleeping on the floor in the living room."

Skye let her uncle's words wash over her. She didn't really care about the sleeping arrangements for Faith Easton's crew. Her main concern was where she would stay. As she had been pointing out for the past month, all the rooms in the area had been rented.

As if reading her thoughts, Dante said, "You can stay at your folks' house. I already talked to your mother."

Skye quickly considered the options. Staying at Simon's was impossible, even though he'd be out of town. While he was gone, he was having all new copper pipes put in, so there'd be no running water. Her brother Vince's studio apartment was barely big enough for him and his drum set. That left her best friend, Trixie Frayne, but Trixie and her husband, Owen, were renting all their empty bedrooms to people coming for the yard sale.

She sagged against the door. She loved her parents, but her mom and dad hadn't been getting along with each other this summer, and the prospect of living with them for nine days, listening to them bicker, made her want to slit her throat. Was five thousand dollars really worth it?

Skye jerked upright in bed and saw Bingo, her black cat, jump off the mattress and race out of the room. *What's that awful noise?* She sank back down and pulled the covers over her head, trying to block out the high-pitched squeal. *Why is someone using a dentist's drill in my bedroom? Shit! It's that stupid alarm clock from Simon.*

He had bought it for her after she had slept through her old one once too often. He had proudly told her that it was guaranteed to wake up even the deepest sleeper. She hadn't had the heart to tell him how much she hated it. Maybe it would have a terrible accident in the move from her cottage to her parents' house.

Skye swatted the loathsome object until it shut up. The snooze alarm would allow her ten extra minutes of much-needed sleep, though now that she was awake, her mind had started to race like a gerbil on an exercise wheel.

Her head emerged from under her pillow and she groaned. She had been up until three in the morning frantically cleaning the cottage, doing laundry, and packing for her eviction. Slowly she eased out of bed.

Fumbling her way to the kitchen, she switched on the flame under the teapot, then emptied a can of Fancy Feast into Bingo's bowl. As she sipped a cup of Earl Grey, she wrote a list of what she had to accomplish before moving in with her parents that afternoon. At the bottom of the paper she wrote: "Figure out how to buy Xanax without a prescription." She would need strong drugs to make it through the next ten days.

After a quick shower, she threw on a pair of denim shorts and an orange University of Illinois T-shirt, then scraped her hair into a ponytail. There was no use bothering with makeup; the weather was supposed to be hot and windy, and she'd be outdoors most of the day checking on the various booths and tables along the five-mile stretch of Scumble River's portion of the Route 66 Yard Sale.

The sale started in the north at Scumble River Road and followed Route 66, which became Maryland Street as it wound its way through the business district. Then it passed Up A Lazy River Motor Court, Brown Bag Liquor Store, and Great Expectations Hair Salon before exiting onto Rolling Water Road and heading into Brooklyn, the next small town along the legendary highway.

As Skye drove to work down Basin Street, Scumble River's business district glowed watercolor bright in the morning sun. The old redbrick and wood-framed buildings with their snapping banners and just-swept sidewalks glistened, ready for the guests that would arrive the next day.

She noted the preparations for the Yard Sale. The police had already placed sawhorses across the intersection at Adams Street. Merchants were setting up tables in front of newly painted storefronts, and city crews were stringing WELCOME posters from one side of the freshly cleaned road to the other. Scumble River was putting its best foot forward. Skye just hoped the town wouldn't trip and fall on its face.

When she reached the city hall, she exchanged her Bel Air for one of half a dozen golf carts that the town had rented when Mayor Leofanti had realized that Scumble River's downtown would have to be closed off to vehicular traffic for the duration of the event.

As she transferred her supplies to the basket behind her seat, she caught sight of a tall, lean woman dressed in jeans and a short-sleeve chambray work shirt crossing the small parking lot. Her nut-brown hair was cut sensibly short, and her hazel eyes sparkled with intelligence.

Skye was supposed to meet the health inspector at eight-thirty and drive him around to the various food booths, toilets, and trash facilities so he could give them his final approval. Could he be a she? Was the twenty-first century catching up to Stanley County?

Skye straightened and asked, "Inspector Pantaleone?"

"Yes. Call me Andrea." The woman held out a tanned hand. "You must be Skye."

"That's me. Nice to meet you." They shook. "Where would you like to start?"

The inspector checked her clipboard. "The Lemonade ShakeUp stand."

"Great. I know that one's in good shape." Skye smiled. The lemonade stand was sponsored by the high school's *Scumble River Scoop* newspaper; in her real life as a school psychologist, Skye was one of the faculty sponsors. Her best friend, Trixie, the school librarian, was the other. She and Trixie had spent several evenings the past week helping the student staff assemble the booth and prepare for today's inspection. "Hop in. It's on the corner of Maryland and Basin." Which was, not coincidentally since Skye had assigned the sites, a prime location in the heart of downtown.

Once Andrea was settled, Skye put the cart in motion and said conversationally, "Have you been a health inspector long?"

"No. I started out as a math teacher, but quit to raise my kids. The youngest started school last year and I was bored, so I began looking around for a teaching job. Before I found one, my uncle mentioned this opening. I took the test and here I am."

"I'm working for my uncle, too." Skye and Andrea exchanged a mutually knowing glance.

Skye stopped the cart a little way back from a hot pink and bright yellow booth. As the women walked toward it, an argument could be heard coming from behind the canvas walls. Skye winced. She recognized the voices as belonging to Frannie Ryan and Justin Boward, the school newspaper's star reporters and coeditors.

When they were a few steps from the booth a tall, sturdily built teenage girl burst through the screen door in the back of the stand and raced past them with tears streaming down her face.

Skye turned to Andrea, "Excuse me a minute. I need to see if she's okay."

Without waiting for a response, Skye hurried off. She caught up to the girl around the corner. Frannie was sitting on a concrete bench staring at the river.

Skye sat next to her and asked, "What happened?"

"Nothing."

"Is there anything I can do?"

The girl shrugged. "Can you make someone be different?"

"Probably not." Frannie sniffed and Skye dug a tissue from her pocket and handed it to the distraught teen. "But I could talk to him. Sometimes a neutral third party can help two people hear each other better."

Frannie gave her a sharp look. "How do you know it's a 'him'?"

"Just a good guess." Skye smiled. "What was the argument about?"

"Justin's taking Bitsy to the concert in the park Sunday night."

Skye made a face. She was afraid something like that might be the problem. Frannie and Justin were best friends, and although Skye suspected that they had deeper feelings for each other, neither of them seemed ready to take the risk and explore those emotions. Unfortunately, one of the other girls on the *Scoop*'s staff had set her cap for Justin, and either he liked her or he was too oblivious to realize that she was reeling him in like a fisherman with a prize trout.

"He asked her out?" Skye questioned cautiously.

Frannie brushed back a strand of long, wavy brown hair. "Not exactly."

"She asked him and he said yes?"

51

"Not exactly."

"Then how?"

"Justin is going with Brandon and his girlfriend. I can't go because I have to go with my dad to my great-aunt's birthday party." Frannie stood and yanked up her jeans. The current low-riding style was a challenge for the teen's rounded shape. Having a similar curvaceous figure, Skye understood Frannie's urge to fit in with the size twos and fours of the rest of the high school class, so she resisted the temptation to suggest that Frannie buy more flattering pants.

"Okay. But how does Bitsy fit into the picture?"

"Brandon's girlfriend invited Bitsy to go along and make it a foursome." Frannie's brown eyes narrowed. "Or so Justin says."

"Don't assume treachery for what stupidity can explain."

A twist of Frannie's lips expressed her skepticism.

Skye was at a loss for what else to say. She couldn't suggest that Frannie skip the family party and tag along with the kids to the concert, although that would probably be the best advice. She couldn't suggest that Frannie ask Justin to miss the concert or go with some other friends, although that, too, would be a solution. She was stuck with option number three, the one that would make her look like a stupid grown-up who didn't understand anything. "It sounds like this isn't his idea, so maybe the best thing would be to let it go. If you make it seem important, it might become more significant than it really is."

"Whatever." Frannie blew out an exasperated breath. "It's just that Bitsy is such a Slinky."

"A what?" Skye hadn't heard that expression before.

"A Slinky is someone who's not really good for anything, but you still can't help smiling when you see one tumble down the stairs."

Skye struggled not to grin. Not that she agreed with the sentiment, but it was darn funny.

"Anyway, it's not like I care what Justin does."

Skye patted the girl's arm. "Of course not."

"But some of his new friends make me feel like I'm less than nothing."

"No one can make you feel inferior without your permission. So don't give it to them."

Frannie's brow furrowed while she considered what Skye had said. Then she nodded. "Got ya."

Skye glanced at her watch. Shoot! They had been gone nearly thirty minutes. "Ready to go back?" She hoped the inspector wasn't too upset at the delay.

Frannie nodded again and led the way.

When Frannie and Skye returned to the lemonade stand, they found Justin, Andrea, and Trixie sipping from paper cups and laughing.

Justin was saying, "So, uh, then would it be okay for me to follow you around sometime and do a story about being a safety inspector?"

Skye smiled. Justin was interested in everything and a keen observer of what went on around him. That, paired with the ability to blend into the woodwork and the tenacity of a mule, made him an excellent reporter.

"Sure. Here's my card. Give me a call," Andrea answered, then caught sight of Skye. "But right now we have to get going."

Skye hurried over. "I'm so sorry to keep you waiting." She lowered her voice. "A teen emergency."

"I understand. I have one of my own."

Before leaving, Skye pulled Trixie aside and asked, "Where were you?"

"I had to pee. What happened?"

Skye filled her friend in on her conversation with Frannie.

Trixie's response was not reassuring. "Maybe she's right to be upset. You just can't trust men."

As Skye turned to join Andrea, she wondered if everything was all right between Trixie and her husband, Owen.

She sighed and continued toward the golf cart, but Justin stopped her. "Hey, Ms. D, do you know who that woman over there is?"

"Where?" Skye squinted across the road.

"By Cookie's Collectibles."

Skye scanned the area but didn't see anyone near where Justin was pointing. "I don't see anyone."

"She's gone now."

"Why did you want to know who she is?"

"Just curious." Justin twitched his shoulders as if an insect was buzzing around him, then muttered into his chest. "I've seen her around Ms. Caldwell's before, and she's not from town."

"Probably a friend." Skye briefly reconsidered her previous thoughts about Justin. Maybe his reporter's instincts were getting out of hand. Should she say something? Maybe later. Right now she had an inspector to show around.

Chapter 5
Wild Kingdom

Skye and Andrea spent the next couple of hours visiting every public restroom facility and trash can along the yard sale's five-mile path through Scumble River. The initial inspection was an eye-opener for Skye, who'd had no idea the whole process would be so involved.

First Andrea walked around the outside of the Port-A-Potty cubicle looking for any leakage. Then she opened the door and sniffed, made a note on her clipboard, and turned to ask, "How often is maintenance scheduled for these?"

Skye consulted her own clipboard and answered, "The owners will service them at the end of each day, and I've hired teenagers to restock them with toilet paper, paper towels, and liquid soap at noon and at four p.m."

"I'd like to see how much toilet paper you have on hand."

Skye fought a grin, recalling her uncle's encounter with the Charmin. Was it really as squeezably soft as the ads claimed? "Sure. It's at the city hall."

"Okay, then I'll look at it when we go back there."

They finished the last trash can a few minutes past twelve and made a quick stop for lunch at the Feed Bag, the only real restaurant in town. After they ate, they examined a hot dog stand, an ice cream counter, and a trailer that would be selling cotton candy, elephant ears, and taffy apples. Food concessions needed to meet a variety of requirements to pass Andrea's scrutiny, including the use of hair restraints, leakproof garbage bags, and a five-gallon container for wastewater.

When they got back into the golf cart, after checking out the Altar and Rosary Society barbecue dinner tent, Andrea glanced at her list and said, "The last two sites are the Doozier Family Petting Zoo and the goat cheese stand."

Skye took a deep breath and nodded. She had been dreading this inspection. Nothing that had to do with the Dooziers, one of Scumble River's most unusual families, ever went smoothly. In a town surrounded by railroad tracks it was impossible to say someone lived on the wrong side of them, but the Dooziers came mighty close. Skye took another breath, forced herself to smile at the inspector, who was looking at her questioningly, and started up the golf cart.

The Dooziers had set up their concession on a sliver of family-owned land east of town, where State Road curved into Route 66. Skye steered the cart around the barricades at the corner of Maryland and Kinsman streets, which marked the end of the city limits. The rest of the sale's path was open to automobiles.

Skye was concentrating on avoiding oncoming cars when Andrea said, "A petting zoo is a little atypical for this type of event, isn't it?"

"Yes, but then so are the Dooziers." Skye struggled to explain. "Have you heard the term 'red-raggers'?"

"Yes. I know it's derogatory, but I've never quite figured out what it meant."

"It's people who live a different sort of life. Mostly they live in those shacks by the river. It isn't that they're poor, although they are. And it isn't that they live in squalor, although they do. It's more that they seem to enjoy living that way." Andrea looked puzzled, and Skye summed it up with, "They're the original out-of-the-box thinkers."

"Ah." Andrea smiled. "And that's what scares you."

"Exactly."

Loud voices and barking dogs greeted them as they approached the Dooziers' corner. Their property was shaped roughly like a long, skinny triangle, and Skye parked at the tip.

She said to Andrea, "Are you ready for this?"

"Ready as I'll ever be." She got out of the cart and Skye followed suit.

The women picked their way gingerly across uneven ground covered with weeds and rocks. Several feet back from the road various pens and cages had been arranged in a rough oval.

To one side of the makeshift entrance, a folding table with a sign reading ADMISSION $5.00 duct-taped to the front edge teetered on crooked legs. Sitting with his cowboy-boot-encased feet propped up on the table's surface was a scrawny, densely tattooed man wearing a pair of jogging shorts and nothing else.

Beyond him, among the pens and cages, were two nearly naked boys wrestling in the dirt, a woman in a skimpy denim miniskirt and a shiny orange halter top, and a teenage girl dressed in black from head to toe, with waist-length ebony hair and dark maroon lipstick.

Andrea murmured, "Oh, my."

Skye opened her mouth but could think of nothing to add. These were the Dooziers. There was no explaining them. It would be like trying to make sense out of an IRS document.

When the man saw Skye, he jumped up, nearly knocking over the card table, and said, "Miz Skye, you're early. We're not quite ready for that there inspection you told us about." She tried to edge past him to get a closer look at what was going on behind him, but he scooted in front of her and said, "Who's this pretty lady?"

Skye gave up trying to see what he was hiding and introduced them. "This is Andrea Pantaleone, the health inspector. Andrea, this is Earl Doozier."

Earl hitched up his shorts and stuck out his hand. "Pleased to meet you, ma'am. We've got some mighty fine animals to show the nice people." He leaned in close and confided, "I figure these city folk probably never touched a mule or a rabbit or such before, so I thought to myself, Earl Doozier, you need to help those poor people."

Skye narrowed her eyes. "Help them for a price, right, Earl?"

He tried to look hurt, but couldn't quite disguise the avaricious twinkle in his muddy brown eyes. "Miz Skye, I got to feed and house all those animals. That don't come free now, does it?"

"Nothing in life does."

Earl looked confused, scratched his butt, then took both women by the arms. "You and your friend come sit in the shade. Glenda will come get us dreckly." He led them to a couple of rusted lawn chairs set up under an olive green tarp.

Skye sat down cautiously. The plastic webbing on the seat looked frayed, and she was afraid it might split under her weight. Andrea didn't seem as concerned, but then, she probably didn't weigh more than a hundred pounds.

Andrea clicked her pen and said, "Mr. Doozier, let's use this time for you to give me a list of the animals you'll be exhibiting."

Earl screwed up his face in thought. "Well, now, let me see. We got us three sheep, a cow, a whole passel of rabbits — you know, it's hard to keep count. Those rascals make babies faster then I can pop open a beer. It ain't human."

Skye hid her smile behind her hand.

Andrea snickered, turning it into a cough, then asked, "Any other animals?"

"Some chickens, a litter of piglets, and a mule."

"Good." Andrea made a note. "Sounds nice and tame."

Skye saw a flicker in Earl's weasellike eyes. What was he up to?

Before she could figure it out, Andrea looked at her watch and said, "I'm sorry, Mr. Doozier, I really can't wait any longer. I need to make my inspection now or you won't be able to open tomorrow."

"Sure, sure. I understand. Just give me one more little minute and we'll get started." As Earl loped away, he yelled over his shoulder, "I don't want to interfere with the duly constipated authorities."

For a split second, Skye wondered if Earl had a spy camera set up in the city hall bathroom to monitor the officials' toilet habits.

Luckily, before Skye's mind could go too far down that path, Andrea said, "He's hiding something."

"Yep." Skye got up and edged toward the pens. "Probably some scam he doesn't want us to know about." She moved closer to where Earl stood talking urgently to his wife, Glenda. "He's not the sharpest hook in the tackle box, but he's caught a lot of fish in his time."

After Glenda turned and scurried away,

Earl sauntered back to the lawn chairs. "Okay, ladies. You ready?"

While Andrea took note of the condition of the pens, feeding areas, and other details, Skye kept an eye out for Glenda. She and the children had mysteriously disappeared. Andrea was going over a list of violations with Earl when Skye spotted activity over by a small U-Haul trailer.

She strolled casually in that direction. As she got closer an incredibly foul odor assaulted her. She stopped a few feet away, her eyes watering. At first the terrible smell distracted her, but then she heard low voices. Suddenly there was a distinctive roar and Skye stumbled backward. Where had the Dooziers gotten a lion, and what were they planning to do with it?

Earl had explained they'd gotten the idea for the lion from some movie they'd seen last summer.

Skye couldn't believe that the inspector had not been able to make the Dooziers get rid of the wild creature. Andrea had explained that it was an old circus animal, and they had all the correct paperwork, so as long as they didn't allow people to actually pet it, there was nothing she could do.

She'd be back the next morning before

the sale opened to make sure the Dooziers had corrected the violations she could enforce. If they hadn't, she could shut them down. Otherwise, Skye was on her own.

The last stop on the inspector's list was the goat cheese stand. It offered quite a contrast to the petting zoo. Here the goats were housed in enclosures nicer than the dorm room in which Skye had spent four years, and cleaner than her present cottage. The owner, Burnett Parnell, clearly doted on the creatures, and he earnestly explained the special diet they required to produce the milk to make the cheese. He eagerly showed them every step of his operation.

After escaping Burnett Parnell, the two women returned to the city hall. Andrea checked out the toilet paper supply before leaving, and Skye wrote her uncle a note about the Dooziers' main — or should she say "mane" — attraction, then returned to her cottage, where she loaded her suitcases and a box of cat supplies into the trunk of the Bel Air.

She had just sat down on the steps to wait for the TV star to arrive when a silver Porsche zoomed into the driveway. The top was down, but all Skye could see of the driver was a stream of raven black hair blowing in the wind.

A Land Rover with a picture of an old trunk half open and spilling out treasure — the TV show's logo — painted on its side, an Audi, and a Honda Civic stopped in a line behind the convertible. Faith and her entourage had arrived.

Skye got up and dusted off the back of her shorts, wishing she had taken the time to change clothes.

The TV star stepped out of the Porsche, and her staff rushed to follow suit, nearly trampling each other to be the first to reach her side. Faith ignored them and adjusted her amethyst off-the-shoulder minidress before marching toward the cottage.

Skye squinted at the approaching celebrity. Her right sleeve appeared to have a fluffy tan cuff that covered her arm from her wrist to the elbow. *Why is she wearing a fur muff in the middle of August?*

Faith stopped in front of Skye, flicked a dismissive glance up and down her body, and said, "Skye Denison is supposed to be meeting me here."

"I'm Skye."

"Oh." Faith gave a brittle little laugh. "Sorry, it's just that Skye is such a pretty name." Her tone left no doubt that the slur was intentional.

Skye felt herself flush but said coolly,

"Why, thank you. My mother will be so relieved that you like it."

Faith narrowed her eyes, then snapped, "Well, I haven't got all day. Show me the house."

"After you." Skye held open the front door and Faith swept past her into the foyer, leaving a trail of lavender scent in her wake. Skye followed, and the TV star's entourage trailed her. So far none of them had spoken, not even to offer introductions.

Faith spared a fleeting look at the guest bath, which opened off the entryway to the right, and an even shorter glance at the kitchen to the left, before striding into the great room.

Standing in the middle of the space, she turned in a half circle, then gestured to the built-in bookshelves lining the outer walls on either side of the glass doors that led out to the patio, which overlooked the river. "This is nice. I could do a lot with this. Have you ever thought of having it professionally decorated?"

Before Skye could reply, the muff on Faith's arm transformed itself into a barking and growling Pomeranian that leapt onto the couch. Bingo, who had been asleep on the sofa cushion, jumped to his feet, arched his back, and hissed a warning.

Faith screamed, and Skye, without thinking, made a grab to save her pet. One of the TV star's entourage pulled her back just before the dog's teeth came down on her wrist. Her rescuer whispered urgently in her ear, "Don't. That little rat will tear your arm off. It's gotten a piece of each one of us at one time or another."

The canine whined in frustration at having missed a chance to rip into Skye's flesh. Bingo saw his opportunity and swiped his enemy across the muzzle. The dog yipped and backed away. Bingo advanced, but the Pomeranian turned tail and bounded back into her mistress's arms, where she glowered at the cat, Skye, and the room in general.

Faith exploded. "What do you mean by having a vicious animal on the premises?"

Skye glared. "Bingo is not vicious, and he'll be coming with me."

"I want him out of here right now. Put him in your car until you're ready to leave."

"No," Skye said in an even tone. "It's too hot for him to wait in the car."

Twin spots of red blazed on Faith's high cheekbones and she turned to the man who had saved Skye from being bitten. "Nick, darling, do something or I'm walking out right now."

"I'll handle it, sweetheart." The man patted Faith's shoulder, taking care to avoid the dog's reach. "Why don't you look at the rest of the cottage?"

The TV star shook her head. "I'm staying right here until this problem is solved to my satisfaction."

The man walked over to Skye. "Hi, I'm Nick Jarvis, the producer/director of *Faith's Finds*. Would it be alright if Jody — she's Faith's personal assistant — sits with your cat in the Land Rover?" He gestured to a nondescript girl in her early twenties dressed in jeans and a T-shirt with the show's logo on the front. "She'll keep the AC running."

Skye nodded. "I'll get his Pet Taxi."

After Skye returned with the plastic crate, put the protesting Bingo inside, and turned the container over to Faith's personal assistant, Nick said, "Shall we continue the tour?"

Faith stuck out her lower lip. "No. Lovie is still too upset."

"Lovie?" *Talk about a misnomer.* Skye raised a skeptical eyebrow. "She looks fine to me." As far as she could see, the dog had wrapped itself around Faith's arm and gone back to sleep.

"That shows how much you know." Faith

raised her chin and looked down her nose. "According to Lovie's Bow-Lingual Dog Translator, she is still very sad." The TV star thrust a small blue receiver at Skye.

Displayed on the tiny digital screen were two closed eyes, a round nose, and a tear-shaped mouth. Skye felt her jaw drop open and it was a while before she managed to ask, "And this device does what exactly?"

Faith pointed to a matching blue microphone/transmitter attached to the dog's collar. "It picks up her barks and sends them to this walkie-talkie thingy. Using the Animal Emotional Analysis System, the device translates the barks into pictures that tell me how she's feeling."

"Now I've seen everything," Skye muttered to herself. She watched as the face on the screen changed. Now the eyes were wide-open ovals and the mouth was curved upward with a tongue hanging out.

Nick took the receiver and turned it back toward Faith. "Look, darling, Lovie's happy again. Let's finish up so she can get settled in."

Without acknowledging Nick, Faith moved into the bedroom and flung open the closet door. She whirled around and announced as if a great tragedy had occurred, "It's not empty."

Skye explained, "I cleared out half the space for your use."

"But I need it all."

"Sorry." Skye shrugged. "This is the best I can do."

Faith's impossibly violet eyes locked onto Skye's emerald-green ones. Neither blinked.

Nick immediately stepped forward. "Five hundred dollars if you remove your clothes."

Skye spun around and sputtered, "I beg your pardon?"

Nick frowned. "I meant the ones in the closet."

Skye thought quickly. Where could she stash them? "Okay, I'll put them on the rod in the utility room." She held out her hand.

"It's a deal." He peeled five one hundred-dollar bills from his money clip and placed them in her palm.

Faith hadn't stuck around for the transaction. She was now in the master bath, standing next to the two steps that led up to the oversized soaking tub and frowning at the oval window that was set high on the wall, positioned so the tub's occupant could lie back and look outside. "That needs to be covered."

"Right." Nick made a note on a small

leather-covered pad. He pointed his Mont Blanc pen at Skye. "You can clean out that closet while we unpack the cars."

While Skye transferred armload after armload of heavy winter clothes to the utility room, she saw Faith's staff bringing in cases of wine and liquor, bags of food, a seven-piece matched set of leather luggage, and an old-fashioned steamer trunk. It looked as if they were moving in for at least a year.

As Skye cleared out the last of her things from the bathroom, she noticed that her everyday white towels had been replaced with expensive plum-colored ones, and on one of her trips to the bedroom she watched as a young man stripped the bed and replaced all the linens with lilac satin sheets and huge down-stuffed bolsters.

He noticed her interest and blushed. "Jody would usually do this, but since she's with your cat . . ." He trailed off, then said, "I'm Kirby Tucker, the head writer."

"That must be interesting." Skye smiled.

He shrugged. "It's a start."

Skye nodded and returned to her task.

She had emptied the closet and was back sitting on the front step when Nick, Kirby, and Faith emerged. She noted that while the others were red-faced, sweaty, and smudged,

Faith looked as if she were ready to step in front of the camera. There wasn't a wrinkle in her dress or a drop of perspiration on her forehead. Skye bet she hadn't lifted a finger except to point to where she wanted something placed.

After the rental agreement was signed and Nick handed Skye the five-thousand-dollar check, she turned over the keys to her cottage, got in the Bel Air, and headed to her parents' house. As she turned the corner onto Basin Street, it dawned on her that she had left something important behind — the confidential files from the high school.

The school board had decided to spiff up the high school by painting the walls and laying new carpeting over the summer. Skye had been directed to pack up everything in her office, so the custodial staff could store it all in the gym. Uncomfortable with allowing confidential files to be set out for three months in just a cardboard box, she'd had her father come by the school with a dolly and his truck and move the office file cabinet to her utility room at home.

Should she turn back and get the cabinet? It was locked and the key was on her school key ring, which was in her briefcase, which was in the trunk of her car.

Surely the files would be safe. Probably no

one would even notice the cabinet. The TV people didn't look like the type to do their own laundry. And if they did see the cabinet, it was locked and they had no reason to care what was inside. She was silly to worry; certainly none of them would break into it just out of idle curiosity.

Chapter 6
Let's Make a Deal

Skye wiped the sweat from her forehead with the bottom of her T-shirt. Wasn't it supposed to get cooler as evening approached? She fumbled in her purse with one hand, searching for the super-sized bottle of Tylenol she had put there the day she took the job as the Route 66 Yard Sale coordinator. The rattling of the few remaining pills reminded her that she needed to buy a replacement before the opening ceremony tomorrow.

After dry-swallowing a couple of caplets, she looked into the rearview mirror at two glowing golden eyes and begged, "We'll be there soon. Please, please, be quiet. I've had a really bad day."

Bingo ignored her entreaty and continued to yowl. He hated his Pet Taxi, he hated riding in the car, and he hated change; and he was currently being subjected to all three.

Skye's head throbbed, and as she turned the Bel Air into her parents' driveway, the ache became worse. It wasn't that she worried about her own welcome; she knew that her mother's second dearest wish in the world was for Skye to move back home (her first wish was for Skye to get married), but May had an unreasonable dislike of animals, especially house pets. Skye was pretty sure that when Dante had arranged for her to stay with her parents for the next ten days, he hadn't mentioned the cat. And when May had agreed, she'd forgotten all about Bingo.

The pea gravel glimmered whitely in the dusk as Skye parked in front of the left side of the large garage. She made sure the right side was unobstructed so her father could get his truck out for his daily six a.m. visit to his mother.

Skye took a deep breath. The night air smelled tantalizingly of freshly mowed grass and hamburgers frying on the grill. Her parents were sitting on the patio near the back door, and the voice of the Cubs' announcer floated up from the portable radio on the table between them. Chocolate, her father's Labrador retriever, lay by Jed's side.

For a minute, the scene looked like a picture painted by Norman Rockwell. Then

75

May spotted the Pet Taxi in Skye's hand and snapped, "You're not bringing that animal in the house. Bad enough I have to put up with Chocolate jumping all over me every time I come outside to empty the garbage or hang clothes on the line."

Skye looked at her father, thinking he might take her side. He shrugged, a sheepish expression on his face. "Up to Ma."

Skye put down the Pet Taxi and Chocolate lumbered to his feet. Skye watched in apprehension as the dog pressed his nose against the wire door. Would Bingo react as antagonistically to Chocolate as he had to Faith's Lovie that afternoon? She held her breath as the animals stared at each other for a moment, then Bingo started to purr and Chocolate flopped down with his head resting on the cat carrier.

While Bingo and Chocolate were reenacting the Peaceable Kingdom painting, Skye's mind was busy. She said to her mom, "If Bingo can't stay here, then I can't either."

May scowled. "Animals do not belong in the house."

"Fine." Skye crossed her arms. "Let's see. What are my options? The motor court is full, Trixie's rented out all of her spare rooms, Vince hasn't got the space for me, and Simon's having the pipes replaced while he's away."

Simon had left that morning for a funeral directors' convention in Sacramento; afterward he was staying with a college friend who lived in the area while he toured Northern California. He'd be gone until a week from Tuesday.

Skye felt a twinge of guilt. She had barely taken time to say good-bye to him the night before. He had wanted Skye to accompany him on the trip, but there was no way she could leave her job just as the sale was about to start.

May's voice broke into Skye's thoughts. "You should have gone with him. What if he meets someone out there?"

Skye refused to be drawn into that discussion. "Let's stick to the real problem rather than worrying about one that could happen." She sighed dramatically. "If Bingo isn't welcome here, I guess we'll have to live in my car."

May gave her daughter a sharp look. "You can't do that. People will talk."

"What else *can* I do if you won't let Bingo stay here?"

May exhaled noisily. "Okay. The cat can stay, but you have to keep him in your bedroom at all times. No roaming."

"Thank you, Mom." Skye reached down for the Pet Taxi, box of supplies, and her suitcase, then hurried into the house before May could change her mind or think of more restrictions. Chocolate woofed his good-bye to Bingo and the cat purred loudly in return.

After settling Bingo with bowls of water and food and filling his litter box, Skye joined her parents on the patio. She sat on the step next to her mother's concrete goose. Skye had long since stopped trying to dissuade May from dressing up the statue, and instead now played a game with herself, predicting May's mood on the basis of what she had chosen for the goose's outfit.

Today it wore little mechanic's overalls and held a wrench in one wing and a tiny placard in the other. The poster read: WHAT'S GOOD FOR THE GOOSE IS GOOD FOR THE GANDER.

Skye whistled under her breath. It could mean only one thing. Her parents were still feuding over the time Jed was spending helping Bunny get her car running. Come to think of it, he'd been working on the project for more than two months. Maybe she should have a talk with her father and find out what was going on. Not tonight, though. After the yard sale. She'd take care of everything after the yard sale.

While Skye was lost in thought, Jed announced from the grill, "Hamburgers are about done, Ma."

May walked over to the bright yellow picnic table Jed had built from scraps of lumber and black pipe. "Skye, grab the potato salad and baked beans from inside, and get yourself something to drink." She tore open a package of paper plates. "I'll be in to get the other stuff in a minute."

After a pleasant but mostly silent dinner they went inside and Jed climbed into his recliner, grabbed the remote, and promptly fell asleep. As soon as the dishes were done, May sat in her chair and followed suit.

Skye curled up on the couch and read her book to the music of her parents' snores. At ten o'clock she pried the TV control from her father's fingers and turned to ABC for the news. She had just settled back into the sofa when the phone rang. Neither of her parents stirred, so after the third ring Skye answered it.

Her Uncle Dante's voice boomed from the receiver, "Get your ass down to the police station right this minute. Wally just arrested Faith Easton."

"I've told this cretin numerous times that I was not trespassing." Faith Easton paced up and down the interrogation room at the Scumble River police station, her mauve high-heeled sandals clicking on the worn linoleum. "I just popped into a few booths to establish the best place to begin filming in the morning. I'm warning you, if I'm not released immediately, I may decide not to do the program after all."

Skye turned to Walter Boyd, the police chief, who stood aloof, ignoring Faith's complaints. Skye and Wally had an unsettled relationship. Due to circumstances beyond their control, they had never dated, but there was a strong underlying attraction between them that influenced their interactions. Since Skye had helped to solve some of Scumble River's most notorious crimes, their relationship had turned downright volatile.

She chose her words carefully. "Wally, what exactly happened?"

He moved closer to her and lightly pushed a stray curl from her cheek to behind her ear. "You requested that I assign extra personnel to the yard sale area, so I had Officer Quirk in the cruiser and borrowed Deputy McCabe from the sheriff's department to patrol on foot."

"Yes, I was afraid that there might be some petty thievery or vandalism." Skye moved back, just out of his reach. She didn't like the way her heart raced at his touch.

For a moment, Wally's shoulder sagged beneath his crisp uniform, but he continued, "About half an hour ago, McCabe radioed dispatch that he was about to investigate a suspicious person skulking around the booths on Basin."

Faith wheeled around. "I was not skulking." Her slight British accent became thicker. "Are you all daft?"

Wally disregarded her. "He found Ms. Easton with the tarp off several tables, taking pictures of the items."

"There. You see." Faith's face glowed with righteous indignation. "That proves I wasn't stealing anything. Now discharge me immediately or I shan't be responsible for the repercussions."

Skye made a scornful noise and asked Wally, "So what happened?"

"McCabe cuffed her and brought her in. Then he called me and I called the mayor."

Skye was tempted to dump this mess back in her uncle's lap, but the thought of the money he was paying her and the chance of owning her own cottage stopped her. Instead she said, "And Uncle Dante called me because he didn't want to be bothered at this time of night."

"Looks that way." Wally's warm brown eyes crinkled in amusement. He had turned forty the previous winter, but if anything he was more handsome than the day he had arrived in Scumble River as a twenty-three-year-old rookie. He radiated a vitality that drew Skye like the powdered sugar on a donut to a black sweater. "We have her on trespassing, but I leave it up to you whether we charge her or not, since the yard sale is your baby."

"Gee, thanks." Skye ignored the flare of attraction, focusing on the matter at hand and considering her options. Dante would kill her if she screwed up the televising of the sale. They couldn't afford to buy advertising like that. On the other hand, she hated to let the insufferable Faith Easton get away with breaking the rules just because of her fame and influence. "Who owned the booths that she was caught messing with?"

Wally consulted his notebook. "Ye Olde Junque Emporium and Cookie's Collectibles."

"Were the owners contacted?"

"Yes. Neither wants to press charges." Wally grinned. "I think they were both thrilled to be singled out by the famous *Faith's Finds* and hope to get on TV."

"Fine. If they don't care, I don't care."

Skye made a washing motion with her hands. "Let her go."

"It's about time." Faith looked around. "Someone will need to fetch my car."

"I'll give you a ride." Skye picked up her purse and turned toward Faith. "You should thank Chief Boyd for handling this matter so diplomatically."

Faith was halfway through the front door but turned back, smiled sweetly, and said, "Bugger off!"

Wally's face froze and Skye wondered what he'd do, but before she could say anything he burst out laughing and said to Skye, "I don't know what her problem is, but I bet it's hard to pronounce."

While Skye giggled at Wally's wisecrack, she examined him closely. The brief return of his ex-wife in February and his milestone birthday in March had been hard on him. There was more silver in his black hair than before, and the lines around his eyes had become permanent. He was still recuperating emotionally from those incidents, but he seemed to have regained his sense of humor, so Skye was hoping for a full recovery.

"Guess I'd better go drive the queen to her carriage." Skye walked to the door and pushed it open.

"Good luck. She probably turns into a pumpkin or maybe a vampire bat at midnight," Wally cautioned.

"Thanks." She looked back and saw the heartrending tenderness of his gaze. Something intense flared through her, but she cleared her throat and pretended not to be affected. "Uh . . . bye. See you later."

"You are so lucky to be out of town this week. Talk about excellent timing." Skye wound the telephone cord around her finger. Thank goodness for the two-hour time difference between California and Illinois. She had nearly forgotten her promise to call Simon, but it was only nine-thirty in Sacramento.

"What's been going on?" Simon's soothing voice washed over her. "We didn't get a chance to talk much last night, since you had to get your cottage ready for that TV star. Are you having a hard time?"

"Oh, no more than usual." Skye tried to sound amusing rather than whiny. "Let's see. So far the mayor's been buried in toilet paper, the TV star has been arrested for trespassing, and I think Mom and Dad may be getting a divorce."

"Boy. You could probably pitch that as a sitcom out here." Simon chuckled. "So tell me how all that has happened in the twelve or so hours I've been gone."

Skye launched into a detailed explanation, ending with, "I forgot to mention that Frannie and Justin are fighting, and I have my suspicions about Trixie and Owen, too."

"Wow. Not a good time for couples in Scumble River. Glad you and I are okay."

"Thank goodness. I couldn't take another crisis right now," Skye declared. She felt comfortable with Simon. Maybe some of the highs had ebbed from their relationship, but there weren't any emotionally draining lows, either, and that was the kind of relationship she wanted. Wasn't it? Her thoughts strayed briefly to the attraction she still felt for Wally, but she firmly shut that door and concentrated on Simon.

"Speaking of a crisis, I think Bunny may be up to something," Simon said. "I hate to ask since I know you're so busy, but if you get a chance, could you drop by the bowling alley and check up on her?"

"Sure. Any idea what she might be doing?" Skye rolled her eyes. Simon always thought his mother was up to something, and of course, he was usually right. She had reentered his life in November after a twenty-year absence and had already managed to become involved in several adventures.

"No." Simon paused. "She just seemed unusually wound up the last time I spoke to her, and there doesn't seem to be a reason for her to be that excited."

"Okay. I'll stop by when I get a chance, and since Dad's been working on her car, I'll see if he's noticed anything." Skye added "check on Bunny" to her mental to-do list. "So, how's the convention?"

"Okay. I spent most of this afternoon at the customized casket show."

"Huh?"

"It's the newest thing in California. Everyone is ordering caskets that reflect their 'essence.' "

"You're kidding."

"No, they have ones that are shaped like various cars — the VW Beetle is very popular, I understand. I also saw ones that looked like swimming pools, pianos, and canopy beds."

"I can just imagine what the people in Scumble River would request." Skye giggled. "They'd want a John Deere tractor, an accordion, and a La-Z-Boy recliner."

Simon chuckled just as the doorbell rang. Who would be ringing her parents' bell at midnight? Scumble River officially closed at ten p.m.

Skye said a quick good-bye to Simon and went to find out.

Chapter 7
Mission: Impossible

"I'm so sorry to bother you at this time of night, but I didn't know who else to turn to and you remind me so much of my daughter, Sterling." Alma Griggs stood on the front steps, wearing a faded rose-print housedress and, despite the heat, a white cotton sweater.

Her face was pale, and when Skye took her hand to guide her inside, her skin was clammy. What in the world had happened? "Don't worry about the time. Please, come in and sit down." Skye settled the old woman on one of the living room chairs. "Let me get you a glass of water."

"That might be a good idea." Mrs. Griggs rested her head on her hands. "I am feeling a bit dizzy."

"Put your head between your knees," Skye suggested as she ran into the kitchen.

When she returned with the drink, Mrs.

Griggs had rested her head on the back of the chair and her eyes were closed. It looked like she was sleeping, or . . . Skye's heart thudded. Surely Mrs. Griggs hadn't died during the minute or so she'd been gone. She cleared her throat. "Uh, here's that water."

The older woman's eyelids fluttered and she straightened, reaching for the glass. "Thank you." After taking a healthy swallow, she said, "I really am sorry to bother you. Did I wake you up?"

"No, not at all. I'm a night owl." Skye pulled up the ottoman and perched at Mrs. Griggs's side. "Now, tell me what's wrong."

"It's that woman. I know it's her, and the police won't do anything about it."

"What woman?"

"Cookie Caldwell." Mrs. Griggs's voice grew stronger with each word. "She's been after me ever since I told everyone about her little scheme to cheat me."

"Really?" Skye knew Mrs. Griggs had *said* she was going to spread the word but Skye'd been so wrapped up in the yard sale the whole summer she hadn't heard a thing. "Let's get back to that later. What happened tonight?"

"Like I do every Friday, I left my house at five on the dot to meet my friends for the

KC fish fry, then after that we went to the GUMB Assembly Hall to play bingo. It starts at seven, and we're usually home around ten, but we were a little earlier tonight because we didn't stop for ice cream. Peg's stomach was upset."

"Okay." Skye wasn't sure where Mrs. Griggs was going with the story, but she decided to let her tell it in her own way. "So, you got home early, and . . ."

"And someone was in my house! I could hear them clomping around upstairs."

"Oh, my." Skye hadn't been expecting that. "What did you do?"

"I know I shouldn't have, but I went in." A faint look of embarrassment settled on Mrs. Griggs's features, but she said defiantly, "I've lived in that house for seventy years, and I have to protect it."

Skye knew that this wasn't the time to argue that wood and bricks were not worth a life, so instead she asked, "What happened then?"

"I grabbed my rifle from the front closet and yelled that I had a gun and wasn't afraid to use it — I've been hunting since I was ten years old, bagged my first deer at twelve." Mrs. Griggs paused to take a sip of water. "Well, whoever was in the house must have gone out the second-story balcony and climbed down the trellis — it's wrought iron and was installed to be used as a way out in case of fire. Anyway I heard more footsteps, then the balcony door squeak — I keep meaning to oil it — then some rustling, and a thud."

"Then you called the police?"

"Well, first I went around back to see who it was."

Skye made a sound of dismay in her throat at the older woman's foolhardiness, realizing at some level that she might have done the same thing herself given the circumstances. Mrs. Griggs reminded Skye a lot of herself. "And who was it?"

"I didn't see her, but it was Cookie Caldwell. I'm sure of it." Mrs. Griggs leaned forward. "That woman has been pestering me to let her look at my things since June when I showed her my vase."

Skye didn't want to get distracted from the chronological events. "Let's hold on to that thought for a minute." She was having trouble following the older woman's story. "After the intruder disappeared, you called the police, right?"

"Right, but it turns out my house is no longer in the city limits, so I had to call the county sheriff's office."

"Did they send a deputy?"

"Yes, someone named McCabe. Seemed about as sharp as a bowling ball. I told him what happened and we looked around, but since nothing was vandalized and the only thing missing was a piece of cheap costume jewelry — but my husband had given it to me for our first anniversary — McCabe said there wasn't much he could do. He filled out a report, but I could tell that it would end up filed under 'Senile Old Woman.' "

"Mmm. So the intruder hadn't messed anything up?"

"Not really. I could tell things weren't where I had them, but my house is pretty full of stuff, so to the police it probably looked just fine."

Skye wasn't sure how to ask the next question. "Um, how were you thinking I could help you?"

"Well, you've solved some crimes in the past, and since you already know Cookie Caldwell, and what she's capable of, I was hoping you'd look into this matter for me. It's obvious the police won't do a thing." Mrs. Griggs suddenly looked every year of her age. "The pin may not have any monetary value, but it was from my husband and it means a lot to me." Before Skye could answer, the older woman continued, "And she's starting to scare me."

Mrs. Griggs's last statement caught Skye by surprise. She would have bet big money that the old lady wasn't afraid of anything. "How?"

"She's relentless." Mrs. Griggs's shoulders slumped. "It started right after the incident with the vase. At first it seemed harmless enough. She came around to the house and apologized. I accepted, but refused her request to take a look at my other things."

"That was probably best."

"Right. Fool me once, shame on you. Fool me twice, shame on me." Mrs. Griggs drained the glass of water. "After that, she started calling me, leaving me notes, following me around downtown."

Skye frowned. "That's terrible."

"And this last week it's gotten worse. Monday, somebody cut my clothesline and all my clean laundry fell into the dirt. Tuesday, when I went out to get my mail, all that was in the box was a pile of ashes. Wednesday, someone put sugar in my gas tank." Mrs. Griggs suddenly grabbed Skye's hand, her nails digging into the palm. "And Thursday, the Virgin Mary disappeared."

"Oh, my." Skye blinked. She was fairly sure Mrs. Griggs was referring to a statue of the Madonna. In Scumble River and the surrounding towns, the figurines were placed in upright bathtubs whose interiors had been painted blue. These homemade shrines were then inserted into the ground as a yard decoration.

"This morning I got a call telling me I was next." Mrs. Griggs released Skye's hand and collapsed back in her seat.

"Then tonight someone broke into your house." Skye brought the chain of events to its alarming conclusion.

"Yes."

"Did you tell the deputy all this?"

Mrs. Griggs nodded. "McCabe said they'd keep an eye out, but he didn't seem too impressed."

"Is there anyone you could go visit for a while? A friend or relative who lives out of town? How about your daughter?" Skye was trying to figure out what she could do. Maybe after the yard sale she'd have time to watch Cookie and catch her in the act.

"No! I'm not running away." Mrs. Griggs shook her head. "Besides, I don't have anyone. Neither Mr. Griggs nor I had any siblings, so no nieces or nephews. He had a few distant cousins, but I stopped hearing from them years ago. I'm sure they must all be dead by now. And my daughter, Sterling, was killed in a car crash in 1969. I don't have anyone."

"I was born in 1969," Skye murmured without thinking.

"I knew it." Mrs. Griggs straightened. "What month?"

"December."

"That's the month she died." Mrs. Griggs took Skye's hands and stared intently into her eyes. "You're going to think I'm a silly old woman, but you have the same hair, eyes, body type; even your voice sounds the same. I'm sure you're Sterling reincarnated."

"Now, Mrs. Griggs, really, I'm not your daughter come back to life." Skye gently removed her hands from the woman's grip. "You don't really believe that, do you?"

"Yes, I do." A stubborn expression had settled on Mrs. Griggs's face. "And that's why you're going to help me."

Skye knew she'd be sorry, but she said, "I'm going to help you because I like you, not because I'm your dead daughter." Before Mrs. Griggs could protest, Skye continued, "I'll talk to Wally tomorrow and try to convince him to speak to Cookie, even though it isn't his jurisdiction. If that doesn't work, I'll have a little chat with her myself. But I really can't do much more until the yard sale is over."

"I understand, dear." Mrs. Griggs got up.

"You do what you can, and give me a call when you have a chance."

"Would you like to stay here tonight?" Skye asked. "My bed has fresh sheets and I could sleep on the couch."

"No, I'll be fine."

Skye walked the old woman to the door. "I'll call you sometime tomorrow, but you can phone here anytime. My mom will track me down."

"Thank you, dear."

As Mrs. Griggs went down the front steps, Skye abruptly wondered how the woman had known she was staying at her parents and called out, "How did you find me?"

"That TV star moving into your cottage was the talk of the KC fish fry, and your grandma mentioned at the bingo game you were staying with your folks for the duration." Mrs. Griggs waved. "Good night, Sterling."

Skye shook her head as she watched Mrs. Griggs climb into an ancient Lincoln and drive off. Imagine Mrs. Griggs thinking that Skye was her reincarnated daughter. Still, Skye had felt an immediate connection with the older woman, almost a sense of having known her before. Skye shook her head again. No, that kind of thinking was silly.

Mrs. Griggs was just a lonely old lady who missed her daughter. Skye felt sorry for her. There was nothing supernatural in that.

The Route 66 Yard Sale officially started at eight a.m. Skye was in her office and on the phone by six. Her first calls were to all the other towns participating. No one was officially in charge of the whole sale; each town had its own coordinator, who took care of his or her section, but Dante had been the driving force behind the idea, so keeping an eye on the entire event fell to Skye.

By seven-fifteen she had talked to the people in charge in Elwood, Wilmington, Braidwood, Godley, Braceville, Gardner, Brooklyn, Dwight, Odell, Pontiac, Chenoa, Lexington, Towanda, and Funks Grove. The larger cities of Joliet and Normal had declined to participate, although their hotels and restaurants were happy to accommodate the people pouring in for the sale.

When Skye finished her last phone call, she stood and adjusted the official Route 66 Yard Sale black-and-white baseball cap on her head, then tucked the matching T-shirt into her black shorts, made sure her tennis shoes were tied tightly, and clipped her walkie-talkie to her belt.

Before leaving for the sale's grand opening, she went next door to the police station to talk to Wally about Alma Griggs and Cookie Caldwell, but she was told Wally was already out patrolling the yard sale. She would have to catch him sometime later in the day.

During the short golf cart ride to the ribbon-cutting ceremony, Skye went over her mental to-do list. After the opening, she wanted to make a circuit of the booths to see that they were having a smooth start. She especially needed to check on the Doozier Petting Zoo. She just knew that lion would cause trouble. Her only hope was that the Dooziers had not made the necessary improvements and the inspector had closed them down.

As Skye pulled up to the black-and-white-checkered ribbon stretched across Maryland Street at Kinsman, Skye caught her breath. Behind the barricades, as far as she could see, was a wall of people. She looked at her watch. It was only seven-thirty, half an hour before the sale would open. How long had these people been gathering, and what had they done with all their cars?

Skye had gotten permission from the owner of the out-of-business aerosol can factory on the corner of Scumble River Road and Route 66 to use that site as a parking lot, but would that be enough? And if it wasn't, what would happen?

Although the main opening ceremony was to take place in Scumble River, most of the small towns along the route were having their own ribbon cuttings. Skye wondered briefly what kind of crowds had gathered for them, and would consequently be wending their way toward Scumble River later in the day.

Her thoughts were interrupted by one of the part-time policemen that Wally had called in for the sale. "Ma'am? You're in charge here, right?"

"Yes, officer." Skye smiled at the young man, even though she hated being called "ma'am." He didn't look much more than eighteen and seemed extremely uncomfortable in his uniform. "Can I help you?"

"We're diverting traffic around Maryland by taking them north on Kinsman, then west on Springfield, and back south on Rosemary Road."

Skye nodded, wondering why he was giving her a geography lesson.

"Well, the sale hasn't even started yet and traffic is already backed up as far as Brooklyn. The police there just called and asked us to kindly get the galldarn cars moving. What should we do?"

Skye chewed her lip. She had no idea what to suggest. First of all, her sense of direction was awful, and second, she had not considered this scenario. "Have you checked with the chief?"

"Yep. He said to see what you wanted to do."

Great. Depending how you looked at it, either she had Wally's full confidence or he was throwing the whole mess in her lap. She made a snap decision. "Okay, instead of diverting them all to the north, have every other car go south on Kinsman, west on Stebler, and take the old bridge over to Rolling Water Road. Then if they want to go on to Dwight they can go south, and if they want to come back toward Scumble River they can go north."

The officer looked doubtful. "That old bridge can only take one vehicle at a time."

"Yes, I know, but one is better than none."

He pulled on his cap. "Yes, ma'am."

Before she could reconsider her decision, Dante pulled up in his own golf cart. Beside him, his wife, Olive, sat as if someone had stuck a pole down the back of her dress. Her short ash blond hair was sprayed into a helmet that the NFL would have envied.

Her pink shoes and handbag precisely matched the flowers in her dress and the pearls on her ears, throat, and finger.

Olive looked around anxiously before getting out of the cart. She had moved to Scumble River from Chicago more than forty years ago when she married Dante, but she still seemed ill at ease among the natives.

Dante waddled up to Skye, Olive trailing him, and demanded, "Is everything ready?"

"Good morning to you, too, Uncle Dante." Skye smiled sweetly. "Yes, it is a lovely day, even if it is a little on the hot side, but we are so lucky it isn't raining."

"So, is everything ready?" Dante repeated, raising his voice.

Obviously her uncle was not learning from her attempt to model courteous behavior, so Skye tried another behavior-management technique — ignoring him. "And how are you today, Aunt Olive? You look lovely, as always." Skye leaned forward and kissed her aunt's soft cheek. Olive smelled of old-fashioned face powder and attar of roses.

Olive patted Skye's hand, then cut her eyes at her husband before stammering, "Thank you, dear. I'm fine."

Dante gritted his teeth and snarled,

"Good morning. Now will you tell me if everything is ready?"

Skye nodded. "We're all set." She guided her aunt and uncle to the small portable platform and helped them onto it, then handed Dante a microphone. She turned and nodded to a high school boy she had recruited from the audiovisual club to run the PA system. He flipped the switch and held up his thumb.

Skye looked at her watch. The second hand was just sweeping the twelve. It was precisely eight o'clock. She turned to Dante and cued him. "Now."

While Dante started with the usual thanking of everyone and their dog for helping, Skye scanned the audience. Faith and her TV crew were in the front row taping the mayor's welcoming speech. Skye wondered idly how much of his talk would end up on the cutting-room floor. She spotted her parents and brother near the middle, and not too far from them was Trixie. Mrs. Griggs sat off to one side on a lawn chair with several other Scumble River senior citizens.

Directly behind the seniors was a group of the town's merchants, including Cookie Caldwell. Skye grimaced and looked around. Several police officers were scattered through the throng, but no sign of the chief. As soon as Dante finished, she really had to find Wally and talk to him about the Cookie/Mrs. Griggs situation.

Although by a quirk of rezoning Mrs. Griggs now lived outside the city limits, Skye knew she would have better luck persuading Wally, rather than the sheriff, to do something to protect the old woman. Besides her personal relationship with Wally, he regarded the town's citizens as his people, while Scumble River was only one small part of the sheriff's kingdom.

Dante paused and the spectators applauded. He then began his closing. "Route 66 is no longer an official highway, and perhaps because of this, it has gained an aura that attracts hundreds if not thousands of people every year to try and follow it from beginning to end. Much like Marilyn Monroe and James Dean, it is more revered now than when it was 'alive.' The legend is more than the reality. The invented past has more meaning to people because it can be anything you want it to be. Because of this, we who live along a small stretch of this magic thoroughfare want to honor it, and we do so today by welcoming you to the First Annual Route 66 Yard Sale. A hundred miles of fun, entertainment, and treasures."

The crowd went wild, clapping and whistling. Skye was stunned. The one thing her uncle had not ordered her to write and, in fact, wouldn't let her see, had been his welcoming speech. She had been sure it would be boring and self-congratulatory, and the first half had lived up to her expectations, but the closing was amazing. Who knew her uncle had that kind of romantic oratory in him? It was a reminder that she should try to be less judgmental about people.

Feeling chastised, she went to help her aunt and uncle step down from the platform. Once they were safely on the ground and she had given orders for the dais to be moved away, she hugged Dante and said, "That was a wonderful speech. You brought tears to my eyes."

He stiffened in surprise, then hugged her back and said, "Never forget, there's a fine line between bull's-eye and bullshit, and I am a master archer."

With that, Dante and Olive walked over to the ribbon. Skye handed him a huge pair of gold scissors and stepped aside. He cut the ribbon and welcomed everyone again. Then, before the police moved the saw-horses, he and Olive got into their golf cart, waved, and drove away.

Skye stood on the sidelines as the crowd

was allowed through the barricade and onto the rest of Maryland Street. After the majority of the horde had spread out among the sale tables, Skye got into her own golf cart and started to make the rounds. The Lemonade ShakeUp stand was already doing a brisk business and she waved to Justin, who was manning the window.

People were three-deep at most of the tables, and the vendors were working frantically to both sell to and keep an eye on the buyers. Skye noticed that Cookie's table was mobbed and she was working it alone.

Everything seemed to be running smoothly downtown, so Skye headed over to the bridge to check out the west side of the sale. Her godfather, Charlie Patukas, had allowed the Boy Scouts to use the front part of his motor court parking lot for their booth. Across the road and down a little, Skye's brother, Vince, had set up a table in front of Great Expectations, his styling salon, and was selling hair care products.

So far, so good. Skye turned the cart around to go back through town and examine the other side of the sale — the many booths and stands outside the cordoned-off area that were spread from Scumble River Road to Kinsman Street. Included in that group were both the Dooziers' Petting Zoo and Skye's own family's Denison/Leofanti Farm Stand.

The Dooziers were like a pair of children's scissors — eye-catching and colorful but not too sharp. When one added Skye's own family to the mix, many of whom were a beer short of a six-pack, it was clear why she had dubbed this the Wild West, even though geographically it lay east of town. As she crossed the barrier, she felt as if she should strap on a six-shooter and grab her rifle before venturing into such untamed territory. In her head she could hear an ancient warning: Beware! Past this point there be monsters.

Chapter 8
Survivor: Scumble River

Skye felt herself relax. Everything seemed fine as she rode through the sale. The fields on either side of the road were full of sellers, and people wandered from table to table, browsing through the merchandise. Many vendors were locals, peddling crafts, homemade and homegrown goodies, and the contents of their barns and attics, but an equal number were professional dealers who had rented space from the land-owners.

Cars were inching forward, many pulling small trailers intended to haul the loot they purchased back home. The yard sale organizers had hoped to attract ten thousand people; if today was any indication, they might double their goal.

Skye tensed up again as she steered her golf cart around the big curve. On her right was the Doozier Petting Zoo. She knew that family would be up to something. The question was what?

She squinted, not believing her eyes. Where was the chaos? Where was the commotion?

Earl Doozier sat at the card table calmly taking money for admission. He was dressed in a respectable pair of shorts and his shirt actually had a collar. He had even combed his hair, although the part was crooked and he had enough hair grease on it to lubricate a semi.

Everything was in order. This couldn't be right. But it was. The people coming out of the attraction seemed as happy as those going in. Skye listened intently; there was no screaming or yelling — the scene was almost . . . bucolic. She frowned. Should she stop and check things out more closely? No. Why press her luck? She waved at Earl and kept going.

She had just taken a gulp from her water bottle when she approached the Denison/Leofanti Farm Stand. The liquid spewed out of her mouth and down the front of her T-shirt as she saw her mother smash an entire blueberry pie into Faith Easton's face.

For an instant Faith froze, blueberries oozing down her cheeks and onto her white silk blouse. Then she wiped the fruit and crust out of her eyes, flinging the mess into the spectators who had crowded around to watch the excitement. There were screams, and people jumped back as if the TV star had hurled acid into their faces.

Uttering a high-pitched war cry, Faith grabbed a pitcher of iced tea and emptied it over May's head.

May's hair clung to her like a rubber swim cap, and her white tank top was now transparent. She pulled the soaked cotton fabric away from her breasts and turned from side to side, looking for a weapon of mass destruction.

Skye stomped on the golf cart's brake and was off and running before the vehicle had come to a complete halt. As she raced toward the food fight, she looked frantically for reinforcements. Someone else from the family should be manning the stand along with May. Her relatives had agreed to work in pairs.

Skye spotted one of her cousins backed as far away from the fracas as possible. At first she wasn't sure which identical twin it was, but since Gillian had just had a baby in the spring and still carried a little extra weight, Skye was pretty sure the coward deserting May in her time of need was Ginger.

Just before she reached the mêlée, someone grabbed her arm and said, "Hold on there. You don't want to mess up our shot, do you?"

For the first time, Skye noticed that the TV crew was taping the scuffle. Nick Jarvis, Faith's producer/director, gave her a half-smile.

"Yes, I do," she stated, trying to wiggle out of his grasp. "If you show this on TV, my family will —"

"Sue us? Just try."

She gave him a mocking look. "City people sue. Here in Scumble River we like our revenge a little more personal. Every man has a shotgun and knows where all the abandoned mine shafts are. We won't sue you, we'll just make you disappear."

Nick dropped her arm as if it had turned into a python and backed away, yelling, "Cut!" to the cameraman.

By the time Skye had elbowed her way to the table, the two women had come to a standoff. Each held her chosen missile, a coconut cream pie for May and a double fudge rum cake for Faith. Skye knew she had to say something quickly before the desserts became airborne.

She yelled, "Put down your weapons and no one will get hurt." Neither combatant paid the least attention to her. She tried again. "Come on, now. You don't want to do this." Not a flicker of an eyelash from either warrior. Skye played her trump card. "Faith, you do realize that your crew is taping this and you look absolutely ridiculous?"

The TV star risked a glance to her side, and when she saw the camera she shrieked, "I'm going to murder that swine!"

Faith lowered the cake and May followed suit, but Skye felt it would still be a good idea to separate the two. She had just stepped between them when May said, "I don't see how she ever got on TV. She's about as bright as a twenty-watt lightbulb and as pretty as a dust bunny."

Faith glared. "Is that right? Well, you people seem to think that the four major food groups consist of beer, chips, sugar, and Jell-O salad with marshmallows."

Skye closed her eyes. Trust her mother to snatch controversy from the jaws of compromise. Suddenly she realized her own ill-advised position and her eyes flew open, but it was too late. The desserts had already been launched and Skye became a casualty of friendly fire as her mother's pie hit her full in the face.

After Faith's entourage finally pulled the TV star away, Skye turned to her mother and demanded, "What in God's green earth were you thinking? Do you realize they were filming you? You're lucky if you don't end up on *America's Funniest Home Videos*."

May paused in scooping ice out of her cleavage. "That woman has been bugging the crap out of me since she got here."

Skye raised an eyebrow. "She's only been here for one day. When did you see her?"

"She was here yesterday morning while we were setting up the booth. She kept trying to buy things before we could even get the stuff on the tables. She wrestled a marble-topped table right out of your Uncle Wiley's hands. For a tiny little thing she's strong as an ox."

"Oh." Skye had thought Faith had arrived in Scumble River in the afternoon. Now she wondered when exactly the TV star had entered the town.

"And she was trying to cheat us." May finished de-icing her chest and started to towel-dry her hair. "I looked all the really old stuff up, just like you told me to, and made a list of what it should sell for. She offered us five dollars for all those silk pillow shams your grandpa got in World War II, and according to that *Antiques Roadshow* book, they're worth from fifty to a hundred bucks a piece."

Skye soothed. "I warned you that everyone's going to try and get a bargain."

May's expression was mulish. "Well, we told her no and then I found her here nosing around this morning before the yard sale even opened up. She was trying to convince your cousin Ginger to let her have a whole box of salt and pepper shakers for ten dollars, and I know each pair is worth more than that."

"Mmm." Skye knew May would never get mad enough to throw baked goods over mere money. "What did she really do to tick you off?"

"She said my piecrust wasn't flaky." May's lower lip thrust out. "And she said it in front of everyone."

Skye nodded. She should have guessed. There were only two things that would make her mother lose her temper to that extreme. One was to insult her culinary skills. Still, she thought there had to be something more for May to waste good food. "What else?"

May suddenly found the area she had began to sweep fascinating. She answered without lifting her gaze from the broom. "She called you fat."

Ah, the second thing that would cause May to lose her temper — an insult to one of her children.

Skye put her arm around her mother and teased, "Then she has to die. Shall I take care of it or will you?"

May shook with giggles. "I think that's a mother-daughter activity. We'll do it together."

It took Skye a good hour to calm her mother, help clean up and restock the booth, and then stop at her parents' house to wash and change clothes. It was nearly eleven a.m. by the time she returned to the sale.

She still had not spoken to either Wally or Cookie about Mrs. Griggs. Her walkie-talkie was connected only to Dante and the high school kids she had hired for toilet paper patrol, so she couldn't contact Wally by that method. She decided to head back downtown, make a quick stop at the police department, and then go on to the Cookie's Collectibles table.

Wally was not at the station, but the dispatcher agreed to radio him to meet Skye at the Lemonade ShakeUp. That way she could check up on the school newspaper's stand at the same time, and as an added bonus it was directly across the street from Cookie's.

Skye enjoyed zipping around on a golf

cart rather than having to maneuver her bulky Bel Air. As she rolled around the corner onto Maryland, she waved to a flock of teenagers who stood in a blankly staring row, too cool to wave back. It was always interesting to see if anyone would acknowledge her presence. No luck today. None of them so much as twitched a muscle or flicked a lash.

She was shaking her head at the thought that these were all kids who had snuck into her office to talk to her at one time or another but who wouldn't admit her existence outside of school, when she heard the first howl. It sounded like it was coming from farther down the street. She stepped on the accelerator, and the little cart shot forward.

The noise grew as she neared the end of the block. There, once again, in the middle of a free-for-all, was Faith. She had changed clothes after the food fight and now, dressed in a fresh suit, stood in front of a table constructed from sawhorses and pieces of plywood.

It was clearly a makeshift stand where a local was selling items from his attic or basement. There was no rhyme or reason to the stuff being offered — bedpans were stacked next to strings of Christmas lights, and old doorknobs filled beer steins.

Faith and a woman wearing a Harry Potter T-shirt, green polka-dot shorts, and laceless tennis shoes, and sporting a fluffy red bow in her hair, were in a tug-of-war over what looked like a life-size plastic statue of Dennis the Menace.

People had chosen sides and were cheering for their favorite. Faith had the numbers behind her, but Miss Red Bow's supporters were more vocal.

One of that faction screamed, "Give it up, TV star. Ain't you got enough stuff? Let one of the little people have something."

Faith never lost focus, and with one mighty tug she pulled the prize from her opponent's hand. In doing so she landed on her derrière in the dirty street, but she quickly hopped up, dug a roll of money from her pocket, and shoved a five-dollar bill at the awestruck seller. Yelling "Keep the change" over her shoulder as she hurried away.

Skye could see the price tag clearly marked "$3". She could also see the huge dirt stain on the seat of Faith's expensive lilac skirt. Now Skye understood why the celebrity traveled with so much luggage; she obviously went through an outfit an hour.

No one appeared to be hurt, and Miss Red Bow's followers were consoling her, so

Skye ran after Faith. When she caught up with her, the TV star was stashing the treasure in the back of the Land Rover, one of the few vehicles allowed on the closed-off street.

"What was that all about?" Skye asked.

Faith's tone was cool. "It's nothing. A misunderstanding."

"Wrestling someone for a plastic doll is nothing?"

"I had my hand on the piece when that creature tried to steal it from beneath my very nose."

"So, you both tried to pick up the same item at the same time," Skye persisted. "What's so important about it?" She could see a struggle going on behind Faith's eyes. "Go ahead. You know you're dying to tell me."

Faith gave a tiny shrug and said, "Alright. Why not?" She brought out the article in question and pointed. "This is an original 1950s fiberglass statue of Speedy, the Alka-Seltzer boy. Smaller figurines similar to this one routinely go for three hundred to five hundred dollars. I can easily get four or five thousand for one this size."

"And you only gave the seller five dollars?"

"It was nearly double what he was asking for."

Skye shook her head. She knew she'd never be able to explain morality to Faith. "Did the other woman know its value?"

"Please." Faith gave her a mean smile. "Considering her appearance, no doubt she thought it was a garden gnome."

Skye decided not to go down that path, considering her own mother's predilection for dressing a concrete goose. Instead she said, "Look, if I catch you disrupting the sale one more time, I'll have to bar you from it."

Faith sneered. "I rather doubt your mayor would allow that." She turned to her crew, who had gathered while she and Skye were talking. "I'll meet you back here after lunch," she told them. "I need to go change."

As the star left, Kirby Tucker, the writer, stage-whispered to Jody Iverson, Faith's personal assistant, "I thought she had to wait for a full moon to do that."

Jody snickered and they strolled off.

Skye had finally connected with Wally and they were strolling among the mob that engulfed the corner of Maryland and Kinsman streets, taking in the sights. So far they had seen a guy with a dining room table strapped to his back and a woman trying to pile the matching chairs on top, an elderly man screaming at his wife, who was in the midst of selling his dentures, and a child standing on a sale table with a sign around his neck that read, MAKE ME AN OFFER!

Skye really hoped that last one was a joke, but since Wally didn't seem concerned, she didn't investigate. Besides, she had to concentrate on getting Wally to help Mrs. Griggs.

"And after the Virgin Mary disappeared, Mrs. Griggs got a call saying she was next." Skye paused to take a bite of her hot dog. After she chewed and swallowed, she demanded, "How can you say she's not in any danger?"

"I didn't," Wally replied. "What I said was there isn't much I can do about it. Her house is outside my jurisdiction." Stopping to inspect a group of teens who had surrounded one of the sellers, he caught the eye of their leader and shook his head. A moment later the kids had miraculously melted into the crowd, and he continued, "McCabe suggested she stay with someone for a while, but she refused to budge. The sheriff's department can't very well put a guard on her twenty-four seven, especially with the yard sale going on."

Skye knew Wally was right. "So, there's nothing the police can do?"

"Not until a crime has been committed." Wally took a gulp of his lemonade. "The county dispatchers were told to keep an eye out for her number, and the deputies were told to take extra swings by her house, but that's about it."

"Did anyone talk to Cookie?"

"Of course, but she denies everything."

"I have a bad feeling about this."

"Me, too." Wally ran his fingers through his hair. "Mrs. Griggs isn't the only one who has complained about Cookie."

"Really? What else has she done?"

"Mostly it seems she gets obsessed by something and can't let it go. I don't think she's very stable." Wally's attention was drawn to the line in front of a Port-A-Potty, where several men were shouting at each other. "I'd better go break that up." He gave her an affectionate smile and a one-armed hug before sprinting off.

Skye frowned. Why had Wally suddenly started touching her so much? And why didn't she tell him to stop? Was her attraction to the police chief growing? She'd thought she had those feelings under control. And what about Simon?

Before she could figure out an answer, she noticed someone familiar in the center of the toilet dispute. Wait a minute. Wasn't

120

that Nick Jarvis? She shook her head. Those TV people couldn't even go to the bathroom without causing a commotion.

Skye's talk with Wally had increased her determination to have a chat with Cookie, but once again the shop owner's tables were swamped with customers and she was manning them alone. Skye bit her lip. She'd just have to wait. In the meantime, maybe she could fulfill her promise to Simon and check in on Bunny.

Skye retrieved the golf cart from its parking spot near the Lemonade ShakeUp stand and headed down Basin Street toward the bowling alley. As she neared the Altar and Rosary Society barbecue tent, she heard a familiar British accent and slowed down.

Faith had cornered Alma Griggs between the cashier and the entrance.

Skye pulled up just in time to hear the TV star say, "But, my dear, it is of paramount importance that you allow me a glimpse of your fabulous home. I have it on good authority that you have some spectacular objets d'art from around the world."

"No." Mrs. Griggs frowned and seemed to be staring at Faith's chest.

"I could pop in for just a moment, any time that's convenient."

"What part of 'no' don't you understand?" The older woman craned her neck, still appearing to be looking at the celebrity's chest.

"But —"

Skye hopped out of the cart and cleared her throat. She tried to make out what Mrs. Griggs was looking at, but all she could see was a lilac suit jacket and Faith's long black hair.

Faith glanced at Skye, then thrust a card into the older woman's fingers. "I implore you, ring me up before you allow anyone else to make an offer." With a pious look she said, "You know, there are some unscrupulous dealers around who won't play fair with you as I shall."

Skye snorted, and Mrs. Griggs let the bit of pasteboard fall to the ground. Faith's face flushed an unbecoming shade of terra-cotta before she stomped off.

One of the unsuspecting Altar and Rosary ladies called to her as she walked in front of the cashier's counter, "Miss, wouldn't you like a nice barbecue lunch?"

The TV star turned on her. "Are you mad? I wouldn't eat this slop if you offered me an original N. C. Wyeth. You people seem to think the only spices in the world are salt, pepper, and ketchup." Her expression furious, she stormed off.

"Oh, my." The church lady picked up a paper fan and waved it vigorously in front of her face.

Skye asked Mrs. Griggs, "Are you okay?"

"I'm fine. I just wish I knew why everyone is suddenly so interested in my things."

"Maybe it's time to bring in a professional appraiser."

Mrs. Griggs nodded. "I've made an appointment for a week from Monday."

"Good." Skye waved good-bye. "I'll see you later."

Skye glanced at her watch. It had been nearly an hour since her last attempt to talk to Cookie; maybe she'd be a little less busy now. Bunny could wait.

Making a three-point turn, Skye went back down Basin and turned onto Maryland. Cookie had a prime location on the corner in front of her store. The crowd had thinned a little, but there were still quite a few people browsing.

While Skye parked the golf cart, she made a decision. This time she would wait and nab Cookie the second she had a free moment.

At the booth, Skye scanned the length of the tables and spotted Cookie near the far end talking with someone. Although Skye couldn't quite see who the other person was or hear what was being said, she was pretty sure they were arguing, since Cookie was shaking a finger and her face was beet red.

Skye tried to edge around the large man obscuring her view, but as he turned and saw her, recognition dawned in his eyes. "Miss Denison, I haven't seen you since February. Where you been keeping yourself?"

She groaned to herself, but pasted a smile on her face and tried to gauge his mood. Nate Turner was one of the more volatile parents she worked with. "Oh, here and there. How's Nathan doing?"

"Great. That program you recommended straightened him out. He'll be back at school this year."

"Good." Skye tried once again to get past the man's bulk. "Tell him if he needs anything, just stop by my office or put a note in my box."

"I'll do that." Nate awkwardly patted her shoulder. "Thanks." He waved and moved on.

Skye scooted into the space he had vacated, but whoever had been quarreling with Cookie had gone, and all Skye saw was Cookie sitting alone with tears streaming down her face.

Chapter 9
Car 54,
Where Are You?

"It was so frustrating." Skye twisted the telephone cord as she lay across the bed in her old room at her parents' house, talking to Simon. "When I finally got to speak to Cookie, all I ended up doing was consoling her."

"Why? What happened?"

Skye had already told him about Mrs. Griggs's break-in and the older woman's fear of Cookie. "It was sad. After how awful Cookie was to me in June, I never thought I'd feel sorry for her, but I do." Skye pictured the shop owner huddled on a folding chair, sobbing. "She just kept saying over and over, 'Everyone I've ever loved or trusted has betrayed me.' "

"But what does that have to do with Mrs. Griggs?"

"That's the frustrating part. All Cookie would say about her was that sometimes

125

when she really wants something, like to see the contents of Mrs. Griggs's house, she can't stop herself from going after it, again and again, even when she knows it's useless and she should quit."

"She sounds a little unstable."

"That was definitely my diagnosis, and that's what Wally said, too. Seems Mrs. Griggs isn't the first person she's done this to in Scumble River."

"But the police can't arrest Cookie for anything?"

"Nope. It's doubtful Mrs. Griggs could even get a restraining order. And it complicates matters that her house is now outside the city limits." Skye carefully phrased her next statement. Simon had gotten a lot better about her investigations, but she knew he still worried about her. "You know, the sheriff won't take the same kind of personal interest Wally would take. That's why Mrs. Griggs wants me to help her."

There was a long pause before Simon asked, "What are you going to do?"

"I really don't know, but after the yard sale I'll figure something out."

"I'll help you when I get back."

"Thanks." Skye stroked Bingo's soft fur as he nestled against her side and he started to purr in his sleep. Somehow Simon's kindness was making her feel worse. Maybe it was because she'd been feeling more and more attracted to Wally.

"You've certainly had a busy day, what with that TV star's antics and Mrs. Griggs's problems." Simon's voice dropped a notch. "Too bad I'm not there. I'll bet a massage or a moonlight swim would lower your stress level."

"Now you're just being mean, tempting me with something I can't have." Skye's thoughts flew to a few weeks ago when Simon had borrowed a friend's cabin in Wisconsin and they had spent most of a long weekend indulging in those activities. She'd had a good time, but even then, deep in her heart, she'd felt something was missing.

"Do you want me to come back? You said you didn't mind me being gone, but if you need me . . ." Simon's voice trailed off.

"Like I said before, we wouldn't have any time together. Anyway, where would you stay? Your house is uninhabitable by now. And I know you've been looking forward to seeing your old friend. Besides, you promised to be Spike's partner in that bridge tournament next weekend. You can't back out on that."

The words rushed out, surprising Skye. She paused. Didn't she want Simon to come home? Of course she did. It was just . . . just that she didn't want to ruin his trip. That was the reason. She was almost sure of it. Realizing the silence was growing awkward, she hurried to fill it by changing the subject. "Are you having a good time at the convention?"

"It's always interesting to see the new merchandise that's being offered," he replied. "Today I bought a license plate holder that says MY OTHER CAR IS A HEARSE."

"You aren't going to put that on your Lexus, are you?"

"Maybe," Simon teased, then turned serious and asked, "You didn't get a chance to check on Bunny, did you?"

"No, I'm sorry. I tried a couple times, but kept getting waylaid." Skye felt guilty. She knew Simon was worried about his mother. "Before I knew it, it was five o'clock and I had to meet Mom for Mass, since we'll both be tied up tomorrow morning and won't be able to go then."

"That's okay. I know you're busy. Whenever you get a chance is fine."

"I'll do it sometime tomorrow for sure."

They talked for a while longer, then Simon said, "I better let you go so you can get some sleep. It must be nearly midnight there."

Skye swallowed a yawn. "Yep, it'll probably be another long day tomorrow. But I'm sure things will go better."

Six a.m. Skye heard the back door snick closed as her father left the house on his way to his daily visit with his mom. A half hour later, the door shut again. This time it would be May leaving to help set up the Denison/Leofanti booth, which was opening at seven rather than eight like the rest of the sale. The two families had decided to sell coffee and homemade donuts to the presale crowd, which consisted mostly of vendors and a few buyers who would also arrive early to beat everyone else to the treasures.

Skye turned over and snuggled into her pillow; she could sleep another half hour. She didn't have to be anywhere until eight today.

"Meow." Jed's departure had woken Bingo, who stood by his food bowl, demanding breakfast.

"Go back to sleep."

Thump. Bingo had jumped on the bed. A few seconds later his cold nose pressed against Skye's warm one. "Meow."

After several more attempts to persuade the cat it wasn't breakfast time yet, she threw back the sheet and got up. A can of

Fancy Feast tuna later, Bingo permitted Skye to leave the room.

She adjusted the hot water of the shower so it pummeled her back. Moving so the spray could reach her sore derrière — the golf cart seat was not well padded — she sighed and tried to block out the to-do list that was dancing in her head.

Today she had promised to take shifts at both the Lemonade ShakeUp booth and the family farm stand. Skye wondered if Frannie and Justin were on speaking terms, and decided that since the disputed concert was tonight, they probably weren't.

Skye abandoned all thoughts about Scumble River's teen romance when the bathroom door slammed open and May burst into the room. Even through the fogged-up and water-splashed glass door of the shower, Skye could see that her mother's face was ashen and her breathing irregular.

"What's wrong?" Skye leapt out of the shower and grabbed her mother, who was swaying as if she was about to pass out. Skye looked anxiously for a place to sit May down. She finally closed the toilet seat with her foot and eased her onto it.

"She's dead."

"Grandma?" Cora Denison was eighty-four, but she was healthy.

May shook her head, then suddenly vomited into the trash can next to the toilet.

"Aunt Kitty?" Skye thrust a washcloth at her mother, anxiously trying to remember who was on coffee and donut duty this morning at the family stand. She thought it had been only been her mom, her aunt, and her grandmother.

"No." May wiped her mouth and mumbled, "Cookie Caldwell."

"What?" Skye nearly screamed the question.

"She fell on Grandma, but we shoved her back in." May reached for the trash can and was sick again.

"Back in where?" Skye demanded.

"The liquor cabinet."

Skye was beginning to feel like maybe she had never woken up, and this was one of those stress dreams where no matter how hard you try, you can't make sense of what's happening. After all, she was standing there naked, and nudity was often an element in such nightmares.

Maybe if she had some clothes on it would all make sense. She grabbed her robe and struggled into it, her wet skin sticking to the cotton, then said, "Are you all right, Mom?"

May nodded and wiped her mouth again.

"Are you sure she's dead?"

May's complexion took on a greenish cast, but she only swallowed loudly and said, "Yes. There was blood all over her, and she was stiff as an ironing board."

"Oh, my God." Skye forced down the bile rising in the back of her own throat. "Tell me what happened, from the beginning."

"Grandma, Kitty, and I met at the stand a little past six-thirty. Grandma was going to make the donuts, and we were going to make the coffee and do the selling. First we set up the deep fryer, got the coffeepot going, and took the batter out of the ice chest."

Skye nodded. It sounded logical to her.

"Then we went to put out the paper goods and plastic spoons. We had stored that stuff in that old liquor cabinet Grandma's trying to sell. The shelves are missing, but it has a lock."

"So, Grandma had the key?" Skye asked.

"No. The key was lost before I started dating your father. We've been using a hairpin."

Skye shook her head at the logic of locking something that could be opened with a hairpin. "So Grandma unlocked the cabinet?"

"Yes. Kitty and I were standing right next to her."

132

"And Cookie Caldwell fell on Grandma?"

"Right. Grandma screamed, and Kitty and I shoved Cookie back in and closed the cabinet door."

"Then you called the police, right?"

May's tone was exasperated. "How could we do that? There's no phone at the stand."

"Where are Grandma and Aunt Kitty now?" Skye didn't bother to ask about a cell phone. She knew none of the women owned one.

"They're at the stand, waiting for you."

"What? Why?" Skye ran out of the bathroom, and across the hall into her bedroom, where she frantically started to throw on clothes. As May trailed behind her, Skye yelled, "Call Wally right now!" She pulled a comb through her wet, tangled hair, wincing at the pain as she jerked at the snarls. "You're a police dispatcher, for heaven's sake. You know better than this."

"No." May's expression was stubborn. "We decided you need to handle this."

"Me?" Skye hopped on one foot, trying to tie her tennis shoe. "Why?"

"You have experience." May crossed her arms and thrust out her lower lip.

Skye stopped hopping and limped out of the room in the direction of the kitchen. "Fine. I'll call Wally." She knew that expression on her mother's face, and it meant there was no changing her mind. "But he'll want to talk to you."

"Tell him to meet us at the stand." May followed her. "I'll be in the car."

Skye watched her mother disappear out the back door. Should she call 911 or use the private line? She decided on the latter and punched in the familiar number. "Thea? This is Skye. I need to talk to Wally. It's an emergency."

Thea was the day dispatcher. "He's just pulling into the garage. Hold on a sec."

The 5th Dimension sang half of "Going Out of My Head" before Wally got on the line. "What's up?"

She should have been thinking of what to say instead of listening to the Muzak, no matter how appropriate the song. "Ah, well, it looks like, maybe, Mom, Aunt Kitty, and Grandma Denison have found a body at the family's farm stand."

"That's at the corner of Scumble River Road across from the old factory, right?"

"Yes."

"Then that's out of my jurisdiction. You need to call the Stanley County Sheriff's Department." Wally's voice was troubled. "The county took that area over a few months ago. Remember, I told you about the rezoning when you asked me about Mrs. Griggs?"

"Couldn't you call them and say you'll handle it?" Skye pleaded.

There was a short silence before Wally said, "No, I'd like to, but I really can't. Buck Peterson would never let me take over, and my asking would just cause hard feelings. It's an election year, and he'd be afraid it would make him look bad."

"Damn! Damn! Damn!" Skye pounded the wall in frustration. Things were going from bad to worse. She forced herself to take a deep breath and calm down. None of this was Wally's fault. After grabbing a pencil and a pad of paper, she struggled to keep her tone even. "Do you have the sheriff's number handy?"

Chapter 10
Name That Tune

In rural locales, officials don't arrive at the scene as fast as they do in the city or suburbs. After all, the sheriff's office can be located anywhere from the neighboring town to forty-five miles away.

On the other hand, word of mouth travels a lot quicker in the country, and Dante pulled into the parking area in front of the Denison/Leofanti farm stand right behind Skye and her mother.

Skye wasn't sure who had informed him. It could have been Wally or Thea, or anyone else who had been around the police station when she made the call. This was big news, and someone would have rushed to notify the mayor.

Others also turned up almost immediately — some to buy donuts, not knowing that a body had been found; some attracted by the growing crowd; and some who just happened to be in the right place at the right time to scoop the competition — such as Faith Easton's TV crew, who had come for breakfast and stayed to film the breaking story.

At first, Skye tried to keep everyone a good distance away from the stand, especially Dante, who kept poking around and showing things to the TV people, but the crowd grew restless long before the sheriff arrived.

By the time an ambulance finally drove up to the stand, the lack of siren and lights making it clear that the EMTs had gotten the message that there was no reason to rush, Skye had lost control of the situation. And when the sheriff got there a few seconds later, he was just in time to see Dante and Skye playing tug-of-war with what turned out to be Cookie's purse.

Skye had wrapped the straps around her hands and was trying to keep the huge leather tote upright.

Dante had grabbed the bottom and was yelling, "Give it to me. The TV people want to take a picture of it."

Skye shook her head. "We need to wait for the authorities. Quit touching stuff."

"I'm in charge here." Dante gave a mighty yank.

"What in Sam Hill are you two idiots doing?" Sheriff Peterson thundered, every inch of his six-foot frame quivering with irritation.

Dante whipped around to face his accuser, leaving Skye literally holding the bag, and blustered, "What took you so long, Buck? We could've had a couple more murders here in the time you took."

The sheriff started to answer back, but eyeing the TV crew, he slammed his mouth shut and turned to his deputies. "Get them out of here. Then run the crime tape back about a hundred feet all around the stand." After the deputies left, the sheriff turned to the EMTs, who had opened the cabinet but not removed the body. "What do you have?"

"DOA. We called for the deputy coroner." As the EMTs filed back to the ambulance, the one in charge said, "You're in luck. He was visiting his mother in Brooklyn, so he should be here any minute."

Skye hadn't thought about it, but with Simon out of town and him being the county coroner, they'd have to send for the next person in line to come to the crime scene. The deputy coroner Simon had appointed was a pediatrician at Laurel Hospital, more used to vaccinating kids than examining dead bodies. But he'd had some training as a forensic pathologist and so was the best choice among a limited field of candidates.

The sheriff turned his attention back to Dante and said, "You'll have to wait outside of the taped-off area."

Dante protested and cursed, but allowed himself to be led away.

When the sheriff returned, he said to the women, "Okay, who discovered the body?"

All eyes turned to Skye. She shrugged and stepped forward. "Sheriff Peterson, I'm Skye Denison. My family is running this stand during the yard sale."

"Did you find the body?"

"No. My grandmother did." Skye pointed to the older woman, who sat limply on a brightly colored lawn chair. "Cora Denison."

"Were you present?"

"No. Just my mother, May Denison, and my aunt, Kitty Denison."

The sheriff took off his hat and scratched his bald head. "Then why in blue blazes am I talking to you?"

"Uh, my family asked me to speak for them."

Buck frowned. "Why? Are you a lawyer?"

"No. I'm a school psychologist."

"A shrink. Even worse." The sheriff narrowed his eyes. "I've read about you in the paper, haven't I?"

"Maybe." Skye didn't meet his gaze. She certainly wished that the local newspaper hadn't done that feature on her, calling her the Scumble River Nancy Drew.

"Well, listen up. I'm not Wally Boyd, and I won't have you messing around in my investigation. Do you hear me?"

Skye nodded, her face flushing with anger. She did not mess around. She helped.

"Good." Sheriff Peterson turned, leaving her standing there, and yelled to one of his deputies, "Ed, put these women in separate squad cars." He pointed to May and Kitty. "And don't let them talk to each other." Under his breath he muttered, "At least not any more than they already have."

Skye made a move to go to her grandmother, but the sheriff stopped her. "Why did you call the police rather than an ambulance?"

"My mother said Cookie was dead, not injured."

"How did your mother know? Is she a doctor?"

"No, but she said the body was stiff as a board."

Buck nodded to himself. "Ah, rigor Morris."

Skye fought desperately to keep her face expressionless. Surely, the sheriff didn't think Cookie was a dead cat.

After ordering Skye outside the crime scene tape, the sheriff went over to her grandmother. As he tipped his hat, Skye heard him say, "Ma'am, I need to talk to you about finding the body."

When Sheriff Peterson finished with her, Cora walked over to Skye, who was hovering just outside the restricted area. "Did you hear all that?"

Skye nodded.

"We're in big trouble here." Cora tsked. "Buck Peterson has always been four pennies short of a nickel, and it looks as if he just lost his last cent. With him in charge, I'll end up in jail before the murderer does."

Sheriff Peterson towered over Dante. "You need to close down the Scumble River part of the yard sale."

They, along with Skye, were in the mayor's office in the city hall. Dante was backed up against the front of his desk, while Skye leaned against the wall near the door, ready for a hasty retreat. The sheriff had not been pleased when Dante had insisted on her presence, saying she was his assistant.

"No way am I doing that, Buck." Dante angled his head back and glared at the sheriff. "I just talked to the city attorney, and he says we don't have to."

"People are trampling all over my crime scene."

Skye offered, "Sheriff, you've closed down the farm stand, and it's pretty isolated. The only thing near it is the parking area across the street. The petting zoo and the guy selling goat cheese are half a mile down the road."

"Fine." Buck shook his head. "But you got a fox running around in a whole henhouse full of chickens. You'll feel mighty bad when he kills the next one."

Skye bit the inside of her cheek so she wouldn't laugh. The sheriff was certainly sure this was fowl play. "Why are you so certain there'll be a next one?"

The sheriff frowned. "I'm not. But I don't want to take the chance." He looked at her suspiciously. "Why do you think there won't be?"

"It seems like a crime of passion to me. Someone kills her in the heat of an argument, then stuffs her in the nearest available hidey-hole." For a moment Alma Griggs's face flashed into Skye's mind — she certainly had been mad at Cookie — but Skye pushed that thought aside. No way would such a nice old lady kill someone.

Buck harrumphed and turned back to Dante. "It's on your head if someone else gets hurt."

Dante stared the sheriff down. "No. It will be my fault if Scumble River loses all the money it's invested in the Route 66 Yard Sale. It will be your fault if you don't find Cookie Caldwell's murderer and he kills again."

Skye gave her uncle a thumbs-up. Dante kept surprising her.

Buck's face turned so red that Skye almost expected steam to come out of his ears like on a cartoon. He spun on his heel and stomped out the door, saying over his shoulder, "In that case, I'd better take a good look at your kin, since the victim was found at your stand, by your relatives."

Skye shot Dante an inquiring look. Their family didn't have anything to hide, did they? He shrugged. Who knew?

After the sheriff left, Dante ordered Skye to field calls from the media about Cookie's death. The phone stopped ringing by noon, so he allowed her to take her afternoon shift at the Lemonade ShakeUp booth, as planned. The stream of people ordering drinks was endless — if she never saw another lemon it would be too soon.

While working the lemonade stand, Skye had received a message about a family meeting being held at her folks' house at four. When she pulled into their driveway a few minutes past the hour, her parents' garage was already full of her aunts, uncles, and cousins, all engrossed in several animated conversations. The men clutched cans of beer, and the women sipped iced tea from clear plastic cups.

An ancient black fan rotated on the top of her father's tool bench, trying unsuccessfully to cool the overheated building. A hot breeze fluttered the striped curtains on the small windows, and the yellow walls glared brightly. An old refrigerator hummed in a corner next to a shiny white freezer, and Jed's collection of toy tractors festooned the shelves that ran along three of the four walls.

Skye found an empty lawn chair and sat, half listening to her relatives argue, too tired to join any of the discussions. Not surprisingly, her parents were on opposite sides. Her brow puckered. She really had to do something about that soon.

Her brother, Vince, dropped into the seat beside her. "What do you think? Should we forget it or find another location to set up the stand?"

"Well, the whole family did put in a lot of work gathering the stuff from basements and attics to sell, not to mention growing and canning the extra produce."

"True. But isn't it a little disrespectful to go on as if nothing has happened?"

"Maybe, but none of us really knew Cookie." Skye paused to listen to her mother and father bicker. "That reminds me, since your hair salon is gossip central, did you hear who in town *was* close to Cookie?"

"Nobody." Vince shrugged. "She got her hair done at my shop, but she never talked about anything personal — mostly just her tennis game and her business."

"And no one else talked *about* her?"

"No." Vince screwed up his face in thought. "It was almost as if she was a ghost or something. The people in town just sort of ignored her."

"How odd." Skye considered how hard it was to fly under the radar in Scumble River. She had tried — and failed almost immediately. It took a lot of effort not to be noticed. Had Cookie been hiding something?

Vince and Skye sat in companionable silence while their families argued toward a verdict. They knew none of their uncles or aunts would listen to them. No one under the age of fifty got a vote.

It was finally agreed that they would re-open the farm stand in front of the bowling alley. Bunny had called earlier and offered them that space, since it was currently not being used. May pouted, not wanting to take anything from that "horrible woman," but the decision had been made.

The men hopped into pickups, intent on building a new stand while it was still light, since the sheriff had cordoned off the old one. Luckily, most of the items that they were selling had not been left at the old stand overnight, so only a few of the really large pieces were now off-limits.

The women retreated to the kitchen to begin baking for the next day's sale. Skye's offer to help was rejected. Her reputation for burnt cookies, fallen cakes, and lead-crusted pies had preceded her.

Skye felt insulted, but also relieved to be dismissed. It was already past six, and the concert in the park was supposed to start at seven. She needed to get over there and make sure that the night's entertainment, a rock gospel group called the Godly Crüe, was ready to go.

Scumble River Park was a small finger of land that extended into the river for about half a mile. It was accessible by vehicle only from Maryland Street, and that entry point had been shut down because of the yard sale. That left the footbridge that extended from the apex of the Up A Lazy River Motor Court parking lot as the only real entrance, although a few people chose to arrive by boat.

Skye threaded her way through the meandering crowd until she reached the bandstand, located at the farthest tip of land, and she was reassured to see amplifiers scattered around the perimeter and people settling into lawn chairs and spreading blankets.

Skye spotted the musical group's manager and lead singer, Will Murphy, an angelic-looking young man in his late twenties. "Will, good to see you again. Is everything set for your show?"

"I believe so, Sister Skye." The singer ran his fingers through his curly blond hair. "We were real sorry to hear about that lady being killed. We weren't sure if we should perform or not."

"Sorry. I should have contacted you and let you know that the mayor has decided to keep events going as scheduled." Skye smiled in encouragement. "You know what they say. The show must go on."

Murphy nodded halfheartedly, his baby blue eyes troubled. "Let me introduce you to the rest of our group." He took her arm and propelled her toward three women who were tinkering with instruments. "Everyone, this is Sister Skye Denison, the person who hired us."

They all said hello.

"Sister Skye, this is Sister Mirabel Elliott on drums, Sister Rosalind Gallen on guitar, and Sister Delilah Forsythe on keyboard."

Mirabel had a halo of red hair and a sweet smile. Rosalind's black hair fell like a veil around her shoulders, and she looked as if she should be cradling a baby instead of a guitar. Delilah was the odd woman out in the heavenly quartet. Her long brown hair was scraggly, and acne bloomed on her cheeks and chin.

They all made small talk for a bit, and then Skye excused herself to wander around and check out the crowd. As she strolled, her stomach growled, and she headed toward the Lions Club pork chop supper.

After filling a plate, she looked around for a free seat and heard someone call, "Skye, over here."

Trixie was sitting alone at one end of the long row of tables.

Skye joined her, plopping her tray down, then climbing over the attached seat. "Hey, what's up? Where's Owen?"

"Not much." Trixie grimaced. "He's at home. One of the cows is sick. I knew it was a mistake to add livestock to the farm."

"Yeah, you don't have to babysit corn or soybeans." Having grown up on a farm, Skye was well aware of the pitfalls of the occupation.

"It's almost as if he deliberately bought the animals so we'd be even more tied down."

"Really?"

"Yeah. It's not as if I'm asking him to get into life's fast lane. I just want to occasionally get out of the driveway."

Skye nodded sympathetically, but she didn't have any suggestions. Instead, just before taking a big bite of grilled pork chop she asked, "How's the bed-and-breakfast business going?"

"Not bad. The two couples are great. You'd hardly know they were there, but the single guy, Montgomery Lapp, is a pain in the you-know-where."

Skye swallowed and asked, "How come?"

"First off, he's an antiques buyer for a bunch of stores in Chicago — calls himself a picker. Anyway, the first day he's with us I catch him snooping through the house, making a list."

"A list?"

"Yeah. Turns out some of the stuff we got when Owen's mother died is antique."

"Make sure you check around about prices if you decide to sell," Skye cautioned, thinking of Mrs. Griggs's experience with Cookie and her mother's encounter with Faith. "What else did he do?"

"He's just so darn persnickety. He demanded that his sheets be ironed. He only eats a special kind of cereal, and has to have soy milk. We had to put the cats in the barn because he claims to be allergic, but, you know, if he really was allergic he'd still be sneezing, because cat dander is still all over the house. You can't get it up even with a thorough cleaning." Trixie heaved a dramatic sigh. "Worst of all, I'm the one at his beck and call. Owen promised to help if we took in paying guests, but now he's always too busy."

"This Lapp guy sounds like a real pill." Skye took a sip of her lemonade, not commenting about Owen. No way was she getting in the middle of that fight.

Trixie shrugged. "Enough of my problems. What's the scoop about the murder?"

Her brown eyes sparkled with interest; she was not one to wallow for long in her own unhappiness.

Skye swallowed a bite of biscuit. "With Simon out of town and Wally not on the case, I don't know a thing."

"But she was found at your family's farm stand, by your mother." Trixie twisted a strand of short brown hair around her finger. "You must know something."

"I don't even know how she died." She forked a piece of roasted potato into her mouth. This was heaven. She hadn't eaten all day.

"Oh, oh!" Trixie bounced in her seat like a drop of water on a hot griddle. "I know. I know."

"Really? How?"

"How do I know, or how did she die?"

"Both." Skye made an effort to keep the impatience out of her voice. Trixie was Trixie, and there was no hurrying her.

"Monty, the pain-in-the-butt antique guy, said he heard that she was stabbed to death with a piece of jewelry."

"How could someone be killed with a piece of jewelry?"

Trixie smiled triumphantly. "That's exactly what I said."

"And?"

"It was an old brooch. A huge, four-inch bar pin in the shape of an arrow with two intertwined hearts in the middle. He said someone stabbed her in the carotid artery with it, and when she pulled it out of herself, she bled to death."

"How awful." Skye frowned. Hadn't she just heard something about a pin? She couldn't remember. She'd seen and heard about too much junk in the past few days to recall anything in particular.

"They found the brooch clutched in her fist," Trixie said with a shiver. "It reminds me of an Edgar Allan Poe story. 'The Tell-Tale Arrow' instead of 'The Tell-Tale Heart.' "

No longer hungry, Skye pushed her plate away. She didn't want to imagine Cookie locked in a cabinet and dying alone. It was too distressing. And Skye felt somehow guilty, as if she could have done something. But what?

Cookie had banished Skye from her store, and she deliberately kept herself aloof from the people in Scumble River. Even yesterday afternoon, when she had been crying and Skye had offered her comfort, Cookie had been talking to herself more than to Skye. She hadn't really shared anything. Still, Skye found it hard to accept that she couldn't help everyone.

After their meal, Skye and Trixie walked back to the bandstand and listened to the Godly Crüe play.

"They sound pretty good," Skye commented.

"They do. I wondered what a rock gospel band would be like."

"So did I, but Dante insisted on squeaky-clean family entertainment, which is a lot harder to find than you might think."

"It always amazes me that people like Dante can be so sanctimonious and still maintain a straight face." Trixie's grin was wicked. "How many coordinators did he sexually harass before the family talked you into taking the job?"

"Five." Skye didn't want to discuss Dante's peccadilloes, so she looked around at the audience. They all seemed to be enjoying themselves.

"Hey, look over there." Trixie jabbed Skye in the side with her elbow and pointed to an area near the bandstand. "Isn't that Simon's mother? But who is she with? He's young enough to be her son."

Skye's gaze followed Trixie's finger. "Oh, no. That's the writer from the TV show. This can't be good."

"Are you going over there and find out what she's up to?"

"I'd better not. It's never smart to talk in front of a writer. You might find yourself in his next script. I'll have a private chat with Bunny tomorrow."

They walked a few steps farther, and then it was Skye's turn to nudge Trixie in the ribs. "Catch what's happening over to the right." She had spotted Justin and his friends. Bitsy was clinging to Justin like the plastic wrap on a cheese slice.

Trixie whistled under her breath. "Frannie will certainly be unhappy if she finds out about this."

"If?" Skye grimaced. "What do you mean *if* she finds out? Someone has probably already left her a message on her answering machine. What is Justin thinking?"

"Thinking?" Trixie scowled. "I swear, the entire male intellect is rivaled only by that of garden tools."

Skye nodded distractedly. Frannie would be destroyed.

Chapter 11
Meet the Press

"No, don't fly back." Skye was once again lying across her childhood bed, petting Bingo and talking to Simon in California. "There's no reason for you to come home."

His smooth tenor was edged with concern. "I should be there for you. You sound pretty stressed out."

"I'm fine. Sheriff Peterson is being a jerk, so I doubt I'll be involved in the murder investigation." Simon didn't comment, but Skye could feel the disbelief radiating from two thousand miles away, so she reiterated, "I'll just carry on with the yard sale and let the sheriff take care of the murder."

"Okay. But if you change your mind, just call and I'll be on the next plane back."

"I will." Skye tried to change the subject. "What have you been doing?"

"The usual — attending lectures and

having business dinners. Oh, I did get to play the Funeral Director Feud game."

"What's that?"

"It's like *Family Feud* on TV, but the questions are all related to the funeral home business. Like, 'Name a stupid question the bereaved always asks.' And, 'Which hymn will make you gag if you have to hear it again?' "

"That's awful." Skye snickered. "Did you win?"

"No, the other team buried us."

"Ew. That one's older than dirt." Skye giggled. "What else have you been doing?"

"Missing you."

"That's so sweet. I miss you, too." After Skye said the words she wondered if they were true. In a way, it had been nice not to worry about fitting Simon into her busy schedule. She quickly suppressed that thought and asked, "Have you given your talk yet?"

"No, my panel is tomorrow."

"Are you nervous?"

"Nah. Panels are easy. If you have something to say, you can talk. If you don't, you can let someone else talk."

"Oh, well, that's good," Skye said, before changing the subject again. "It looks like there will definitely be a problem between Frannie and Justin." She described Bitsy and Justin's behavior during the concert.

"That's too bad." Simon's tone was somber. "It's a shame when you can't appreciate what you already have."

"True." Skye felt a twinge, and an image of Wally flickered through her mind. She pushed it away. Simon was a terrific man, and she wasn't going to throw her relationship with him away just because she had some chemistry with the police chief — okay, not just *some*, a *lot*. Still . . .

Simon's next question drew her attention back to the conversation. "Any news about Bunny?"

Skye had been putting off telling Simon about his mother. "Sort of. I saw her tonight at the park."

"And?"

"And she was with one of Faith Easton's TV crew."

"Was it a date?" It was no secret that Bunny liked men and they liked her.

"He's in his twenties, but knowing Bunny, maybe . . ." Skye trailed off. "Look. Come hell or high water, I'll definitely speak with her tomorrow."

"Good." Simon sighed. "I just have a really bad feeling about this. Bunny and show biz are not a good combination. That lifestyle offers way too much temptation for her."

Bunny had arrived in Scumble River a few months ago, addicted to the painkillers she had been given when she hurt her back and on probation for trying to forge prescriptions to get more of them. To keep out of jail, she'd had to attend Narcotics Anonymous meetings, find work, and establish a permanent address. Simon had helped her with the last two.

Skye agreed to speak with Bunny tomorrow, without fail, and she and Simon said their good-byes.

After hanging up the phone, she yawned. Time to go to bed. But first she needed a cold drink. She padded into the dark kitchen, careful not to wake her parents, who had gone to sleep at least two hours ago, although not together. Her mother was in their bedroom, but her father was sleeping on the couch in the living room.

Skye frowned. She had better find out what was going on with them and do something before the situation got worse. Neither of her folks was very good at apologizing. May was able to pout longer than it took the state to repair a pothole, and Jed figured it would all go away if no one talked about it.

As Skye was taking a glass from the cupboard, she heard a noise from the utility room and stiffened. She stuck her head around the swinging doors. Nothing but the washing machine, dryer, and furnace lined up on one side and the bench and coatrack on the other. She was about to turn back to the kitchen when she heard the sound again. Her gaze flew to the back door. Peering through the glass was a triangular white face. Alongside it was a finger tapping the windowpane.

Skye flipped on the yard light and stared. Trixie stood on the back patio, dressed only in lime green baby doll pajamas and flamingo pink flip-flops.

Skye threw open the door, and Trixie said, "All men are idiots, and I married their king."

Without answering, Skye hustled her friend inside, through the kitchen, down the hall, and into her bedroom, closing the door behind them. The last thing she needed was to wake up her mother, who would make things worse by agreeing with Trixie's assessment of men.

Trixie threw herself across Skye's bed.

"Okay, what happened?" Skye asked.

"I told Owen to do one thing to help out before I left for the concert tonight." Trixie wiped away a tear edging its way down her cheek. "One thing! And did he do it? No!"

Skye was amazed that Trixie was able to shout at the volume of a whisper. "What did you ask him to do?"

"I'm making these special muffins and coffee cakes for breakfast tomorrow, and you have to add this liquid 'starter' to the batter every four hours for twenty-four hours before you make them. I asked him to add the seven o'clock portion." Trixie sat up and hugged her knees. "When I got home at nine, I went to check, and he hadn't done it. The whole batch is ruined!"

"Oh, no."

"And I have nothing else to give the people for breakfast unless I toast some Wonder Bread."

"Mom probably has something in the freezer you could use," Skye offered.

"No, thanks." Trixie stretched out, her head pillowed on her arms. "It's not my problem anymore."

"Really?"

"Really. When I confronted Owen, he shrugged it off like it was too trivial to bother with. Said he couldn't leave a sick cow because of a recipe."

Skye winced. What had that man been thinking? "What did you do?"

"At first I just walked out of the barn and went to bed. But then I kept thinking how everyone would be looking at me tomorrow during breakfast. Like I was a failure. So, I got up, wrote Owen a note saying he could be the one to face our hungry guests in the morning, and left."

"Wow." Skye wondered how long it would take Owen to A — find the note, B — figure out where Trixie had gone, and C — come banging on Skye's parents' door asking for her. "So, you want to stay here with me?"

Trixie nodded like a little girl. "Is that okay?"

"Sure. There's one empty sofa left." It was actually a love seat, but Trixie was short.

"Point me to it. I'm exhausted." Trixie trailed Skye to the den.

Skye gave her a fresh set of bed linens and a pillow, hugged her good night, and went back to her room. After she had slid between the sheets, Bingo edged his way out of the closet, where he had been hiding since Trixie's emotional entrance, and jumped up on the bed.

Skye scratched him behind the ears, making a mental list of her chores for Monday with each stroke of her fingernails. Talk to Bunny. Find out why her parents were fighting. Work her shift at the family's stand. And check on Mrs. Griggs. She'd been okay Saturday when Skye had phoned, even though she had called Skye Sterling, but Skye hadn't had a chance to phone the older woman on Sunday and she was worried about Mrs. Griggs's reaction to Cookie's death.

But the best-laid plans of cats and women rarely work out. As Skye fell asleep, she never dreamed what she'd really be doing the next morning, or that she would only accomplish one of the tasks on her list.

"No comment," Skye repeated for the hundredth time as she fought her way from the parking lot to the entrance of the city hall. Another microphone was shoved in her face, and she batted it away, snarling, "Put that thing in my face again, and you'll draw back a bloody stump."

One of her larger second or third cousins on the Leofanti side of the family was guarding the front door, which he opened a crack for her to slip inside. She leaned against the glass for a moment to get her breathing back to normal. The media people were relentless.

The morning had already started out on a bad note when Skye's parents had decided to use her as an interpreter, since they were now officially not speaking to each other.

To add to her woes, Trixie had refused to go home, and sent Skye there to pick up some clothes for her to wear that day. Owen had greeted her with a stoic expression and hadn't asked about Trixie's whereabouts. Skye had peeked in the dining room and found the guests eating coffee cake, muffins, and donuts that looked suspiciously like the ones sold in the grocery store's freezer section.

The two couples seemed happy enough with the food, chatting about what they were hoping to find at the sale and commenting on the concert the night before, but the man sitting alone at the other end of the table was clearly displeased with the situation and sat crumbling the pastries on his plate rather than eating them.

When he spotted Skye, he raised his voice and said, "We were promised homemade country cuisine, not grocery store rejects. Everybody *does not* like Sara Lee."

Skye had pretended not to hear him and backed out of the room, thinking that he must be Montgomery Lapp. She wondered how he would handle the predicted ninety-degree heat dressed in a long-sleeve fuchsia silk shirt, black jeans, and an elaborately embroidered vest.

Skye's morning had gone further downhill when she dropped off Trixie's suitcase and reported that Owen had managed to feed their guests. Trixie's reaction had not been pretty. Comments concerning Lorena Bobbitt's handling of a badly behaved husband had filled the air, and Skye wondered if she should call Owen and warn him to hide the butcher knives and protect his privates should his wife show up looking for him.

Now the media were howling at Skye's door, but not as loudly as Dante was screaming from behind his. Skye escaped into her office before her uncle spotted her, stowed her purse in the desk drawer, and checked her watch. Hard to believe it was only five to eight. It felt more like high noon.

Her phone rang. She warily picked it up. "Route 66 Yard Sale. May I help you?" She listened for a moment and said, "No comment."

After she hung up on the reporter from the *Chicago Sun-Times*, she noticed that her message light was blinking like a Christmas tree bulb about to burn out. Pulling up the desk chair, she sank into it and pushed PLAY. Only two communications were from someone other than a newspaper reporter or TV station. One was from Frannie, her voice shaky, saying not to bother to call back, she'd catch up to Skye later. The other was from the sheriff, wanting to talk to her immediately.

Skye sat back and contemplated the ceiling. There really was no contest. She dialed. On the fourth ring a machine picked up and a male voice said, "The Ryans are not available to take your call at this moment. Please leave a message after the tone."

She left the required information and added a sketchy idea of where she could be found throughout the day. Skye was worried. Where could Frannie be at eight a.m. on a summer morning?

Just as Skye picked up the receiver to phone the sheriff, Dante bellowed, "I can hear you in there. Get your ass in here right now."

Skye contemplated ignoring her uncle, but knew he would get worse until she took the thorn out of whichever paw was hurting him.

Dante didn't look up as she entered his office. He finished shouting into the telephone and banged down the handset. "Where the hell have you been?"

Skye considered a smart retort, since her day didn't officially begin until eight, but instead listed her morning's itinerary, concluding with "Then I risked life and limb to fight my way through the media mob to come here."

"We have to stop this." Dante abruptly stood up, knocking his chair over. "Between those stupid reporters and the idiot cops, they'll ruin my yard sale."

For once her uncle had a point, but Skye wasn't sure what he expected her to do about it.

"You know, if my sale is ruined, you don't get your bonus."

"But this isn't my fault," Skye protested. She had worked hard for that money, and she needed it or she'd lose her chance to buy the cottage.

"I didn't say it was your fault. I said I was going to *blame* you for it."

Skye didn't normally react well to coercion, but as she watched Dante pace, an idea started to form. She grabbed a legal pad and pen from his desk and plopped down on a nearby chair.

What seemed like only minutes later, she noticed a shadow looming over her and looked up.

Dante was straining to see what she was

writing. Finally, he demanded, "What? What? You got an idea?"

"Maybe." Skye pursed her lips. "Sit down and let me go through the whole thing before you comment."

Dante grumbled, but sat down. "Yeah. Go ahead."

"There's nothing much we can do about the deputies, but at least there aren't many of them, and I bet they'll mostly be gone after today. The sheriff may stick around, but not for long." Skye sat forward. "As for the media, I think you should hold a press conference this afternoon. Right now they're in a feeding frenzy, trying to scoop each other, but if we give them all the information we have, let them take their pictures of you and the crime scene and Cookie's store, maybe they'll be satiated. Then tonight we have a little memorial ceremony for Cookie, and that should signal closure to them." Skye had one last idea. "And if that isn't enough, we tell them that although we don't have any more info, maybe they should talk to the sheriff's department or the deputy coroner."

Dante nodded as Skye spoke, and when she finished he said, "I like that. Both the sheriff's office and the deputy coroner's are way the hell over in Laurel. It will get them out of here."

"I am curious about one thing." Skye wrinkled her brow. "Why are the media so interested in Cookie's murder? We've had murders here before without this kind of attention."

"That's a good question. Maybe you should ask the sheriff when you tell him about the press conference."

"Me!" Skye squeaked. "I mean, I think *you* should talk to him — head man to head man."

"Maybe." Dante crossed his arms. "But he wants to talk to you anyway, so you're elected." He looked at his watch. "You'd better call him right now. Otherwise you'll be late for your shift at the family farm stand." He sighed, an expression of martyrdom on his face. "Since you'll be so busy, I'll arrange the press conference and memorial myself."

"Fine. Don't forget to invite the *Scumble River Star*'s owner, Kathy Steele, and Vickie from the *Laurel Herald News*. We don't want to insult the local papers." Skye hoped her school newspaper staff didn't get wind of the conference, as this wasn't really an appropriate story for a school paper, but she'd bet good money that either Frannie or Justin or both would show up.

When Skye went back to her office and

called the sheriff's department, she was told that Sheriff Peterson had set up a temporary office in the Scumble River Police Department, and she was to report to him there immediately.

She ducked out the back door of the city hall and into the PD's garage, using that entrance so she wouldn't have to deal with the throng of reporters waiting out front. One of the part-time dispatchers Skye didn't know very well was on the phone. She buzzed Skye inside and pointed to the interrogation room.

Buck Peterson was sitting at the table smoking a cigar, drinking coffee, and reading the *Laurel Herald News* as she walked in. He looked up and ordered, "Sit down, shut up unless you're answering a question, and tell the truth."

Skye sat, but made no additional promises.

The sheriff took a last slurp of coffee, folded the paper and pushed it aside, then blew a noxious cloud of smoke in her direction. "You didn't mention to me yesterday that you had been fired by the victim earlier this summer. Why?"

"I never thought about it." Skye coughed out her answer.

"That's funny, because I hear it was real

bad. That she even struck you with a sword."

"Who told you that?" Skye had never mentioned to anyone that Cookie had hit her.

"An anonymous tip. How bad was it? Did it make you mad enough to want to kill her?"

"No!" Skye drew in a sharp breath. Did the sheriff really think she had killed Cookie? "Look, we had a disagreement about business ethics, she fired me, and I got a better-paying job that same afternoon." Skye calmed down, and reason flowed back into her thinking. "Besides, if I'd been mad enough to do her harm, it would have been eight weeks ago, not yesterday."

"Ah, but that same tipster said they saw you talking to Cookie at her table the day before, and she was crying." The sheriff leaned forward and waved the lighted cigar in Skye's face. "So, what was that all about?"

No way would Skye implicate Mrs. Griggs. Technically the sheriff should already be aware of her problems with Cookie, but if he couldn't put two and two together, Skye would certainly not be the one to give him a calculator. She thought fast. She would tell the truth, just not the whole truth.

"Well?"

Skye met and held his gaze. "I'm the yard sale coordinator. I check on every table, booth, and stand throughout the day. When I got to Cookie's she was having an argument with someone. By the time I made it through the crowd, whoever she was fighting with was gone and she was in tears."

"Who was she fighting with?"

"I didn't see."

"How convenient."

Skye shrugged and waited. The sheriff smoked in silence. Finally, she asked, "Do you have any idea why the media are so interested in this murder? We've had murders here before, and no one but the local papers paid any attention."

Peterson took his time before answering. "Turns out the vic was married to some big-shot politician in Chicago who died in bed with a hooker a few years ago. He was dressed as a nun and the hooker was dressed like a Catholic schoolgirl. The media went wild. Cookie disappeared. Now she turns up murdered in Scumble River using her maiden name."

Skye nodded. Yep. That would make the

media go crazy, all right. "Was she hiding from something or someone?"

"Just reporters. Those bastards made her life so miserable she had to leave Chicago in order to get any peace." Sheriff Peterson shook his head, a look of sympathy on his gruff face. "Her family knew she was here."

"Oh." Skye felt a ripple of guilt. Once again she had judged someone too harshly without knowing the whole story. After Cookie's awful experience with her husband, no wonder she was aloof and standoffish. Of course, that didn't excuse her trying to swindle little old ladies out of their assets. "By the way, the mayor wanted me to tell you he'll be having a press conference this afternoon and a memorial for Cookie tonight."

Peterson stalked out of the room without responding, but once he left Skye could hear him screaming. She couldn't tell whom he was yelling at or what he was saying, but she didn't think he was complimenting anyone on having done a good job.

When he came back, he made Skye tell him about being fired again. He kept her for another hour, making her repeat what she had already said several times, then he let her go with the admonition not to leave town. All through the rest of the interroga-

tion she kept wondering who the anonymous tipster could be and how he knew
things that only she and Cookie could have
known.

Chapter 12
Jeopardy

The press conference was a success. Justin hadn't shown up, but Frannie had, though Skye hadn't been able to talk to her. The teen kept to the back, and Dante wouldn't let Skye stray more than a few feet from his side.

By late afternoon it looked as if the yard sale would continue as planned. Skye was relieved that the event seemed to be saved. She hated to be mercenary, but she really needed the bonus Dante had promised her. If she lost her cottage, she didn't know what she would do.

They held the memorial in front of Cookie's store. She had not attended any of the local churches, so Dante read a passage from the Bible and the president of the Scumble River Merchants Association gave a brief eulogy. The ceremony was well attended, but afterward the crowd broke up quickly, and it was only five to eight when Skye started her drive home.

She used her key to let herself into her parents' darkened house. Where was everyone? She walked through the utility room and flipped on the lights in the kitchen. On the counter was a place setting with a note in the middle of the plate:

Skye, Trixie and I have gone to Joliet for supper at Applebee's and then we're going to a movie. There's fried chicken, mashed potatoes, and biscuits in the oven. Coleslaw is in the fridge. This is for you. Don't give it to your father! Love, Mom and Trixie.

Skye whistled under her breath. Things really were getting bad between her folks if May had stopped feeding Jed.

Before having dinner, Skye checked on Bingo, who was curled up asleep in the middle of her bed. She gave him fresh water, cleaned his litter box, and put dry food in his bowl.

Having taken care of the cat's needs, Skye checked the answering machine. Simon had phoned a few minutes before she got home and said he would be tied up the rest of the night. He'd talk to her tomorrow.

Skye exhaled noisily; in truth, she was a bit relieved to have missed his call. She was really beat, and welcomed the silence of the empty house. After a quick shower, she put on her nightgown and robe and sat down to eat.

Only then did she realize that there was still no sign of her father. She got back up and checked the house, but he wasn't there. She flipped on the outside lights and walked across the driveway to the detached garage. Jed's truck was missing and so was he.

Skye chewed her lip. Where could he be? He rarely left the house on a weeknight. Her best guess was that he was at the tavern having a beer and commiserating with the other men about the women in their lives, or at his brother's having a beer and commiserating with Wiley about the women in their lives, or at the Moose Lodge in Laurel having a beer and commiserating with his brother Moose about the women in their lives.

She just hoped he got back before May did. Skye did not want to play marriage counselor tonight, especially after the day she'd had — although she knew that sometime real soon she would have to do just that.

As she ate supper, she remembered she

hadn't called Mrs. Griggs or talked to Bunny. She really should call them tonight. It was close to nine-thirty, but if she called right now it would still be okay, as ten was the official witching hour in Scumble River.

Skye sighed, pushed her plate away, and laid her head on the counter. She'd rest for just a second while she figured out what she wanted to say to Bunny and Mrs. Griggs. Then she would call them.

Two hours later, the doorbell's harsh chime woke her up. Skye shot off the stool and looked around, dazed and confused. The back of her neck hurt, and it seemed she had taken a nap in her dinner — the left side of her head was encrusted with mashed potatoes.

The doorbell rang again, and Skye grabbed a dish towel, trying to remove the food caked in her face and hair. In mid-wipe it dawned on her. Where was everyone? A quick glance at the clock informed her that it was past eleven-thirty. Her parents and Trixie should be home, but surely they hadn't walked past her snoozing facedown in her supper plate and left her there.

A third peal of the doorbell sent Skye flying into the utility room. The outside lights were still on from her earlier trip to the garage, so she could clearly see who was standing on the patio — and how hard she was crying.

For a nanosecond Skye wondered how her parents' house had turned into Heartbreak Hotel, but she squashed that thought as she flung open the door and drew the weeping girl inside.

"He's gone!"

"What?" Skye guided Frannie into the living room, settled her on the couch, and sat on the coffee table facing her. "Who's gone?"

"Justin. We had a huge fight this morning, and I didn't see him all day, and now his mother called, and he's gone."

Skye felt her chest tighten. She had seen Justin for counseling from the middle of eighth grade until the end of his sophomore year this past June, when she'd dismissed him from services. She was sure he had made sufficient progress with his self-esteem to handle his dysfunctional family and the other problems in his life without her assistance. Had she been wrong?

Skye patted Frannie's hand. "Take a deep breath and tell me what happened from the beginning."

There was a hitch in Frannie's voice as she started to talk. "When I got home last night from my great-aunt's birthday party, one of my friends from the paper called and told me she saw Justin and Bitsy making out at the concert."

"I wouldn't exactly say they were making out," Skye murmured before she could stop herself.

"So, you saw them, too." Frannie pounced on that detail. "Anyway, this morning Justin showed up at my house and tried to act like nothing had happened."

"Maybe nothing did happen."

The look Frannie gave Skye could have cooked bacon faster than a microwave. "I couldn't let him make a fool out of me, so we had a huge fight and I told him to get lost."

Skye winced at the girl's choice of words.

"I didn't see him all day, which didn't surprise me, but about an hour ago the phone rang, and it was his mother. She wanted to know if he was at my house. I said no, she should check with Bitsy, but then I got to thinking, so I sneaked out and drove by Bitsy's house, and there weren't any lights on. I don't think he's there." Frannie ended with a sob.

Skye moved to take the teen in her arms, but stopped. She was alone with an underage girl and had on only a robe — this was one of those situations they warned you about in school psychology classes.

Instead, she patted Frannie's hand and said, "Let me get you some water. I'll be right back."

Skye detoured into her bedroom and changed into shorts and a T-shirt, then grabbed a glass and filled it from a pitcher in the fridge.

She handed it to Frannie and sat back down. "Did Mrs. Boward say if she had called the police?"

Frannie took a gulp of water and shook her head. "No. I don't think this is the first time Justin's disappeared, but he hasn't done it in the past year or so."

"Do you have any idea where to look for him?"

Frannie chewed on the end of her ponytail. "Well . . ."

"Yes?"

"I know a couple of places where he went before."

"And they are?" Skye prodded.

"Sometimes he'd camp out at the Recreation Club, and sometimes he'd stay at the old aerosol factory."

"I'm guessing he had a way into these places other than the front door?"

Frannie nodded without looking up.

Skye considered the options. Both of the places Frannie mentioned were outside the city limits, thus under the jurisdiction of the county sheriff. No way was she calling Buck Peterson. If he found the boy, he'd probably arrest him for trespassing. "I'll call Justin's mom and see if he's come home."

"Okay."

Frannie hadn't moved when Skye returned from talking to Mrs. Boward. "He's still not back, and you were right about her not wanting to call the police. She'll give him twenty-four hours."

Frannie moaned.

Skye argued with herself, but finally caved in. "First, you call your dad and tell him where you are. Then, if he's okay with it, we'll go check out Justin's usual hideouts."

This time Frannie's moan was more of a whine, but she dutifully got up and walked toward the kitchen phone. From Frannie's end of the conversation, Skye gathered that Xavier, Frannie's dad, wasn't pleased to hear she had snuck out of the house, but he agreed she could show Skye where Justin might be.

The carriage clock in the living room was striking midnight, but Skye didn't feel like Cinderella as she struggled with what to say in the note she was writing to her parents — another good reason for living on her own with only a cat for a roommate. Bingo did

181

not require a full accounting of her where-abouts every second of the day.

Before she could finish, her father's pickup pulled into the driveway, and he ambled into the kitchen with a goofy grin on his face. A cloud of cigarette and beer fumes followed him like a dog on a leash.

Skye shook her head. Jed never, ever grinned — except when he'd had too much to drink. She turned to the teenager hovering behind her and said, "Frannie, wait for me in my car, okay?"

The girl opened her mouth to protest, but quickly closed it when she saw the expression on Skye's face. "Yes, ma'am."

After Frannie left, Skye said mildly, "Pretty late for a weeknight."

"Yep. Ma'll be sore."

"She's not home."

"Oh?" A look of confusion crossed his features. "Where's she at?"

"Dinner and a movie with Trixie." Skye knew she should let her parents work out their difficulties themselves, but she hated to see them fight, so she gave in to the temptation to "fix" things. "You need to get into bed before she gets home."

"Right." Jed staggered down the hall toward his bedroom. "What she doesn't know won't hurt me."

Now Skye had to do something about the way he smelled. There was no time for a shower. "I'll be right back."

She ran outside and into the garage, waving as she passed the Bel Air where Frannie was sitting. She grabbed one of Jed's work rags and sniffed. Ah, gasoline, grass, sweat — all the usual Jed odors. Just what she needed.

Back in the house, she hurried down the hall, calling, "Dad? Dad?" Peeking around the bedroom door, she saw him lying across the bed in his underwear, snoring. Quickly, she ran the rag over him until the smell of beer and cigarettes was replaced with the scents of the normal Jed. She then snatched up his clothes, ran back outside, and threw them into the Bel Air's trunk. She'd either wash them or get rid of them — whichever she had time for.

She was just closing the lid when her mother's big white Olds pulled into the driveway. Phew, that had been close. Skye leaned into the Bel Air and said to Frannie, "One more second."

May got out of the Olds and walked toward Skye. "Your father home?"

"Yes."

"Did you give him any of your supper?"

"No."

"Good." May seemed to suddenly realize how late it was and that Skye was fully dressed and getting into her car. "Where are you going at this time of night?"

"How about you? Why were you out so late?"

"We missed the first show and had to go to the nine o'clock." May smiled thinly. "Was your father worried?"

Skye crossed her fingers. May hadn't specified what he was worried about. "Yes."

As Skye explained the Justin problem, Trixie joined them.

When Skye finished, Trixie got into the Bel Air. "I'm going, too."

"Me, too." May claimed the other side of the backseat.

Not having the energy to argue, Skye got behind the wheel and started the car.

There was no sign of Justin at the Scumble River Recreation Club. Lots of people were camping out, in everything from ten-dollar army surplus pup tents to RVs that cost more than Skye's cottage, but no one — at least no one still awake — had seen the boy.

The abandoned factory was a lot scarier to check out, but except for a family that had been unable to find a place to stay for the yard sale and had decided to use the empty building as their private motel, the women found nothing.

It was nearly two when Skye dropped Frannie off and closer to three by the time she got to bed herself.

When Skye dragged herself into the kitchen the next morning, she was shocked to see no sign of the evening's activities on either of her parents' faces. Jed didn't appear at all hungover, and no one would have guessed that May'd had only three hours of sleep.

Skye felt like the portrait of Dorian Gray, her face reflecting her parents' sins. As she flopped into a chair, May brought her a cup of tea. She sipped gratefully, hoping the hot liquid would perform some magic and stop the pounding in her head.

The throbbing crescendoed when May said, "Tell your father that I would appreciate it if he showered before coming to bed. He stunk like —"

Skye froze while her mother searched for the word she wanted. Had May's sensitive nose detected the odor of cigarettes and beer?

"— an old toolbox last night." May completed her thought and went back to doing the dishes.

Jed's gaze met Skye's as they both relaxed.

"Also," May went on from the sink, "tell your father that yesterday was our anniversary."

"Your anniversary is in June," Skye reminded her mother.

"Not our wedding anniversary, the anniversary of our first date. We had dinner at the Riviera, and we always go back there and order the same thing — chicken and spaghetti. We've been doing it for over thirty-five years, but this time he forgot."

Jed got up and walked toward May, his brow furrowed. "Ah, Ma, you know how bad my memory is."

May whirled around and shook a soapy finger at him. "Jedidiah Denison, you know all the words of the F Troop theme song, the address of every model tractor dealer in the country, and the VIN from every truck you ever owned. Don't be talking about a bad memory to me."

Skye's last view of her parents as she fled the kitchen for her bedroom was Jed decorated with soapsuds and May whacking him with the plastic spatula.

After she heard the back door slam twice, indicating that both her parents had left, Skye crept back into the kitchen and phoned Mrs. Boward. Justin still hadn't returned. Skye urged the woman to call Wally, but she refused, saying she was sure her son would be back soon.

Skye chewed her thumbnail. Should she talk to Wally herself? She turned away from the phone and went to get dressed. Although she felt a certain responsibility, she wasn't the boy's mother. There was only so much she could do.

She still hadn't made up her mind as to her next step when Trixie stumbled into Skye's bedroom and sprawled across the bed. "What are you up to today?"

Skye finished putting her hair into a French braid and picked up a mascara wand. "Counting the days until the yard sale is over and I can have my life back."

"How many?"

"Six." Skye finished with her eyes and inserted gold hoops into her earlobes. "What are *you* doing today?"

"Guess I need to go pick up some more clothes."

Skye phrased her next question carefully. "Have you considered making up with Owen?"

"Why should I? He hasn't even noticed that I'm gone."

"I'm surprised you let him drive you out of your own house." Skye tried another strategy. "No wonder he hasn't noticed. *He's* not the one sleeping on a love seat. *He* has all the comforts of home."

Trixie popped up and off the bed. "Hey, you're right. Why should I be the one inconvenienced?"

"Sure. You take the house back." Skye was hoping that proximity might solve Trixie and Owen's problems.

"Right. He can sleep in the barn."

So much for proximity being the answer. Skye finished dressing, walked toward the door, and gave Trixie a little wave. "Call me, or find me around the yard sale, and tell me what happens."

Chapter 13
Animal Planet

Dante had various newspapers spread out across his desk when Skye arrived at the city hall. "Look at this." He pointed to multiple pictures of himself at the press conference and memorial service. "Not bad, eh?"

Skye scanned the photos. "They're great." Dante appeared very dignified. "You're the very picture of a modern small-town mayor." She smiled to herself, doubting Dante would get the Gilbert and Sullivan reference.

"I put Scumble River on the map, just like I said I would." Dante preened. "My press conference and the memorial were on the TV news last night. I bet that'll bring even more people to the yard sale. We couldn't afford to buy this kind of advertising."

Skye shuddered at the thought of profiting from someone's death. Too bad her uncle was probably right. People could be pretty morbid, and attendance would doubtlessly increase because of Cookie's murder.

"Did you notice that there were no media people out front?" Dante asked, as if it had all been his idea. "And Buck said he's done with the crime scene and Cookie's store. We're back in business, stronger than ever."

"Great," Skye said from the doorway, intent on making her getaway. "Well, I'd better get to work." Dante in a good mood was almost scarier than Dante in a bad one.

Dante didn't look up; his gaze was locked on a picture of himself. "Did you hear they found out who owns the pin that killed Cookie Caldwell?"

Skye halted her footsteps. "No. Who?"

"Alma Griggs." Dante tore his attention from his own image. "Hard to believe an old lady like that could kill someone like Cookie."

"Just because she owned the pin doesn't mean she used it. It could have been lost, or she could have sold it, or —" Skye abruptly remembered Mrs. Griggs's break-in. "— it could have been stolen."

"Sure." Dante's focus was back on the newspapers. "Maybe."

"Were there fingerprints on the pin?"

"Nope. Said with the blood and all, they couldn't lift any."

"Did they arrest Mrs. Griggs?"

"No. At least I didn't hear that they did." Dante scratched his chin. "They were questioning her, though."

At that moment Dante's phone rang, and Skye slipped out of his office.

She hurried into her own office and called next door to the police station. "Thea? This is Skye."

"Hi, honey. How are you and your poor family? Imagine finding Miss Caldwell like that. Must have been a terrible shock."

"Yes, it sure was, but Mom, Grandma, and Aunt Kitty are fine."

"Who would have thought someone like Miss Caldwell was really rich and famous. You just can't tell about people, can you?"

"No, you can never tell." Skye doodled, waiting for Thea to wind down so she could ask her question. "So, is Sheriff Peterson still taking up space in your interrogation room?"

"Yes, and he's real mean, not at all polite like Wally."

"How awful." Skye certainly agreed with Thea's assessment of Buck Peterson. "Is that where he questioned poor Mrs. Griggs?"

"Yes. He dragged that sweet old woman here at six in the morning."

"What a creep." Skye closed in on her real query. "Did he arrest her?"

"No, but he's itching to. One of his deputies mentioned that Miss Caldwell had been bothering Mrs. Griggs all summer, and I thought the sheriff's head would explode. He yelled at that poor boy for twenty minutes for not telling him about that sooner."

"Guess maybe he should read the reports made to his own office."

"That's what Wally said." Thea's satisfaction with her boss was evident in her voice. "The sheriff didn't like hearing that at all."

Skye wondered at Wally's motives. He wasn't a stupid man, so he must have had a reason for needling Sheriff Peterson.

When Skye left the office to start her patrol of the yard sale, she was amazed at the size of the crowd. Even though she and Dante had anticipated an increase in attendance because of the publicity surrounding the murder, it was happening sooner than she had expected. It was a Tuesday, for heaven's sake. Didn't anyone work anymore? She found it hard to believe that so many people were taking their summer vacation in Scumble River.

Starting on the west side of town, Skye planned to work her way through the entire yard sale route and end up over by the original location of her family's booth on the eastern boundary. Since the sheriff had released the crime scene, she wanted to take a closer look at it.

On the morning the body was discovered, it had taken all her concentration just to keep her relatives and other spectators from removing or destroying any important evidence, so she hadn't had a chance to carefully inspect the site and get a clear mental picture of what had happened.

Skye's first stop was the new Leofanti/Denison farm stand. It was even better than the first one. The men had rebuilt the booth to resemble the front of a barn. Dante's daughter-in-law was handling the food side of the stall, where business was brisk. People were snatching up homemade baked goods, preserves, pickled peppers, and fresh-from-the-garden vegetables as if they were about to disappear off the face of the earth forever. Skye had never seen the beautiful Victoria so harried.

On the other end of the stand, Jed's older brother was handling the tool and farm implements, which were selling at a slightly less frenetic pace.

Skye approached him and said, "Hi, Uncle Wiley. How's it going?" Wiley looked a lot like Jed, with the same compact build and farmer's tan, but he had inherited his father's Swedish blue eyes and wore his white hair in a pompadour.

"It's going." None of the Denison men were even close to being chatterboxes.

"Did you and Dad have a good time last night?" Skye probed. Jed had evaded Skye's question as to where he had been the night before, and she was determined to find out, just in case he *had* been with Bunny.

"Huh?" Wiley's leathery forehead creased in confusion. "Kitty and I watched TV. We didn't go out. What are you talking about?"

"Oh." Skye knew she had to distract her uncle before he started asking questions she didn't want to answer. "I must have misunderstood." She held up an object that defied description. "Hey, what's this?"

Wiley took off his John Deere cap and scratched his head. "1920s cattle dehorner, I think. Found it in an old barn we tore down last summer."

Before she could put it down, a man in a cowboy hat snatched it from her hands. "I saw it first." His belt buckle was bigger than a dinner plate and held his beer belly in like a girdle. "It's mine."

Wiley raised an eyebrow at Skye, who nodded slightly and grabbed it back. "No. I want it. Finders keepers." She snuck a quick peek at the price tag as she cradled it against her chest. It was marked twenty-five dollars. She said to Wiley, "I'll give you fifty dollars."

The cowboy wrenched it out of her hands. "One hundred bucks."

Skye gauged her opponent's interest. He was sweating and licking his lips. "One-fifty."

"Two hundred."

Skye opened her fanny pack and peered inside, pretending to count her money. "Two-fifty-five."

"Three hundred." The cowboy reached into his jeans pocket and produced a gold money clip. He peeled off three hundred-dollar bills and slapped them into Wiley's hand. "Cash on the barrelhead."

Wiley tucked the money away and said with a sly smile, "Sold to the cowboy."

After the guy walked away carrying his prize in a blue-and-yellow striped bag with a stylized *D* and *F* on its side, Skye said to her uncle, "Well, that was a strange one."

"Maybe." Wiley winked before turning to wait on a new customer. "But everybody is somebody else's weirdo."

Skye's next stop was the Lemonade ShakeUp booth. She hoped Justin would appear for his noon shift, or at least call and say he wasn't coming. Bitsy's mother, Joy, was the adult on duty working the lemon juicer; and Bitsy and a new boy, who had joined the student newspaper staff only a couple of weeks before school got out, were handling the sales window.

"Hi, Bitsy, Rusty." They waved, but were too busy taking orders to talk. Skye walked around back and went inside. "How's it going, Mrs. Kessler?"

"Busy." Joy wiped her forehead with a paper towel. "I'll be glad when the next shift gets here."

Skye looked at her watch. It was ten to twelve. "They should arrive any minute."

Before she could say any more, the screen door opened and Xavier Ryan entered, followed by Frannie. He nodded to the women. "Mrs. Kessler, Miss Skye."

"Hi." Joy whipped off her apron and thrust it at Xavier. "Sorry, I've got to run. I need to get home." She held open the door. "Come on, Bitsy. We don't want Alex to be home alone too long, do we?"

Skye had worked with Joy's son that past school year. He had attention-deficit/ hyperactivity disorder, and his parents had chosen not to medicate him. He had made some gains on the behavior-management program Skye had set up, but he was still a handful, especially in an unstructured situation like being home alone.

While Joy waited impatiently for her daughter to wash her hands and take off her apron, she turned to Skye. "I'm opening up a new business this fall. It's a workout place just for women. You should come try it out. The first session is free."

Skye narrowed her eyes. Was Mrs. Kessler insulting her? She couldn't tell, so she joked, "Thanks, but I get enough exercise just pushing my luck."

Joy looked puzzled, but rushed out without answering.

Skye turned to Xavier and Frannie. "Any word from Justin?"

Both shook their heads.

"I was hoping he'd at least call." Skye chewed her lip. "As soon as I finish my morning check of the yard sale, I'll get Mrs. Frayne and we'll look for him."

Frannie nodded. "I can't believe he's doing this." She appeared to be torn between anger and the urge to cry. Her voice quavered when she asked, "Who's going to help me at the window?"

Rusty had been silent, which was not unusual. In the short period of time he had been a member of the school newspaper staff Skye could barely remember him saying three sentences.

Now he added a fourth. "I can stay."

Frannie hugged him. "Thank you."

Skye looked at Xavier. "Okay with you?"

He nodded.

"Great." Skye turned to go. "Leave me a message at Mrs. Frayne's if Justin turns up within the next couple of hours. After that, call me at my parents' house."

The last loop on Skye's inspection tour was to the east and included Doozier territory. As she steered the golf cart around the curve, she braced herself for turmoil. It was even worse than she'd expected.

Pandemonium stretched out in front of her as far as she could see. Faith Easton's TV crew had set up their camera in the middle of the road, blocking traffic, and people were honking their horns because they could edge past only one car at a time. Others were stopping their vehicles completely and getting out to see what was happening.

It was one giant gridlock, and Earl Doozier stood in the center of it, toe-to-toe with Burnett Parnell, the goat cheese guy. Burnett was heavily muscled and wore a leather vest, jeans, and motorcycle boots. The guy towered over Earl like a Great Dane next to a Chihuahua.

Spittle flew from Earl's semi-toothless mouth and spattered on the other man's bare chest as Earl yelled, "I keep telling you, Burnett, I ain't seen your goats!"

Burnett picked Earl up, his feet dangling several inches off the ground. "Then what are you feeding that mangy lion of yours?"

Skye tensed. Everyone in Scumble River knew you didn't accuse a Doozier of wrong-doing, at least not to his face and without backup, but this guy was from out of town.

Just then, Earl's wife, Glenda, had materialized next to her husband, holding a shotgun. His son Junior and nephew Cletus had crept up behind Burnett; one had a shovel and the other a bow and arrow. Flanking the fighting duo to the right was Elvira, Earl's niece, who flicked open a switchblade as Skye watched.

Skye knew she had to step in before blood was shed. She just didn't want it to be her blood. Maneuvering her cart through the crowd, she pulled up to the left of the two men, snatched a bullhorn from the backseat, and barked in her most authoritative voice, "Put the Doozier down and step back."

Burnett dropped Earl and swung on her. "Are you in charge?" When she nodded, he pounded on the front of the golf cart, causing it to tilt downward. "This guy is stealing my prizewinning goats and feeding them to his lion."

Skye paled at the horrifying image.

Before she could respond, Earl bleated, "No, I ain't, Miz Skye. I loves goats. Honest."

Skye climbed out of the cart and asked Earl's attacker, "How do you know Mr. Doozier is taking your animals?"

Burnett snarled and pointed at Junior and Cletus. "They told me."

All eyes swung to two skinny boys wearing dirty shorts and flip-flops. The redhead froze for a moment, then tried to dart away.

His mother grabbed him as he ran past her. "Junior Doozier, you explain yourself right this minute!"

"Ma." He tried to wiggle away, but Glenda's grip tightened. "Shucks, Cletus and me was just havin' some fun."

"What kinda fun?" Glenda shook him slightly.

"Burnett kept yelling at us to stay away from his goats, so I told him Pa would feed them to the lions if he didn't quit it." Junior finally squirmed free and looked at the muscled man. "We was just funnin' you."

"Then what happened to my goats?" Burnett turned to Skye, a tear on his cheek. "One's disappeared every night this week."

Skye squatted down and gently turned the boy to face her. "Did you have something to do with that, Junior?"

He scuffed the dirt with his toe. "Cletus and me lured them out of their pen, and we corralled them up yonder behind the old barn." He glared at Skye. "They're fine. We made sure they had food and water."

Burnett hurried away in the direction Junior had indicated, but said over his shoulder to Earl, "This isn't settled, Doozier."

Before he could respond, someone screamed, a roar ripped through the air, and Earl took off running toward his petting zoo.

As Skye stood frozen, a man yelled, "Oh, my God, the lion's got Wanda!"

Skye, along with the rest of the crowd, looked toward where the man was pointing. The lion was standing over a middle-aged woman he'd pinned to the ground and was sniffing her. Her brown eyes bulged from their sockets, and she was breathing in shallow gasps.

Suddenly Earl appeared, brandishing what looked like a giant butterfly net and yelling, "Here, kitty, kitty."

The animal glanced at him, gave Wanda one more sniff, and loped away.

Skye rushed up to the woman. "Are you okay? Do you need an ambulance?"

Wanda brushed off her red stretch pants, pulled down her orange T-shirt advertising a nearby bar, and shook her head. "I'm okay."

"Are you sure?"

The woman nodded and poked at her beehive hairdo, dislodging a twig and some gravel. "Boy, that animal's breath was worse than my ex-husband's." She paused, then added, "And he was about as subtle in getting me on my back."

After verifying that Wanda was un-harmed, Skye attempted to follow Earl and the lion, but it was too late. Faith had spotted her and blocked her path.

The TV star spoke rapidly into a micro-phone, not allowing Skye time to answer her rapid-fire questions. "Here is the person in charge, Skye Denison. Skye, can you explain to our viewers why you've allowed a lion to run loose through the Route 66 Yard Sale? Are you a member of some renegade animal rights group? Is this a statement against caging animals or just a publicity stunt?"

"Get that thing out of my face." Skye shoved the microphone away and tried to push past Faith. "Are you nuts? I didn't allow the lion to run free, and I'm not a member of any animal rights group."

"So, you are in favor of animal experimentation?" Faith still blocked her way.

"Yes. No. No comment." Skye finally squeezed past the TV star and ran after Earl and the lion.

Faith and her crew followed.

Skye stopped a few feet from where the animal had paused to sniff and paw at the ground.

She looked around at the crowd that had gathered in a semicircle around the scene, and raised her voice. "Has anyone notified the police or animal control?" No one answered. "Does anyone have a cell phone?" Several small devices were waved at her. "You there in the Cubs hat, dial 911 and tell them to bring a tranquilizer gun."

That taken care of, Skye turned to Earl. "How in the name of all that's holy did that lion get loose?"

Earl moved his skinny shoulders in what might have been a shrug. "Miz Skye, I don't rightly know. Probably some more snafoolery the boys got up to."

"You told me you had a padlock on the

lion's cage and the only key was on a string around your neck." Skye forced her voice to remain calm. "How could this be the boys' fault?"

"I plead contemporary insanity." Earl stared at his feet.

Skye closed her eyes and prayed for the strength to resist swatting Earl upside the head. After regaining control of her urge to do the little man bodily harm, she opened her eyes and asked, "So, how do you plan on getting him back into his cage?"

Earl's face crumpled like a used tissue. "The guy who rented him to me gave me this here net. Said if you put it over old Kitty's head, he's trained to lay down and go to sleep."

Rented? Who rented out lions for a living? The same person who named a lion Kitty, no doubt. As Skye was puzzling out these last bits of information, Earl's wife marched up to him, still carrying the shotgun. "Earl Doozier, you are too stupid to be a moron."

"Glenda, honey, don't you be saying stuff like that." Earl drew himself up straight and attempted to stick his sunken chest out. "That's definition of character. I could sue you."

Although he was right, it was a definition

of his character, Skye kind of figured Earl meant "defamation," but she wouldn't waste her time explaining it to him. It would be like trying to put makeup on a hog — annoying for the pig and frustrating for her.

Glenda grabbed Earl by the ear and screeched, "If you don't get that lion back in his cage in the next ten seconds, I'm going to knock you into the middle of next week!"

Skye stared. When had Glenda found a way to time travel? Skye tore her attention away from the feuding couple to check on the lion.

The animal was ignoring everyone and everything as it ambled down the ditch, stopping occasionally to investigate an intriguing odor or swat at an insect. As Skye watched, he started digging at the mouth of a nearby drainage pipe, growling softly.

Suddenly someone from the crowd shouted, "Look, the lion's found something."

Everyone turned to stare as the animal pulled a blue-and-yellow-striped plastic bag from the drainpipe. Skye's mind raced. Her family had ordered a case of those bags to use at their farm stand. This one bulged interestingly. Could it have something to do with the murder? If it did, and the lion tore into it, whatever evidence it contained might be ruined.

Without thinking, Skye grabbed the net from Earl's hand and advanced on the lion.

Earl, ever helpful, yelled out, "Careful, Miz Skye. Kitty don't know you."

She ignored Earl and stepped closer to the lion, which was now batting the plastic bag around like a toy. Holding the pole at the very end, Skye measured the distance between her and the animal. One more step. She advanced, aimed, and gently lobbed the huge net over him. Bull's-eye. All those games of lawn darts she'd played as a child had finally paid off.

The lion roared and Skye took off running. He pawed at the mesh once, yawned, and settled down for a nap.

When Skye got back to where the Dooziers were standing with their mouths hanging open, she asked, "So, now how do we get him back into his cage?"

Earl's slack expression became even blanker. "Uh, the owner never told me that part."

Before Skye could throttle the little man, the sheriff's squad car arrived, and since she thought it would be a bad idea to be caught in the middle of an assault, she once again restrained herself. *Shit!* She had forgotten that this section of the yard sale was in part of Buck Peterson's new territory, too. The whole rezoning thing was starting to get really annoying.

Chapter 14
Search for Tomorrow

"And then the sheriff shot the lion in the rump with a tranquilizer dart and posed for the cameras like a great white hunter who had single-handedly saved the native village from being destroyed by a savage beast." Skye finished telling Trixie about her morning as they sat on the front porch of Trixie's house, eating tuna sandwiches and potato chips. She took a sip of her Diet Coke. "It was just plain disgusting to watch him put on his good-old-boy act."

There was no sign of Owen, and Skye hadn't gotten up the nerve to ask about him yet. It had been easier to face the lion.

"Buck Peterson reminds me of an old tire — bald and overinflated," Trixie said, shaking her head in disgust. "What did he do when you showed him the plastic bag?"

"After I pointed out to him that the bags were a special order for my family's booth, and would have only been given out since Saturday, which meant that since the lion had dug it out from beneath a pile of dirt, someone had to have deliberately buried it, he said" — here Skye deepened her voice to sound like the sheriff — " 'Well, young lady, I doubt that old bag has anything to do with the murder, but don't you worry your pretty head. My men will look it over real close.' " She returned to her own tone. "The only reason he was even that polite was because of the TV cameras."

"So, what was in the bag?"

"That was the most frustrating part. They took it away without opening it."

"How rude." Trixie crunched a potato chip, swallowed, and then got down to the business at hand. "Where are we going to look for Justin?"

"I wish I knew. Any ideas?"

"He's on foot, unless someone picked him up. Would he take a ride from a stranger?"

"I don't think so. But maybe we should talk to his friends. They all have driver's licenses. Maybe they took him somewhere."

"I thought Frannie already spoke to that group."

Skye smiled grimly. "If he's hiding out because of her, the boys would never tell her. The question is, will they tell us?"

It took them the rest of the afternoon, but Trixie and Skye finally managed to find all the boys on the school newspaper staff. Rusty was the only one who admitted to seeing Justin since the concert in the park Sunday evening. When pressed, he reluctantly told the women he had seen Justin on Monday morning and that he had been looking for Skye and seemed upset.

"Why would he have been looking for me?" Skye asked Trixie from the passenger seat of the golf cart, as they made the day's final yard sale inspection.

"From what Rusty said, it sounds as if Justin had the fight with Frannie and wanted to talk to you about what to do." Trixie was having fun driving — darting in and out of the crowd.

"So, why didn't he?"

"Maybe he changed his mind, figured you'd take Frannie's side, you being a girl and all."

Skye considered Trixie's explanation, but she was soon distracted by a group of middle-aged women walking down the middle of the road four abreast, quarrelling about lunch.

One of the ladies, who looked as if she was wearing a poodle on the top of her head, was saying, "When I go to a yard sale I shop. I don't eat. I shop."

The others argued that they were starving, but Mrs. Poodle Hair kept repeating, "When I go to a yard sale I shop. I don't eat. I shop."

Skye snickered and wondered who would win — the shopper or the lunchers.

As Trixie and Skye zoomed by, narrowly missing them, the women shrieked and scattered, only to reassemble into a solid wall as soon as the cart had whizzed past. Trixie giggled and waved to them.

Skye shook her head at her friend's antics, then resumed their prior conversation. "But even if Justin changed his mind about speaking to me, why would he suddenly decide to run away?"

"Have you talked to his parents recently?"

"I've tried, but his mother's coping with her own chronic depression, and his father's in such poor physical health he doesn't seem to have the energy to deal with anything else. They're both pretty absorbed in their own needs." Skye put her hands over her eyes as Trixie nearly ran down a guy who was too busy balancing three huge wands of bright pink cotton candy to notice the golf cart speeding toward him.

"Where haven't we looked?" Trixie asked.

"We've checked the places Frannie knew about, talked to his friends, asked the campers at the Recreation Club to keep an eye out for him." Skye rubbed her temples, trying to stimulate a brainstorm. "I'm out of ideas."

Trixie turned the golf cart into the city hall parking lot and hopped out. "The problem is, with all these people in town, I don't even know where we should start."

"Me either." Skye followed her toward the Bel Air. "But Justin's mom did promise to call the police if he doesn't come home by nine tonight, so at five after, I'm going over to the Bowards' and make sure she keeps her word."

Skye dropped Trixie off at her house and headed toward May and Jed's. Trixie hadn't brought up her quarrel with Owen, and Skye had been too chicken to ask how things were going, especially since she had to face her parents' bickering once she got home.

It was close to six by the time Skye walked into the utility room. To gauge the atmosphere, she paused at the swinging doors that led to the kitchen, then blew out a breath of relief. Things seemed normal. May was bustling around making supper, and Skye could hear the TV coming from the living room, tuned to her dad's favorite news program.

For just a moment, Skye allowed herself the luxury of imagining that her parents had made up.

Then her mother turned to her and said, "Tell your father that supper will be ready in five minutes, and he'd better be washed up and at the table, or I'm giving it to that precious dog of his."

Skye passed on an edited version of her mother's message before escaping to her bedroom to feed Bingo and clean his litter. She shook her head as she scooped. Things were pretty bad when litter box duty was preferable to time spent with her parents.

She washed her hands and returned to the kitchen to help put the food on the table.

Her father was sitting at his usual place, a frown on his face. He muttered something about supper being late, and things went downhill from there.

Skye made the mistake of attempting conversation during the meal, but any topic she chose turned into a missile that her parents lobbed at each other, using her as their grenade launcher.

While Skye and her mother did the dishes, Skye made her second error by asking, "Exactly why are you so darn mad at Dad?"

"Let me see. Where should I start? He's never home. He goes missing so much I should put his picture on a beer can." May sighed and wiped her hands on the green terry-cloth towel hanging from the handle of the silverware drawer. "He fixes stuff for everyone but me. And instead of talking to me, or taking me somewhere at night, he falls asleep watching *Weakest Link*, and only wakes up in time to catch a few minutes of the ten o'clock news before he goes to bed."

"But that's how he's been for as long as I can remember. I don't understand what he's done lately that he hasn't always done."

May gave her a dark look. "Why do you always take his side? He's not the one who changed your dirty diapers, fed you, and kept your clothes clean."

"I know. I'm not taking his side." Skye tried to put her arm around her mother, but May shrugged it off. "Really, I'm just trying to understand."

"Then figure out why he's spending so much time with that tramp." For a moment May let her mask slip, and Skye could see the pain and confusion her mother was feeling.

"Bunny?"

"How many middle-aged trollops do we have in town?"

Skye wasn't touching that question with a ten-foot mascara wand.

May went on. "Why did Simon ever buy that bowling alley for her? She's nothing but trouble."

"Bunny's not the problem." Skye mentally crossed her fingers, hoping she was telling the truth. "She just bought an old car, and Dad is having a good time fixing it up. Remember how much time he spent restoring my Bel Air?"

"If that hussy isn't the problem, then find out what is." May paused at the entrance to the den. "He could have built her a new Cadillac by now."

"You need to tell Dad how you feel."

"As if he'd care." May slammed the den door behind her.

Her mother's deep unhappiness had shaken Skye, and she decided it was time to talk to Jed. But as May had predicted, he was fast asleep in front of the TV. She tried to wake him by gently shaking his shoulder, but that only succeeded in increasing the volume of his snores.

After several unsuccessful attempts, and in fear for her eardrums, Skye retreated to her bedroom. An evening of petting Bingo and reading a good mystery sounded like just what she needed.

At five after nine, Skye called Justin's parents to see if he had returned. He hadn't. Mrs. Boward had called the police, and they were going to look for him.

Feeling as if she had finally accomplished at least one task, Skye decided to go to bed. She had telephoned Simon earlier, and when he hadn't answered, she'd left a message saying she would talk to him the next day.

Before washing her face and changing into her nightgown, Skye opened the den door and stuck her head in. "I'm going to sleep, Mom. Good night."

May looked up from the newspaper she was reading. "Sleep tight. Don't let the bedbugs bite."

Skye smiled. "You too, Mom." As if any insect would dare to invade her mother's spotless house.

She had already started to close the door when May said, "Shoot. I forgot to tell you that Mrs. Griggs called around four. She wanted you to call her back as soon as you got home."

"Did she say why?"

"No, just that it was urgent that she talk to you, and she wouldn't leave her house till you called." May's expression was sheepish. "I can't believe I forgot to tell you."

"Don't worry about it. I'll call her right now."

"Her number's on the pad by the kitchen phone."

Skye dialed and let it ring until the telephone company's computer voice told her there was no one answering, and for seventy-five cents they would call her when her party was available.

May had followed her and stood wringing her hands. "Isn't she there?"

"All I got was the recording saying to try later." Skye checked the clock. It was nine-thirty. Could Mrs. Griggs be asleep? "I guess she doesn't have an answering machine." Skye had a bad feeling about the whole situation.

"What are you going to do?"

"Telephone the sheriff's department and see if she was arrested. You heard it was her pin that killed Cookie?"

May nodded.

Skye made the call and was told no arrests had been made. She passed that information on to her mother.

"Now what?"

"Guess I'll take a ride over to Mrs. Griggs's house and see if she's okay."

"I'll come along."

Skye couldn't think of a good reason to

tell her mother no, so the two women piled into the Bel Air. They drove over in silence, each lost in her own thoughts.

Mrs. Griggs's house was north of town, along the west branch of the Scumble River on Brook Lane. There were no streetlights and no other homes along the narrow, twisting road. Skye hadn't realized how isolated Mrs. Griggs was from the rest of town.

"The house is dark," May pointed out as Skye turned into the driveway.

"Mmm." Skye got out of the car and May followed. A sense of dread had settled in Skye's chest.

They both mounted the wide front steps and stood on the wraparound porch. Skye rang the bell and they waited. She rang it again and then, after what seemed like an eternity, a third time. There was no answer, and they couldn't hear anything inside. Skye's anxiety level shot upward.

"Maybe we should call Wally," May suggested.

"When we crossed Rood Street, we were out of the new city limits, remember?"

"You're right. I keep forgetting." May tapped her chin with her index finger. "I don't think the sheriff would come out if we called, do you?"

"Well, he certainly doesn't like you and

me, and now he's got his eye on Mrs. Griggs as a suspect, so I'd hate to accidentally get her into more trouble."

"What should we do?"

"I'm going to walk around the house and see if there are any lights on in the back."

"I'm coming with you." May grabbed Skye's arm.

"Why don't you wait in the car?"

"No." May tightened her hold.

"But if you were in the car, you could go for help quicker."

"Okay, you wait in the car and I'll go around the back." May's expression was a cross between stubborn and guilty. "After all, this is my fault for forgetting to tell you about Mrs. Griggs's phone call."

Skye gave up. There was no way she could persuade her mother differently. Instead she put her hand over May's where it lay on her arm, and said, "Then we need to stay together."

The two women followed the porch as it hugged the side of the house. They stopped and peered into each window they passed, but all the curtains were tightly drawn and they couldn't see inside at all.

The porch ended three-quarters of the way around the side of the house, and narrow steps led to a cracked sidewalk that wound out of sight. Skye wished she had brought a flashlight and her baseball bat.

May tsked. "Mrs. Griggs should really get this cement fixed. Someone could fall and break their neck."

Skye didn't answer, trying to concentrate on listening for suspicious sounds. All she could hear was the crickets and an occasional owl hoot.

The grass on either side of the walkway was brown and scraggly, badly in need of both a sprinkler and a lawn mower. It crunched softly as Skye stepped on it.

As they rounded the corner, the backyard exuded a sense of benign neglect. At one time it had contained a formal garden, but now the geometrical plots were merging into the general mess of the lawn. Instead of bright patches of color from the flowers, Skye could see bits of litter and tin cans glittering in the moonlight.

The only item still in good shape was the clothesline, which was white and taut between its two silver-painted poles. A bright yellow cotton pouch of clothespins hung from the center of the line. Mrs. Griggs must have fixed it after it was vandalized.

Farther back on the property as it sloped toward the river, large trees mingled with their shadows, making it appear almost like a fairy-tale woods. Skye could easily imagine the big bad wolf or the witch from *Snow White* hiding in the gloom.

She rubbed the goose bumps on her right arm with her free left hand. The nearly eighty-degree temperature did not stop her from feeling chilled.

May shivered at exactly the same time and tightened her grip on Skye. Her voice quivered when she asked, "Should we check by the river?"

"No." Skye started to walk toward the other side of the house. "I doubt whether Mrs. Griggs would go down there in the dark."

There was no way to see inside through the back windows. Shades were fully pulled down, and no light came from around the edges.

When Skye and May reached the trellis that Mrs. Griggs had mentioned the night she had the intruder, Skye stopped and examined it.

May tugged on it. "This is sure a funny-looking trellis." Although it was covered with vines twined through the wrought-iron rungs, it still looked sturdy enough to support a person's weight.

"Mrs. Griggs said it was designed to act as a fire escape in an emergency."

"That's odd." May wrinkled her nose. She did not appreciate creativity.

Skye looked up at the second-story balcony. The door was ajar, and moonlight glinted off the glass panes. Was Mrs. Griggs peacefully asleep with her door open to catch whatever cooling breezes were available? Or had an intruder once again used that exit as a means of escape?

May had followed Skye's line of sight. "Look, the balcony door is open. Do you think she's up there?"

"Let's see." Skye called out in a loud voice, "Mrs. Griggs. Yoo-hoo, Mrs. Griggs."

There was silence except for the rustling of the leaves on the trees.

The wind had picked up, and Skye could smell rain in the air. She raised her voice and shouted, "Mrs. Griggs, it's Skye Denison. Are you there?"

Not to be left out, Skye's mother added, "It's May Denison, too."

No answer beyond the squeaking of the balcony door, which had begun to swing back and forth in the wind.

Skye turned to her mom, "Let's try together, as loud as you can. One. Two. Three."

Both women bellowed, "Mrs. Griggs!"

They waited a moment, but it was evident

that there was no one conscious in that house.

"I don't think we have any choice. We really need to call the sheriff's office," Skye told May. "Do you have any buddies among the dispatchers there?"

"Betty, but she's on vacation."

"I guess we'll just have to call and take our chances, then." Skye tugged her mother toward the driveway. "Let's go back to your house." Skye was beginning to see why people had cell phones. It wasn't as if Scumble River had a pay phone on every corner, and it was mighty inconvenient to have to run home to use the telephone.

As soon as May got into the car and closed her door, Skye put the Bel Air into gear and reversed out onto the road. Her tires squealed as she threw the vehicle into DRIVE and stepped on the accelerator.

Skye was not altogether surprised to discover that the county sheriff's department did not share their concern about Mrs. Griggs. The deputy that the county dispatcher connected them with said that he would swing past the Griggs house but couldn't do anything else. She wouldn't officially be considered missing for forty-eight hours, and he had to check and see if they could be the ones to file a report since they weren't relatives.

Forty-five minutes later, when Skye called back to see what the deputy had discovered, she was told there was no sign of disturbance and nothing more the deputy could do at this time.

After a heated discussion, Skye and May headed back to Mrs. Griggs's, equipped this time with flashlights, Vince's old walkie-talkies, a pitchfork, and a canister of pepper spray. Neither mother nor daughter was happy with the other.

An hour from when they had gone to use the phone, they pulled into Mrs. Griggs's driveway again. Everything looked exactly as they had left it.

When they got out of the car, May said for the fifth time, "I should be the one to climb up the trellis. I'm a lot lighter than you are."

It had started to rain, and Skye wiped the drops from her eyes. It took all her self-restraint to refrain from bopping her mother over the head and stashing her in the Bel Air's roomy trunk to keep her safe. Instead, she silently counted to ten as she walked to the back of the house.

"I'm in better shape than you, too," May said, trotting behind her daughter and trying to hold an umbrella over both their heads, which the difference in their heights made impossible.

Skye stopped when she reached the trellis-cum-ladder and narrowly avoided getting poked in the eye by an umbrella spoke. "You probably are in better shape, but I'm doing it." She wiped her palms on her shorts to dry them.

"Are you saying I'm too old?" May shook the pitchfork she was carrying at Skye. "I'll have you know fifty-nine is not old."

"I couldn't agree with you more, but I'm still the one who is going inside." Skye tucked the walkie-talkie into her cleavage and the pepper spray into her shorts pocket. She put her foot on the first rung and heaved herself upward, saying to her mom as she did so, "You wait right here. If you hear anything, go get the police. If anyone comes at you, stab them with the pitchfork and ask questions later."

While Skye climbed, she reassured herself that this was not standard gothic heroine foolhardiness. She wasn't dressed in a negligee and high heels, nor was she walking into a basement after hearing a chain saw start up. She had backup. Granted it was her mother armed with a farm implement, but she wasn't going into the dark woods all by herself. It did bother her a little that both the little and the big hands of her watch had moved onto the twelve just as she had started her ascent. Somehow the stroke of midnight had a bad connotation to it.

As she swung onto the balcony, thunder boomed overhead, startling her, and a flash of lightning sizzled in the west, momentarily blinding her. Skye fought to keep her balance. Finally, both feet were on the wooden floor, and after a second to catch her breath she took the pepper spray from her pocket.

She advanced to the door, which was swinging back and forth. The squeaking had gotten worse, and it screeched loudly when she opened it all the way. Skye tensed, but there was no sound or motion from inside, so she stepped forward into the bedroom. She fumbled for the light switch, and when she flipped it on, a small scream escaped her. Lying in the middle of an antique sleigh bed was Mrs. Griggs, with a sword sticking out of her chest.

Chapter 15
The Girl from U.N.C.L.E.

Rain slashed at the windows, and thunder shook the glass figurines on the shelves of the étagère in Mrs. Griggs's front parlor. Skye shivered, convinced that she might never be warm again. She was trying not to think of what was going on above her head, but while she waited to be questioned by the sheriff, it was hard not to go over and over in her mind her last sight of Mrs. Griggs. Who would do something like that to another human being?

Skye closed her eyes and took a deep breath, forcing her thoughts in another direction. Was her mother all right? Was her father worried about their absence? She knew May was similarly isolated in the breakfast room, and neither of them had been allowed to make any phone calls.

She wished the sheriff would come and ask his questions so she could take her mother home, then crawl into bed and pretend this night had never happened.

Her fretting was interrupted by the bellow of an angry voice. She listened intently. It was Buck Peterson, and he was reaming out his deputy at the top of his lungs.

The men were standing in the hall, but the parlor did not have a door, so the sheriff's words were clear. "You jackass! Why didn't you do anything when they called you the first time? It would have been the perfect excuse to get into the house and look around. We might have found something else to connect her with the Caldwell woman."

The deputy was mumbling, and Skye could only catch a little of what he said: "... drove past ... standard operating procedure ... didn't know she was a suspect ... what memo?"

After several more minutes of haranguing, the sheriff's diatribe finally ended and he stomped into the parlor. Showing his teeth in what Skye guessed was supposed to be a smile, he said heartily, "Well, young lady, it looks like you've stumbled into another mess."

Skye nodded warily. She didn't trust him farther than she could throw him, and right now she felt too weak to toss a salad.

Buck flung himself into a delicate Queen

Anne armchair, and Skye winced as the antique creaked in protest. "I have to ask myself, why are there Denisons around whenever there's a murder?"

She bit back a smart answer and instead said, "Well, really, we're only there after the murder has taken place."

He ignored her and tsked. "You all are turning into regular Typhoon Marys."

"Typhoid," Skye corrected automatically.

"Typhoon, typhoid, or typographical, you're going to be watched from now on." His face darkened, and he gave up all pretense at smiling. "I have a feeling you all are the new Manson Family." He sat back and crossed his legs. "Now tell me everything you did since your first visit to Mrs. Griggs."

Skye described her movements again and again. Finally, the sheriff stopped questioning her and left the room, no doubt to talk to May. Once he was gone, Skye grew restless and started to pace. Something she had noticed in the instant she had discovered Mrs. Griggs's body was important. What was it?

She tried to let her mind free-associate by looking around at all the antiques and collectibles in the room. Mrs. Griggs seemed to have enough bits and pieces to open her

229

own store. Skye halted abruptly, nearly tripping on a worn spot in the Oriental carpet.

That was it. The sword that had been used to kill Mrs. Griggs was the same one Cookie had whacked Skye with earlier that summer. She had recognized the stylized handle. So either Cookie had sold the weapon sometime in the past eight weeks, someone had stolen the weapon since her murder, or Cookie had come back from the dead and bumped off Mrs. Griggs.

When the sheriff returned from interrogating May, Skye told him about the sword, leaving out the part that this was the sword Cookie had hit her with. No way was she giving him more reason to think she or her family were the killers.

He seemed less than impressed with her brilliant observation, but finally as the grandfather clock in the hall bonged three a.m., he allowed Skye and her mother to go home. They were once again told not to leave town.

Jed was snoring in his chair when they walked in, and there were no messages on the answering machine. It looked as if no one had found out yet about their night's activities — a stroke of luck Skye was grateful for.

They parted at their bedroom doors. Skye

stripped off her damp clothes and struggled into her nightgown, then slid wearily between the sheets.

"Skye, wake up!"

A hand shook her shoulder roughly, and she shot out of bed. "What? What's happened?"

"You have to do something!" Dante glared at her. "We can't have people thinking there's a serial killer loose. The yard sale will be ruined."

She swept her hair out of her face and squinted at the clock. It was six a.m. She groaned and tried to climb back under the covers.

Dante gripped her upper arm and wouldn't let her lie down. "No. You have to fix things."

"Get out of my bedroom or I'll scream."

"Jesus H. Christ, I've seen you naked." Dante threw his hands into the air. "Olive used to change your diapers."

At least he hadn't claimed he had been the diaper changer. "How did you find out? I thought the sheriff said he would try and keep her murder a secret, let people think she died of natural causes."

"Your mother called me."

"Shit!" Skye rubbed her eyes. She should

231

have warned May not to do that, but she'd thought the sheriff's order to keep their mouths shut would be enough. "So, what do you want me to do?"

"Find the murderer. Keep the media from blowing this out of proportion. And make sure people feel safe."

"Shall I build a replica of the Taj Mahal while I'm at it? Or maybe part the waters of Scumble River?"

"If you have time, be my guest. But first find out who killed Cookie Caldwell and Alma Griggs. Remember, if the yard sale fails, no bonus." Dante turned on his heel and stomped out of the room, adding over his shoulder, "Report to me this afternoon with your progress."

Skye saluted her uncle by putting her thumb to her nose and wiggling her fingers, then lay back down to return to sleep. But the events of the last few days kept gnawing at her. Abruptly it hit her — two people were dead. The tears she had been holding back since discovering Mrs. Griggs's body flowed.

She pulled the covers over her head, hoping May wouldn't hear her sobs. Skye didn't want to be comforted or have to explain her grief. Besides, she knew she'd end up being the one who had to suck up her emotions and comfort her mother. She had always been the strong one in the family, and she doubted things would change anytime soon.

It shocked Skye that she couldn't stop crying. Cookie's death had been bad, but it had somehow seemed surreal, either because of the frantic pace of the yard sale or because the woman herself had kept aloof and never chosen to become a part of the town.

But Alma Griggs had been an active member of Scumble River society for more than eighty years. Whoever had killed her had not only taken her life; he or she had robbed the town of a vital part of the community.

Despite the huge difference in their ages, Skye had sensed a connection with Mrs. Griggs. Skye didn't believe for a minute that she was Mrs. Griggs's reincarnated daughter, but it hadn't seemed strange when the older woman had sought out her help. In fact, it had felt right, like Trixie coming to her for a favor.

Well, the favor had just gotten bigger. Skye wiped the tears from her face with the edge of the sheet and threw back the covers. She would find out who had murdered the two women. Not because Dante had ordered her to, or because she would lose the bonus if she didn't, but because she owed it to Mrs. Griggs. And maybe she owed it to Cookie, too, for not trying harder to understand her.

It was Wednesday — halfway through the yard sale. Only four more days to go. At this point the event was running itself, and except for a couple of inspection tours through the booths during the day, Skye's work was nearly over. Unless, of course, the media latched on to Mrs. Griggs's murder. Then all bets were off. Meanwhile, she would use the time to find the killer.

After Skye had dressed and eaten breakfast, she called Justin's mother. Mrs. Boward reported that he was still missing, but the police had been out looking for him.

Skye briefly considered calling Wally or joining the search herself, but she reluctantly decided there was nothing she could do. She and Trixie had looked everywhere and talked to everyone they could think of yesterday. She was desperately worried about Justin, but could figure out no way to help.

Instead, Skye headed to the city hall. If she could do nothing for Justin, she wanted to be alone, to sit and think about how to approach the murder investigation. Because whether the sheriff liked it or not, she was going to find out what was going on.

In a way, finding a killer was like a referral she would get in her job as a school psychologist. She needed to figure out the stimulus behind someone's behavior. What was the cause? Was it something environmental, or a need that hadn't been fulfilled, or was the person getting some reward from his or her actions?

She settled behind her desk and pulled a legal pad out of the drawer. Where should she start? If this were a case study evaluation she had been assigned at school, she would start with the referral questions. So, what were they?

For several minutes Skye tapped her pen against the paper. Usually the teachers or the parents wrote the questions. She was not routinely involved in this part of the process. Finally she wrote:

1. Who were Cookie's friends? Did she have a boyfriend?

2. How did the murderer get Mrs. Griggs's pin?

3. How did the murderer get the sword from Cookie's store?

4. What does anyone gain from either woman's death?

5.

Skye frowned at the blank after the number five. She knew there was something else she should ask, but couldn't quite put her finger on it. Giving up, she drew a huge question mark and went on.

Now that she had the referral questions, she needed to figure out how to answer them. If this were a true case study evaluation, this would be where she decided what tests to give. But she didn't think even the Rorschach could determine a murderer, no matter what a person said they saw in those inkblots.

She flipped the page over and stared at the fresh yellow sheet. This was not good. She had no idea how to start getting answers. Maybe she needed some caffeine.

As she rooted through her purse looking for change for the soda machine, the phone rang. She picked it up without thinking and then was sorry she hadn't let the call go to the answering machine. With her luck it would be a reporter. "Skye Denison. May I help you?"

"Yes. You can tell me why the heck you didn't call me and tell me about finding Mrs. Griggs dead last night," Trixie demanded. "Was it old age?"

"Mine or hers?" Skye retorted. Then after swearing her friend to secrecy, she explained what had happened, concluding with, "So, then Dante woke me at the crack of dawn demanding I find out who the murderer is."

"What are you going to do?"

"I'm approaching it like a school psych referral." Skye fished out two quarters from the bottom of her purse. "I've written out the questions. Now I just have to figure out how to answer them."

"Read me the questions."

After Skye had finished, Trixie said, "I know who you should talk to about the first one."

"Who?"

"My annoying boarder."

"The antique picker?" Skye asked. "Why?"

"He knew Cookie from the city, and I think he did some business with her here as well."

"That's interesting. How do you know?"

"I heard him on the phone." Trixie's voice dropped. "He seems to be friends with that guy in charge of the TV program."

"Nick Jarvis?"

"Yep, that's the one. I think he knew Cookie, too."

"Wow. I wonder if the sheriff is aware of any of this." Skye let the coins slide from her fingers and picked up the pen, writing down the men's names under the heading "Suspects." "Is Lapp at your house now?"

"No. He left right after breakfast to go over to Odell and Pontiac. The first morning he was here, he explained at great length his method for handling this type of sale. He said he does two sections a day, and then will do a final sweep on the weekend. He's convinced people have been saving all their best stuff and will put it out on Saturday."

"I don't think my family is saving anything in particular. They're just putting out things as other merchandise sells and there's room for it."

"Well, he's really paranoid." Trixie giggled. "He sneaks his buys into the house, and he's afraid someone will see what he's purchased."

"Have you peeked?"

"Not really." Trixie's tone was innocent. "But when I was making up his room a couple of days ago, I did *accidentally* pull the blanket off of the pile, and I did notice a few items."

"What does he collect?"

"Vintage clothes and old jewelry mostly."

"What kind of old jewelry?" Skye asked.

"Gee, I don't know." Trixie paused. "Like you'd see in your grandmother's jewelry box."

"Anything else?"

"Some canes and swords."

Skye's interest sharpened. If Montgomery Lapp collected both jewelry and swords, maybe there was a connection with the murders. "Do you know when he'll be back?" She had to talk to him as soon as possible.

"He usually rolls in around three or four and demands Earl Grey tea and homemade cookies."

"Great. I'll be there at three. You don't mind another guest for tea, do you?"

"Would Watson turn down Sherlock Holmes?" Trixie asked. "See you then."

After hanging up the phone, Skye checked her watch. It was only ten. She couldn't just sit around and wait for Montgomery Lapp to get back. What should she do?

She glanced down at her notes. Ah, Nick Jarvis. In her excitement about Lapp's collecting habits, she had almost forgotten that the TV producer might have known Cookie, too. How could she find him?

She closed her eyes and concentrated, then smiled. Of course. She'd simply do her morning inspection tour. She was bound to run into the camera crew, unless they had gone to one of the other sale sites. Skye suddenly frowned. Or unless Nick had left town after murdering Mrs. Griggs.

Chapter 16
I've Got a Secret

Thankfully, there seemed to be only local media interest in Mrs. Griggs's death. Skye had fielded one call from Kathy Steele, the owner of the *Scumble River Star*, who had heard about Skye's discovery of the body but not that Mrs. Griggs had been murdered. Skye did not enlighten her.

Now, as she threaded her golf cart through the crowds, no one asked her any questions or thrust any microphones in her face. Still, journalists seemed to be a lot like pimples, popping up when you least expected them, and about as welcome. Sheriff Peterson hadn't revealed the cause of Mrs. Griggs's death, and right now few people were even aware it was murder and not just old age, but eventually someone would figure it out.

As Skye passed the corner where the

Cookie's Collectibles tables had stood, she was surprised to see activity. It hadn't occurred to her, although it made sense that someone had to either pack up the booth or run it.

She pulled the golf cart over to the curb and hopped out. Who had taken over Cookie's business? Skye's eyes widened as she spotted Kirby Tucker behind the tables. What was the TV writer doing there?

It took a while to make her way through the browsers, but Skye finally reached the front. She motioned for Kirby to come over, then stood waiting for the young man to finish with the customer he was helping.

When Kirby approached her, she said, "Hi. I'm surprised to see you here. What's up?"

"I have no idea. Nick ordered Jody and me to take turns selling this stuff."

"That's odd. Why?"

He shrugged. "I don't know. I just do what the producer tells me to."

"Do you know where I can find Nick?"

"He might be at the cottage," Kirby offered. "We were supposed to do a segment at some old lady's house today, but we got word this morning that she'd croaked, and I don't think anything else is scheduled until tonight."

"Alma Griggs?" Skye demanded. "Was that the woman whose house you were going to?"

"Yeah. How'd you know?"

Skye ignored his question, her thoughts racing. What was going on here? All of a sudden Nick is taking over Cookie's business, and the TV crew was supposed to tape at Mrs. Griggs's. This couldn't be a coincidence.

After telling Kirby good-bye, Skye returned to the city hall and retrieved her car. It was time to pay Nick Jarvis a visit.

It seemed strange to pull into her own driveway as a guest. Skye felt a flash of annoyance at finding her usual parking spot occupied by Faith's Porsche. As she rang the bell, she wondered how much damage the celebrity and the TV crew had already inflicted on her poor cottage.

After the third ring, the door was flung open by Faith, who stood with her hands on her hips, scowling. "Yes?"

"May I speak to Nick, please?" Skye strained to see past the TV star. Except for boxes stacked everywhere, what she could glimpse of her cottage looked intact.

"Why do you want to speak to my fiancé?" Faith demanded.

"Yard sale business," Skye explained, then

242

said, "I thought you two were keeping your engagement a secret."

"We were keeping it quiet, but we've decided to announce it at the conclusion of this week's show."

"Congratulations."

Faith inclined her head imperially, then stepped aside. "He's in the living room. Please don't take too much of his time."

Nick was sprawled on the sofa, surrounded by a sea of newspapers. He looked up as Skye entered, whipped off his glasses, and tucked them into his shirt pocket before saying, "Skye, what a pleasant surprise. Did you need something?"

"Hi." She sat down on one of the matching director's chairs and flashed him a pleasant smile. "No. Actually I just wanted to ask you a couple of questions, if that's okay."

"Sure, sure." Nick started gathering up papers into a pile. "Excuse the mess. I promise the place will be just like you gave it to us when we leave."

"Thanks." Skye put her purse on the floor next to her and leaned back. "I'm not worried at all," she lied.

"So, what can I help you with?"

"A little while ago, when I was doing my morning rounds of the yard sale, I saw Kirby

243

running Cookie Caldwell's booth, and he said you had told him to do it. As the sale coordinator, I'm wondering on what authority you gave that order."

"Oh, should I have checked with you?" Nick asked.

"Well, technically, yes."

"Sorry. When I found out I was the executor of Cookie's estate, it just made sense to try and sell as much of her merchandise as I could. I figured it would make settling things that much simpler."

"That makes sense." Skye crossed her legs. "I didn't realize you even knew Cookie. How did you come to be her executor?"

Nick straightened a pile of newspapers and didn't look at Skye. "She was my sister-in-law."

Before she could hold the words back, Skye blurted, "Your brother was the one dressed as a nun who died in bed with a hooker?"

Nick looked at her strangely. "That's what the authorities claimed."

"You didn't believe it?"

"Let's just say Harry was no friend of the Chicago Police Department."

Skye processed that information, wondering if it could possibly have anything to do with Cookie's murder. She couldn't think of a connection, but that didn't mean there wasn't one.

Nick and Skye stared at each other for a moment until she said, "I'm still surprised you're Cookie's executor. A brother-in-law seems a little distant. Didn't she have any family of her own?"

"She had a sister, but they weren't close, and her parents are dead." Nick leaned back. "And her son is disabled."

"She had a special-needs child?" The twinge of guilt that Skye had felt when the sheriff told her about Cookie's sad past turned into a full-fledged stab. "How old is he? Where does he live?"

"Ned's twenty-two. He lives in a private group home in the city."

Skye murmured, almost to herself, "That can't be cheap."

"No. And my brother spent every penny he earned, so there wasn't much left when he died." Nick frowned. "Cookie worked hard to pay for Ned's care."

Skye's stab of guilt turned into a shooting pain. When would she learn not to judge people so harshly? "I suppose her estate goes into a trust for Ned, and you're now his guardian?"

Nick nodded. After a moment of silence he asked, "So, is it okay to keep Cookie's booth open for the remainder of the yard sale?"

Skye got up. "As long as the sheriff doesn't mind, it's fine with me."

Nick followed her to the door. "Sheriff Peterson gave his okay yesterday. He's releasing the body later today."

"Where will you have her funeral?"

"I'll have a private service in Chicago. Probably just Ned and me, unless her sister changes her mind."

Skye had already walked outside, but turned back and took his hand. "I'm sorry for your loss."

While Skye drove back toward town, she thought about what she had learned. It seemed she could scratch Nick off her list of suspects. What possible motive could he have to murder his sister-in-law? Unless he thought Cookie had killed his brother. But then, why would he have waited so long to take his revenge?

Glancing at her watch, Skye saw that it was nearly one o'clock. Still another two hours before she could talk to Montgomery Lapp. What should she do in the meantime? Her stomach growled an answer.

Skye parked her car back at the city hall, checked out a golf cart, and headed toward the Altar and Rosary Society food tent. First she'd have some lunch, then it would be time for her long-overdue chat with Bunny — on behalf of both her parents and Simon. When she talked to them tonight, she would finally have something to report.

An hour later, Skye left her golf cart in the bowling alley parking lot and mounted the outside stairs in the rear of the building. The narrow wooden steps seemed flimsy to her, and she hated having to use them. It felt as if they swayed as she climbed, so she clung to the railing.

The wind had picked up, and the hot, dry gusts did not improve Skye's mood. She hoped they weren't in for a storm. Heavy rain could ruin the yard sale in a way that two murders hadn't been able to accomplish, and Dante would no doubt find some way to blame her and withhold the bonus he had promised her. She scowled, hating that she wanted the money so much, but she did. She longed to buy her cottage and finally own something substantial.

Normally, Skye would have approached Bunny's place from inside the bowling alley, but the business was closed during the day for the week of the yard sale, and the entrance was locked. Fighting the wind to stay upright on the small wooden platform, Skye rapped on the apartment's outside door.

Several knocks later, she was ready to admit defeat and leave. Either Bunny wasn't home, or she didn't want to talk to Skye.

Suddenly the door opened and Bunny stood rubbing her eyes, which were bloodshot and smudged with old mascara. She was dressed in a pink satin negligee that was split from just beneath her surgically enhanced breasts to the floor. The cups were embroidered with crystal beads, and matching bikini panties peeked out of the slit every time she moved.

Skye didn't even blink. Bunny had been a dancer in Las Vegas for twenty years, and some things, like her taste in clothing, would never change. Skye just hoped that her addiction to painkillers and her penchant for running away with huge sums of cash had been reformed.

Bunny grabbed Skye in a hug and dragged her inside, saying in one breath and not waiting for answers, "Skye, honey, what brings you here this time of day? I didn't think I'd see you until after the yard sale wraps up on Sunday. Do you want some coffee?"

"No, thanks. I —"

"Well, I sure as hell need a cup." Bunny didn't let Skye go on. "I can't seem to take the late nights like I used to. Before, I never went to bed until dawn. Now I can barely make it to two a.m., when the alley closes."

Skye followed her hostess into the apartment's minuscule kitchen, where there was just enough room for a two-burner stove and a half-size refrigerator. Skye leaned against the doorjamb as Bunny prepared coffee. Looking around the tiny space, Skye didn't think many meals had ever been prepared in it.

After Bunny had had her first sip of caffeine and was settled on the living room sofa, Skye said, "I hear Dad's been fixing your car. Is it about done?"

"That sweet, sweet man. I had no idea it would take so much work to get that old thing running. I feel bad stealing so much of your dad's time. But Jeddy says he's enjoying the challenge."

Skye tried to untangle what had been said from what had been left unsaid. She still couldn't figure out if her dad was just working on a car or if he'd moved on to its owner. She'd have to ask straight out. "Bunny, I don't want to offend you, but my mom is really upset that he's spending so much time over here. Should she be?"

The older woman pushed a tangle of red curls out of her face. "Skye, you should know me better than to have to ask." She took another sip of coffee. "I would never ride another woman's train."

Skye opened her mouth to reply, but Bunny continued, "Of course, if May and Jed are splitting up, I wouldn't mind being the first one in line to toot his whistle."

Skye couldn't think of anything to say in reply. Her only conclusion was that she needed to talk to her father; Bunny was out of *her* control, although hopefully not out *of* control.

Luckily, Bunny did not seem to notice Skye's silence as she chattered away about the bowling alley and the yard sale.

When she started on all the visitors in town, Skye spotted her opening. "Yes, I saw you at the concert the other night with the TV writer. How did you happen to become friendly with him?"

"He was in the bowling alley bar having a drink on Saturday night, and we got to chatting." Bunny fluttered her lashes, which was not very effective since she didn't have her false ones on. "How do *you* know him?"

Was Bunny accusing her of something or just trying to distract her? Skye answered. "I met him when the TV crew moved into my cottage."

"Oh, yeah, he mentioned that. Man, are they crowded. Miss Easton took the bedroom and master bath, and poor Kirby, Jody, and the cameraman are stuck in sleeping bags on the floor in the living room and sharing the guest bath. They flip a coin every night to see who gets the couch." Bunny shook her head. "I told him I spent a few nights on that sofa, and sleeping bags on the floor might not be a bad alternative."

"Really? I thought you said my couch was comfy. As I remember, you didn't want to leave it."

Bunny gave Skye a roguish look. "Well, at the time I didn't have many choices, did I?"

"No." Skye had to admit that when Bunny had been her houseguest, not many options had been open to her. She had been broke, stranded in a snowstorm, and estranged from her only son. Trying to wrest the conversation back to what she wanted to know, Skye continued. "Kirby seems a little young for you — or did you have some other interest in him?"

Bunny smiled coquettishly. "Twenty years isn't all that much."

"Try thirty."

"Oh." Bunny shrugged. "Anyway, I wasn't interested in him that way. I just thought my life would make a great made-for-TV movie, and maybe he'd want to buy the rights from me."

Skye winced. Simon would have a cow if Bunny's story made the airwaves. "Was he interested?"

"Kirby said it might be something he could sell, but my life has been too racy for the Christian network he currently writes for." Bunny teetered to her feet, balanced precariously on three-inch stiletto mule slippers. "He said possibly he could sell the idea to the Playboy Channel, *if* I can come up with a good hook. He's going to talk to the cameraman about maybe making a sample tape, if I think of something."

Yikes! Skye cringed. "Do you have something in mind?"

"Kirby said I need something attention-grabbing, so I'm having a party at the bowling alley Friday night."

"Party?" Skye yelped. "What kind of party?"

"Just a regular party. People buy tickets, and there's open bowling, music, and free snacks. Not only will it be a profit maker for the alley, but it'll give me a chance to do something that will grab Kirby's attention. Right now he's wishy-washy about the idea, so I have to come up with something dazzling to seal the deal."

"Do you really think that's a good idea? People around here are pretty uptight about the sort of show that would be on the Playboy Channel, and Simon would be embarrassed."

"Scumble River could use some shaking up." Bunny frowned. "But I wouldn't want to upset Sonny Boy, at least not too much."

"Maybe you should talk it over with him before you do anything more."

Bunny chewed her lip for a second, then giggled. "Nah, I still look good enough for *Playboy*." She put her empty cup down on the edge of the coffee table, where it wobbled precariously. "Anyway, how could me being a star be a bad thing?"

Absently, while mulling over how to break the news to Simon about his mother's plans, Skye reached out to steady Bunny's discarded mug, and in doing so noticed the publication sitting next to it.

As Skye made her good-byes and left, she couldn't help but wonder what on earth Bunny was doing with *PC Magazine*. The idea of Bunny on the Internet was nearly as scary as the image of Bunny on the Playboy Channel.

Chapter 17
Cheers

Skye checked her watch as she carefully climbed down the stairs outside Bunny's apartment. Shoot. It was still too early for the antique picker to be back at Trixie's. As she sat on the bottom step and contemplated her next move, she heard a loud thud, the clang of a heavy metal tool hitting a concrete floor, and a string of profanities.

Tension settled into the back of her neck like a fifty-pound bag of kitty litter. Reluctantly, Skye looked across the alley. She had seen her dad's pickup parked in the garage's driveway when she arrived, but had ignored what the truck's presence meant.

Skye slowly got up and walked toward the swearing. She really, really, really didn't want to have this conversation with her father, but things didn't seem to be getting any better between her parents, and she felt compelled to try to help.

Chocolate, Jed's Lab, was curled up asleep in a patch of sunshine on the concrete apron in front of the open double door. He opened one eye when Skye approached, then got up and padded over to her as she stood at her father's feet.

Jed's work boots were the only visible part of him as he was lying on a dolly underneath Bunny's 1984 red Chevy Camaro. Like its owner, it had seen better days, and what had once been a hot ride was now showing signs of age and hard use.

Skye petted the dog and waited until there was a pause in Jed's cursing before saying, "Got a minute, Dad?" She had been taught as a child not to bother her father when he was working, and even now that she was an adult, it felt wrong to interrupt him.

The sound of metal grinding against metal was followed by Jed's bellow. "Son of a B!" A moment later he wheeled himself out from under the car and squinted in Skye's general direction, as she stood haloed in the bright sunshine. He then heaved himself to his feet. "Ma send you?"

"No, but I want to talk to you about her."

Jed took a rag from his back pocket and started wiping the grease from his hands. "What about her?"

Skye frowned. He wasn't making this easy. "She's really upset with you."

"She'll get over it."

"Maybe. Do you really want to risk it?"

Jed ignored her question and walked over to an old fridge in the back of the garage. He opened it and took out a bottle of Budweiser. "You want a pop?"

"Sure." Skye smiled inwardly, wondering what it would take for her father to actually offer her a beer. Not that she liked beer, but his offering it would mean he acknowledged that she had grown up.

He snapped open the top of a Mr. Pibb and handed it to her. Skye frowned at the can. The only person she knew who drank this brand was Bunny. Even though the garage was technically hers, or at least belonged to the bowling alley, the fridge being stocked with her preferred soda wasn't a good sign. Skye couldn't imagine a reason Bunny would spend much time out here if it weren't for Jed's company.

Skye's anxiety increased a notch, and when she noticed a couple of lawn chairs with a small white plastic table between them set up on the side, it went up another degree. Things were looking way too cozy for her comfort level.

She sat in one of the chairs, and after a

brief hesitation her father dropped into the other. Chocolate settled at his side, and Jed's free hand automatically started to scratch behind the canine's ears.

Jed took a swig of Budweiser and said, "There's nothing for your ma to get herself in such a state about."

Skye shrugged. "Maybe not, but she is."

Jed slowly considered Skye's answer, then asked, "So, what should I do?"

Skye looked at her father petting his dog and sighed. This was Jed at his happiest — a car that needs fixing, a dog at his feet, and a beer in his hand. How could she tell him he was wrong? She took a deep breath and stiffened her spine. She had to tell him; she was afraid he would lose his wife if she didn't.

"You have to finish up whatever you're doing and not come back here." Skye deliberately made her words vague enough to apply to many different states of affairs.

"I'm waiting for a part. Should be here by Friday or Saturday, then I'll be through."

Skye wanted to scream or at least shock him with the business end of a cattle prod. He just didn't realize how serious the problem was, and obviously she was not conveying the urgency of the situation. "What would happen if you just walked away right now, today?"

Jed was silent. He stared at his calloused, oil-stained hands as they dangled between his knees. When he lifted his head, he said, "Wouldn't be right to leave a job half finished. It'll be done by Saturday or Sunday."

Skye nodded, knowing there was nothing more she could say that might change his mind. Once Jed made a commitment, he was as difficult to move as the lid on a jar of caramel sauce.

They both got up. Jed threw his empty bottle into the cut-off oil drum that served as a garbage can. Skye poured the rest of her Mr. Pibb out on the lawn before following suit. The soda was just too sweet for her.

She felt awkward as she stood in the open garage door next to her father, both of them having run out of words. Finally she kissed him on the cheek and said, "See you tonight, Dad."

"Yep." He lightly socked her in the arm. "Know what your ma's cooking for dinner?"

"Your goose if you don't straighten things out pretty darn soon," Skye muttered as she started across the alley toward her golf cart.

Skye pulled into Trixie's driveway at three-thirty, pleased to see a blue BMW X5 with vanity plates reading LAPOLXY. Trixie had said that Montgomery Lapp's business was called Lapp of Luxury, and that he drove an SUV Beamer, so odds were he was back from his daily foraging.

She took a minute to comb her hair and put on fresh lipstick before getting out of the Bel Air. Trixie's description of Montgomery Lapp's personality convinced her that this was not the time to neglect good grooming habits. As an added measure, she sprayed on some Chanel No. 5.

She was glad she had dressed in nice khaki slacks and a black polo shirt with the words "First Annual Route 66 Yard Sale" embroidered in white above her left breast, rather than her usual shorts and T-shirt. Lapp sounded a little intimidating.

Trixie must have been watching for her, because as Skye got out of her car she came running from the backyard, motioning for Skye to follow her.

"I thought it'd be a good idea for you to come in through the kitchen. It'll seem more casual that way." Once they were behind the house standing at the back door, Trixie said, "Monty just got back a few minutes ago. He's in his room cleaning up, but he should be down for refreshments soon."

"Great." Skye followed her friend into the kitchen, sniffing appreciatively. "Something smells delicious. Have you been baking?"

"I made Snickerdoodles and brownies." Trixie bustled around assembling a tea tray. "Can you grab the creamer from the fridge?"

Skye wondered if the fact that Trixie had baked Owen's favorite cookies meant they were getting along better.

Before she could ask, Trixie provided an answer. "Don't let me forget to give you the rest of the Snickerdoodles before you leave. I want Owen to smell them, but not get any."

"No progress on that front, huh?"

"No. He's as stubborn as baked-on grease at the bottom of an old casserole dish, and he refuses to apologize."

"Have you asked him to?" Skye asked.

"No."

"Have you told him what you're mad at yet?"

"No. He should be able to figure that out for himself." Trixie blew her bangs from her eyes and added the finishing touch to the tray, a small crystal vase containing a few sprays of miniature peach gladioli. "Before we decided to run a bed-and-breakfast for the yard sale, we talked about how much work taking people in for this week would be, and he agreed to do his share. But now that we have their money and they're here, he leaves the whole thing on my shoulders and tells me the cows are more important than I am. He'd have to be pretty dense not to know why I'm mad." Trixie picked up the tea tray and walked toward the kitchen door.

Skye opened it and followed Trixie through the dining room and down the hall. She had a bad feeling that Owen had no idea what he had done to tick off his wife, and unless someone told him, this was another marriage that might implode over a lack of communication.

She just hoped she wouldn't have to be the one to talk to him. It was bad enough having to have that kind of conversation with her dad. She couldn't even picture herself explaining things to Owen. He was an extremely private person, and the whole situation would be beyond awkward.

Skye hurried to catch up with Trixie in the parlor and was just in time to see her set the tea tray on the table in front of a tall, slim man already ensconced on the settee.

He sprawled across the cushions, reminding Skye of a character from an F. Scott Fitzgerald novel. His shoulder-length black hair flowed over the back of the seat, and his fair skin magnified the navy blue of his eyes. He held his pose for several seconds, then straightened and nodded at Trixie, shooting an inquisitive glance at Skye.

Trixie settled into the wing chair facing the sofa, and after Skye took the matching seat Trixie said, "Monty, this is my friend Skye Denison. Skye, this is Montgomery Lapp, our visitor from Chicago."

Skye stuck out her hand. "Nice to meet you, Monty. I hope you're enjoying our sale."

"Yes, I am." He limply squeezed three of her fingers. "I've found some really yummy things. I had no idea you people had so many treasures down here." He leaned forward and lowered his voice dramatically. "In fact, I was led to believe there was only schlock."

Skye raised an eyebrow. "People from the city often underestimate us. Appearances can be deceiving."

Monty nodded, his expression droll. "That's so true. I was driving up I-57 from Missouri and came across a town called Arcola, then a community named Tuscola. I was sure the next one would be Coca-Cola, but instead I got Champaign."

Skye laughed politely at his witticism, then said to Trixie, while continuing to focus on Monty, "Shall I be Mother?" Trixie looked confused, and Skye explained. "I mean, shall I pour the tea?"

Trixie nodded.

"Lemon or milk?" Skye asked. She had deliberately used the British expression, figuring Monty to be an Anglophile. Her ex-fiancé's mother had been fond of that affectation, and she wanted to emphasize to Monty that Scumble River was not the backwater he obviously thought it was.

After the tea and sweets had been handed round, the threesome settled back to chat.

Skye asked, "How were today's pickings?"

"Not bad." Monty smiled enigmatically. "I don't like to discuss my finds."

Trixie shot Skye a look that said, "I told you so."

"I understand. It's always best to be cautious," Skye said. "Until I became yard sale coordinator, I hadn't been around many collectors, but since the sale started I've seen some really appalling behavior."

"You're the coordinator?" Monty's look sharpened. "I'll bet you know where all the good stuff is hidden away."

"Well . . ." Skye didn't, but she thought it might be a smart idea to let Monty think she did.

"You can tell me. I can keep a secret. No one would ever have to know you told me."

As he talked, an idea occurred to her. "Sorry to say, most of the really good stuff isn't even being displayed. It's still in the old folks' houses." Skye held her breath. Would he bite?

Trixie cringed slightly, but didn't say anything.

Monty took a sip of his tea and agreed. "Isn't that the truth."

"It's too bad I couldn't convince some of them to set up a table."

"What a shame." Monty shook his head. "Especially the really old ones with no family. It's not as if they have anyone to leave their antiques to. The state will just auction them off when they die."

Skye decided to go a little farther. "In fact, I knew one lady in her eighties who had a houseful of valuables and needed the money, and I still couldn't get her to show the stuff."

"I heard about someone like that in Scumble River. Was her name Griggs?"

"Yes." Skye feigned surprise. "Who told you about Mrs. Griggs?"

"Cook—" He broke off abruptly and a flush crept up his cheeks.

"Cookie Caldwell?" Skye closed in for the kill. "You knew Cookie?"

Trixie had been watching the action as if

she was at a play, but now she joined in the conversation. "I wondered why you were so interested in her murder."

"Interested? Me?" Suddenly there were sweat stains under the arms of Monty's silk shirt.

"You always knew little tidbits of information about the case before they became general knowledge," Trixie added. "How did you do that?"

"One hears things, as one is out among the sellers." Monty took a gulp of tea and choked, dribbling the brown liquid down his elaborately embroidered vest. "What are you insinuating?"

"I'm not insinuating anything," Trixie replied. "I'm asking you how you knew that Cookie was murdered with a piece of jewelry before the sheriff released that information to the public."

"I told you, I heard people talking." His manner of speaking had lost much of its haughty inflection.

"Who?" Trixie asked.

"How am I supposed to know? They were probably locals. How would I know their names?" He looked to Skye for help, but she kept her face expressionless.

"What were they selling?" Trixie wasn't letting him off the hook.

"I don't remember."

"Really?" Disbelief was thick in Trixie's voice. "I thought you told me that after the first day you had the whole sale mapped out in your mind, that you had a photographic memory. Or did you forget to take the lens cap off?"

"I . . . uh . . . well, that is . . ."

Skye watched him struggle for a few minutes, then said, "Maybe you don't remember what they were selling because they weren't vendors."

"That's it. I must have heard the bits about Cookie's murder from someone who wasn't selling anything." He shot Trixie a triumphant look.

"Right," Skye said, enjoying her role as good cop. "In fact, I'll bet they didn't have anything to do with the sale at all."

"Uh, maybe." Monty's expression was half smile, half frown.

"You know who I think you heard the information from?" Skye asked in a deceptively pleasant tone.

"No." His voice quavered the tiniest bit.

"I think you heard it from one of the TV people." Skye closed in for the kill.

He flinched. "Well, I suppose —"

Skye interrupted him. "You heard it from Nick Jarvis, didn't you?"

A strange look crossed Monty's face, and he quickly said, "No, you're wrong. I didn't hear it from Nick." Monty straightened, and his manner became more confident. "Like I told you two ladies several times before, I don't remember whom I heard the information from. It was just a bit of gossip, not that important to me." He rose from the settee. "Now, if you'll excuse me, I have to get ready for my evening engagement."

After he left, Skye and Trixie sat in silence for a while, then Skye said, "I blew that, didn't I?"

Trixie nodded.

"The first rule of therapy is never interrupt a client, and I broke it."

Trixie handed Skye a brownie on a napkin. "No one's perfect."

"If I had just kept my mouth shut instead of filling in the blanks. But I was sure it was Nick Jarvis who told him."

Trixie bit into a Snickerdoodle, chewed, and swallowed. "What do you think he was going to say before you gave him Nick's name?"

"I don't know." Skye nibbled at the brownie, then said, "Maybe no one told him. Maybe he knew the details because he's the murderer."

Chapter 18
Love Boat

Dante was not happy with Skye's report of her day's activities, or with the progress she was making in solving the murders. Not that she cared. Skye showed up at her afternoon appointment with him only to keep peace in the family, and after his first bellow, she switched on her new favorite daydream, which featured Angel from the *Buffy the Vampire Slayer* reruns she was currently watching. Man, that guy was hot.

She licked her lips, smiled, then frowned. Why was she fantasizing about a TV character instead of Simon? And more important, why did Angel suddenly look so much like Wally?

Skye shook her head; she wasn't ready to answer those questions. Thankfully, she noticed that Dante was finally winding down, and she slipped out of his office, saying,

"Yes, Uncle Dante. Right, Uncle Dante. I'll do that first thing tomorrow."

As she headed toward her parents' house, the exhaustion from the previous night's lack of sleep overwhelmed her. She wanted nothing more than a shower and some mindless time in front of the TV.

It said a lot for her condition that she didn't even consider reading instead of watching television, since she was in the middle of a great book by one of her favorite authors.

The first hint that she was not in for a quiet evening at home was the sight of May, Trixie, and Frannie sitting on the patio with a cooler, a picnic basket, and a pile of beach bags at their feet.

Skye considered throwing the Bel Air into reverse and backing out, but it was too late. Her mother was waving, with a big smile on her face. Skye had no choice but to continue down the driveway toward the house.

Before Skye could get out of the car, the three females ran up to it.

Skye's mom spoke first; her words gushed breathlessly. "Trixie borrowed a pontoon boat. We're going to have a girls' night out on the river. I made a picnic supper, and Trixie mixed up margaritas and mudslides. And Frannie brought her portable CD player."

Skye looked at her friend, who was grinning like an idiot. "Why?"

"Why not?" Trixie heaved the cooler into the Bel Air's backseat. "It's about time we had some fun this summer." The picnic basket followed. "All you and I do is work. Do you realize that we have to go back to school in a week and a half?"

Skye finally managed to open her door and get out of the car.

May ignored her daughter's less-than-enthusiastic response to the plan and hopped into the front seat, yelling, "Shotgun."

Frannie giggled and got into the back.

Trixie attempted to follow her, but Skye grabbed her friend's arm and propelled her toward the house, saying, "Help me change clothes."

As soon as they were inside, Trixie asked, "Since when do you need assistance getting dressed?"

Skye ignored her question. "Okay, I get the part about a girls' night out. Hey, I even understand bringing my mom along since she's been a little down lately. But why is Frannie Ryan coming with us?" Skye continued through the hall to her bedroom and pulled open a drawer.

Trixie frowned. "Well, I ran into Frannie

at the grocery store while I was picking up snacks for tonight, and she seemed so dejected about Justin and all, I thought we could cheer her up."

"You know I love Frannie, and I understand what you're saying, but is it appropriate for her to be with adults in a situation like this?"

"Probably not, but I think she's more comfortable with us than her friends, especially discussing Justin. And she doesn't have a mother to turn to."

While they were talking, Skye had changed into her swimsuit and put on shorts and a T-shirt over it. Now she slipped her feet into flip-flops and stuffed a beach towel into a canvas tote bag. "I see what you're getting at, but shouldn't we be encouraging her to trust her friends and not depend on us?"

"You're right. But this is a very special circumstance. In the future we'll definitely encourage her to be with her friends more."

Skye gave in, tired of always feeling as if she had to be the conscience of the group. "Sounds like a plan." Heck, they were probably tired of her thinking that way, too.

"Great."

Skye fed Bingo and gave him fresh water, then said, "Guess I'm all set."

When Trixie and Skye came out of the

house, May, who was still in the front seat of the car, asked, "So, are we going pontooning, or should I get out and start the laundry?"

"Hold your horses, Mom. We're going." Skye settled herself behind the wheel and started the motor. "Geesh. We were only gone a few minutes."

Frannie giggled and whispered to Trixie when the older woman joined her in the backseat.

Skye eyed them in the rearview mirror as she drove the Bel Air out of Scumble River, wondering what they were up to.

The boat was tied up at the dock of a summer cabin located several miles north of town where the river was calm, with only a mild current.

As they unloaded their gear, Skye asked, "Do you know how to drive a pontoon, Trixie?"

She shrugged. "My friend said it was easy. There are instructions on how to start the engine and how to dock the boat taped up by the wheel. That's about all there is to it. He says it's like driving a lawn mower. Any ten-year-old can do it."

Skye felt her anxiety level go up and was mad at herself. Why couldn't she ever just lighten up? She was not responsible for the whole world. Still, she couldn't help but take inventory. She knew that she and Trixie were strong swimmers, but what about Frannie? And May couldn't even tread water.

While the other two women arranged the picnic basket and cooler just the way they wanted them, Skye quietly asked Frannie, "Can you swim?"

"Sure, Ms. D. Remember, we have lessons in gym class." The teen looked at her questioningly.

"Good. Just checking." Skye was relieved. She knew she could get her mom to shore without any problem if everyone else could take care of themselves.

Trixie must have been reading Skye's mind, because after they were on board and she was maneuvering the boat away from the dock, she pointed aft and said, "The life jackets are back there in that bench. Maybe we should all take one and keep it handy."

Skye flashed her a grateful look, sat back in her lawn chair, and told herself to relax.

They putted peacefully down the river, keeping near the bank and away from faster traffic, until they spotted a quiet area not far from shore.

Trixie stopped the boat and asked, "Anyone want to go swimming?"

Frannie and Skye nodded. May volunteered to get the picnic supper ready. Trixie, Frannie, and Skye swam off the back platform, splashing and dunking each other. Their whoops of laughter drifted on the slight breeze. No one would have guessed that they all had life-changing issues to deal with back in town.

When May had supper ready, she called them, and they clambered back onto the boat. They ate slowly, enjoying the food and the company.

After licking her fingers and tossing the last chicken bone into the trash, Trixie got up and started the motor. "Let's see what's up ahead."

The late-summer night was clear and warm, and there were lots of people out enjoying the water. When they came to a small tributary, Trixie steered them into it, and suddenly they were alone except for the fishes and frogs. The surface of the water was green with algae and clogged with water plants.

The overhanging trees darkened the area and drowned out most sounds. May lit the citronella torches and Frannie started up a jazz CD.

After a few minutes, Skye got up and put on her shorts and T-shirt. It was cooler here than on the main body of the river.

Trixie handed out drinks — margaritas for the adults and soda for Frannie. Skye's weariness was creeping back, and she let the others carry on most of the conversation while her thoughts drifted. When Trixie got up for another round of margaritas, she was surprised and begged off, having hardly touched the one she already had.

May, however, had polished off her first drink and took a big gulp of the second before saying, "When are men going to figure out that there is always free cheese in a mousetrap?"

Skye had officially turned off her brain for the night, and it took her a second to figure out what her mother was getting at, so before she could respond Trixie said, "That's because men are like microwaves." She waited a beat and finished the joke, "They get hot in fifteen seconds."

May chuckled. "Yeah, that doesn't give them a lot of time to stop and think."

Skye laughed, but was too tired to come up with anything witty.

When the giggles died down, Frannie said, "What I don't understand is why boys aren't willing to talk about stuff. Justin just ignores me when I want to talk about how I feel."

Trixie explained, "That's because men

are like mascara, they both run at the first sign of emotion."

They paused in their male bashing for another round of drinks; this time May and Trixie switched to mudslides. Skye, afraid she'd fall asleep if she drank too much on top of her fatigue, took one of Frannie's sodas instead.

After a big gulp, which left a chocolate-milk mustache, Trixie said, "What I don't understand is if they can put one man on the moon, why can't they put all of them up there?"

"That's right." May hiccupped. "The only reason men are alive is for lawn mowing and to fix the car."

The women hooted, but after the laughter stopped, Skye could detect a hint of sadness in their expressions.

May sighed. "I remember the good old days when the worst thing a boy could do to you was give you cooties. Now they all seem to want to break your heart."

Trixie and Frannie nodded in concurrence, then they all turned to Skye, a strange look on their faces.

"Don't you agree, Skye?" Trixie narrowed her eyes and walked over to stand in front of her. "Or have you switched sides now that you're dating Mr. Wonderful?"

When Skye didn't reply right away, May glared and joined Trixie. "Speaking of that, when is Mr. Wonderful coming home? Seems he's been at that conference a long time."

They moved closer to Skye, who had instinctively stood up in order to better defend herself. She backed up until her butt hit the rail that ran around the outer edge of the pontoon. "Mom, you know he's staying afterward to visit with his college friend, Spike Yamaguchi."

"When's the last time you talked to him?" May demanded.

Skye bit her lip. When had she last talked to Simon, and why wasn't she missing him enough to know the answer? Perhaps the reason she hadn't joined in when her mother, Trixie, and Frannie had been complaining about their significant others was because in order to be that upset with someone you had to feel passionately about him. Maybe she no longer felt that way about Simon.

While Skye was trying to sort out her feelings, Trixie and May became more and more agitated about Skye's defection from the sisterhood. They crowded in even closer, breathing alcohol fumes into Skye's face as they argued their points.

Trixie grumbled, "How can you defend men? All they think of is one thing, and once they get that they fall asleep and snore so loud it sounds as if the roof is going to fall in."

May added her two cents. "I didn't raise my daughter to be a traitor to her sex. If you were married, you wouldn't think men are so terrific." She jabbed Skye in the chest with her index finger. "You need to get married so you can be fed up like the rest of us."

Skye was recoiling from her mother's pokes when Frannie squealed and leapt up from her chair. The high-pitched screech and the teenager's sudden movement made Skye jump backward, but there was no place to go. She was already up against the railing. In that instant she felt herself lose her balance and topple over the side of the boat.

As she hit the water she heard Frannie say, "Crap! I forgot. I'm supposed to be home by six o'clock."

Skye bobbed to the surface, chilled and disoriented. Trixie and May were peering down at her. In between giggles they were calling her name and throwing her life preservers, which hit her on the head and bounced away. Frannie had dived into the water to save her and was frantically trying to get her arm around Skye's throat in the classic lifeguard hold.

Skye slapped the teenager away and glared up at her mother and best friend. "That was not funny."

May gave one more burst of laughter before getting herself somewhat under control. Trixie continued to snicker. Frannie wisely said nothing, paddling beside Skye but safely out of her reach.

May and Trixie whispered something to each other, then Trixie leaned over the side of the boat and said, "We've decided you can't come back on board until you tell us a problem you have with Simon."

May crossed her arms. "Yeah. You take that man too much for granted."

Skye sputtered. "You're kidding, right?"

"No." Trixie shook her head. "Tell us something Simon does that bugs you or stay in the water."

Ignoring her mother and friend, Skye swam toward the back of the pontoon, but when she attempted to climb up the ladder Trixie pushed her off.

Skye seethed. What could she tell them? Simon was perfect. Wait a minute. Maybe that was the problem. He was too perfect. Perfection did not encourage passion. There was that word again. When had she started to feel indifferent toward Simon? Okay, she certainly wasn't sharing any of those thoughts out loud while her mother and a student listened. What else could she say that would satisfy them?

"Simon is a morning person and thinks that my liking to sleep late is silly." Skye had started to shiver, and she was close to admitting to anything in order to get back on the boat. "He bought me this darn alarm clock that drives me out of my mind."

Trixie and May conferred, then Trixie shouted, "What else?"

"He thinks punctuality is next to godliness." Skye ground her teeth as thoughts of revenge against her mom and her best friend danced through her head. "He can't stand it if I'm even a minute late."

May snorted. "That's nothing. Your father gets into the car fifteen minutes before we're scheduled to leave and blows the horn until I come out. What else?"

Skye had had enough. "What do you want me to say, Mom, that Simon eats his young?" she snapped.

"Simon has kids?" May looked confused, the margaritas and mudslides having taken their toll. "Are they my grandchildren?"

"Well, they were," Skye retorted. "Before he ate them, that is."

Trixie and Frannie broke up, their laughter loud on the silent river.

Finally Trixie regained her breath and said, "Come on, Skye, surely you can think of something about Simon that really ticks you off."

After a long pause, Skye exploded. "He's always right! No matter what the subject, if we disagree, he's always proven right. And I hate that."

Trixie looked at May, who nodded, then said, "That wins the prize." She gestured for Skye to get back on board.

Frannie followed Skye silently up the ladder.

As Skye toweled dry, picking off weeds and wiping away green slime, she remembered what had caused her dunking and looked at her wrist. It was bare. "What time is it?"

May squinted at her watch. "Nearly nine."

"Shit!"

"Watch your language, Missy," May ordered.

"That means Frannie's three hours late. We'll have to go back ASAP. Xavier will be frantic."

Frannie moaned. "I always ruin everything."

"Everyone makes mistakes." Trixie put

her arm around the teen's shoulders and gave her a quick hug, then turned to the steering wheel.

But before she could start the motor, Frannie yelled, "No! Wait. Dad's cell phone." Frannie dug in her tote bag, then waved a small silver rectangle at them. "When Ms. Caldwell was murdered, he gave it to me for emergencies, but I keep forgetting I have it since I can't use it for anything else."

Skye glanced at Trixie, who nodded. "I think this qualifies as an emergency. You'd better call your dad right away."

Frannie started to punch the buttons, then stopped. "Could you talk to him, Ms. D? He'll just yell at me and won't give me a chance to explain."

Skye fought the school psychologist inside of her; she really shouldn't interfere between Frannie and her father, but her affection for the girl made her say, "Give it to me."

When Xavier answered, she moved as far away as she could from the others, not wanting to be distracted. "Hi, Xavier. It's Skye." She explained the situation, then listened to his reply.

He was not happy, but neither was he the screaming ogre Frannie had portrayed.

When he finished, Skye said, "Thank you. I really do think it was an honest mistake on her part, and we'll keep a close eye on her, I promise."

Skye listened a bit more and said, "Sure, she's right here."

Skye walked back toward where everyone was huddled and handed Frannie the phone. "Your dad would like a word with you."

As Frannie went to the rear of the boat to talk, two pairs of eyes turned to Skye. She gave them a thumbs-up. "Frannie can stay with us as long as she never leaves our sight and is home by midnight."

Frannie clicked the phone off and hurried toward Skye, her face a pale oval in the dim light. "Justin called while I was gone."

"Is he all right?" Skye asked, her heart pounding painfully.

Trixie grabbed Frannie, who was swaying slightly, and seated her in a lawn chair. "Take a deep breath."

Frannie put her hands on her knees, bent over, and inhaled. "Dad said there was a message from Justin on our machine. He played it for me."

"Is Justin home?" Skye couldn't stop herself from jumping in.

"No. He said he had found out some stuff

283

that messed him up and he needed to be alone to think about it. But he was okay."

"What could he have discovered?" Trixie mused.

"That I was mad at him?" Frannie asked with the self-absorption of a typical teen.

Skye put her arm around the girl's shoulders. "I think it was probably something a little more . . ." She struggled for the right word, not wanting to belittle Frannie's feelings. ". . . a little more surprising."

"Yeah, he knew I was mad. That wasn't exactly a stop-the-presses kind of discovery."

"Stop the presses," Trixie reiterated thoughtfully. "Mmm, maybe he was investigating a story for the school paper and found out something."

"Right." Skye thought for a moment. "And what's currently the big story?" She answered herself. "The murder."

May had clearly decided she'd been silent long enough. "Which one?"

"Good point, Mom," Skye acknowledged. "He would have been investigating Cookie Caldwell's murder, but maybe hearing about Mrs. Griggs's death last night was what motivated him to call."

Trixie nodded. "Sure. He's nosing around the first crime and finds out something that bothers him, something he doesn't know what to do with, but when he hears about the second killing, he wants to reassure everyone he's okay." She turned to Frannie. "Can you remember what his message said exactly?"

Frannie closed her eyes and recited slowly, obviously struggling to recall the precise words. " 'Hi, Frannie, this is Justin. I'm fine, but I found out some shit that pissed me off, and I need some time alone to figure out some stuff. Tell my parents I'm okay and I'll be home soon. Hope you're not still mad at me.' "

"Call Mr. and Mrs. Boward right now," Skye directed, feeling guilty because she hadn't thought of that immediately.

While Frannie spoke to Justin's parents, the other three women continued to discuss what his call might have meant.

Frannie rejoined them. "Mrs. Boward said she'd let the police know."

"Good." Skye was silent for a minute, then asked, "Could you tell by the time he left the message — did he expect you to be home, or was he trying to get your machine so he wouldn't have to talk to you?"

Frannie's eyes widened. "That creep! He called when he knew I'd be at my dance lesson. And here I was feeling bad about not being there for him."

May patted Frannie's hand. "Men are like Ziploc bags. They hold everything in, but you can always see right through them."

Skye was glad she hadn't just taken a drink of something, or she would have spewed it all over herself. Trixie was laughing so hard it looked like she was about to pee her pants. And Frannie was giggling, seeming more like her normal self for the first time since she had remembered her curfew and accidentally caused Skye to fall overboard.

Skye had to admit, a girls' night out had been just what she needed. All except tumbling into the river and having her mother and best friend torture her until she told them what they wanted to know. She wasn't forgetting that, and eventually they would be made to pay. It might not be right away, but when they were least expecting it, she would settle the score.

After getting the good news that Justin was okay, even though not back home, the women had decided to continue pontooning. The rest of the evening, they'd laughed, sung, and bonded over the impossibility of ever understanding men. For a couple of hours they had been able to forget the murders, the yard sale, and, more important, their troubles.

Skye and the others dropped Frannie off at ten to twelve and watched until she was safely inside. Trixie was next. Skye was surprised to see Owen sitting on the front porch when she turned the car into the driveway. Skye waved, but either he didn't see her or he was ignoring her.

Trixie hopped out of the Bel Air in a flurry of hugs and good-byes. As Skye backed the car out onto the street, she wondered what Owen would have to say. His expression was hard to read at the best of times, and in the semidarkness, she couldn't tell a thing. He could be about to apologize or ask for a divorce, for all Skye could make out.

Although it was only a few minutes between the Frayne and Denison farms, May was already snoring lightly when Skye parked in front of the garage on her mother's side.

May woke up with a start as the car stopped. "What? Oh, we're home. Good. I'm tired. 'Night."

" 'Night, Mom. Sleep tight." Skye watched as her mom tottered into the house still half asleep. There was little chance Jed was still awake, which was probably for the best. If Jed and May could only get to the weekend without a fight, and he kept his promise and finished with Bunny's Camaro, then maybe they could straighten things out between them.

Skye forced herself to return the cooler and picnic basket to their appointed places in the garage. Then she picked up her tote bag from the car and went inside. Tired as she was, she made sure the back door was locked and the lights were turned out before trudging into her bedroom.

She peeled off her shorts, T-shirt, and the clammy swimsuit underneath, then tried to figure out where her nightgown was. Had she ever been this exhausted before? She wanted to wash her face and brush her teeth, but the bathroom was just too far away. Still wondering what she had done with her nightgown, she fell into bed. She had a vague impression of Bingo curling up on her back, then nothing until morning, when all hell broke loose.

Chapter 19
Twilight Zone

It was tough getting up Thursday morning, but Skye finally dragged herself out of bed at eight o'clock. Actually prying her eyes open and then pulling herself together took another hour.

Upon checking her parents' answering machine, she discovered that she had once again missed Simon's nightly call. His message sounded a bit put out, and after stopping to think, Skye realized that the last time she had actually talked to him had been Sunday evening. She had missed him the last four times he had called. He knew nothing of Alma Griggs's murder or Justin's disappearance.

Simon had left a new number for her, saying he had checked out of the hotel and was now staying with his friend Spike. He also said he would phone Thursday at ten p.m. her time and hoped she would be there.

Skye resolved to be available for the call, even if she had to lock herself and the phone in the bathroom an hour before the appointed time.

Maybe she should try reaching him right now, since for once she was home alone — her mom had the early-morning duty at the Denison/Leofanti booth, and her dad was working on Bunny's Camaro. She reached for the receiver but then hesitated. It was only seven a.m. California time, and while Simon was an early riser, that didn't mean his friend was, too. She'd better wait for his call that night.

She had just sat down with a cup of coffee — tea just wouldn't do *this* morning — when the doorbell started ringing.

Before she could put her mug down, the ringing bell changed to pounding, accompanied by shouting. "Open up. Sheriff's Department."

Skye choked on the swallow she had just taken, and she was still coughing while she fumbled with the lock. As soon as it clicked, Buck Peterson thrust the door open. The glass rattled as the frame banged into the wall. Her breath caught in her lungs as the sheriff, followed by a deputy, pushed their way into the utility room.

Peterson spoke brusquely. "Skye Denison,

we've come to escort you to the sheriff's office. We have some questions to ask you."

She stared at him, her eyes wide with shock. The pulse in her neck felt as if it was beating at ten times the normal rate. "Wha—?"

He grabbed her by the upper arm and started to pull her out the door before she could complete the word. "You can either come with us voluntarily or we'll arrest you and take you in handcuffs," he snarled.

A part of her listened to the sheriff, while the other part noticed that the deputy had disappeared down the hallway toward her bedroom.

"Why?" Skye asked, stalling and trying to figure out what she should do. "Where's your deputy going?"

The sheriff ignored her questions and silently marched her out the door.

"Hey, I need to leave a note for my parents." Skye tried to squirm out of his grasp.

He continued to ignore her and shoved her into the back of his squad car.

Skye briefly thanked God that there were no neighbors close enough to see her being taken away by the sheriff like this. She felt her chest tightening. This was mortifying.

Peterson ordered her to buckle her seat belt, then got into the driver's seat. She leaned forward, threading her fingers through the metal grill separating the front and back, and tried again to ask what was going on.

Peterson cut her off. "Sit still and shut up." He looked straight ahead until his deputy came out of the house and got into the passenger side of the cruiser. Then he asked, "Anything?"

The deputy shook his head, and the sheriff started the engine and slowly backed out of the long driveway.

What had she done? What was happening? The forty-five-minute ride to Laurel, where the sheriff's office was located, was excruciating. Skye's emotions ranged from outrage to fear and back again. The two men didn't speak, and the radio crackled but was otherwise quiet.

After a while Skye noticed that the back of the sheriff's vehicle was a lot different from the back of Wally's squad car. While Wally's was clean enough to perform surgery in, the sheriff's could easily have been mistaken for the city dump.

Fast-food wrappers, newspapers, and cigar butts littered the floor. The seat itself felt sticky, and Skye could only hope it was spilled soda and not some disgusting bodily fluid. Worst of all was the stench, a combination of stale cigarette smoke, urine, and vomit. Since she tended to get motion sick if she rode in the backseat, she was worried she might contribute to both the mess and the odor.

Finally Sheriff Peterson parked in his designated spot in front of the county building and yanked Skye out of the vehicle. Icy fear swept through her as he marched her in silence down the sidewalk and up the stairs. The deputy did not accompany them into the main office; instead he turned off into a hallway on their right.

The sheriff grunted to the dispatcher as they passed by. "Call the jail for a matron."

Peterson deposited her in a stark room with only a table and two chairs and locked the door behind him. Dread twisted Skye's heart. Why had she been brought here? What should she do? Who could she call? Would Wally help her? This was bad. This was very bad. She tried to retrieve the anger she had initially felt over her treatment, but she was too scared. This was even worse than she had originally thought.

On the ride over it had dawned on her that they wouldn't be treating her this way unless they thought she was the murderer. What had made them think that? Skye forced herself to focus, but couldn't come up with anything except that she'd been the one to find Mrs. Griggs's body. Surely that wasn't enough for them to arrest her.

After what felt to Skye like the longest wait of her life, Peterson walked back into the room, a tall woman in a tan uniform following him. The woman wore no makeup and her blond hair was pulled back into a tight bun. She sat on the molded plastic chair she had carried into the room and placed in the corner. Her gray eyes held no empathy as she gave Skye a quick once-over.

The sheriff didn't introduce her; instead he took the remaining seat at the table and scooted close to Skye. The smell of stale tobacco and sour whiskey rolled off him, causing her eyes to water. She twitched her nose, trying not to sneeze in his face.

Suddenly Peterson leaned even closer and shouted, "Why did you kill Alma Griggs? Did she see you kill Cookie Caldwell? Was she trying to blackmail you?"

"What? No! I mean I didn't kill either one of them," Skye sputtered. "Are you crazy?"

"We have evidence that links you to the Griggs murder," the sheriff said, smiling a mean jack-o'-lantern grin.

"That's impossible. Because I didn't do it."

"Which is funny, since we definitely have

evidence you did," the sheriff stated, clearly pleased with himself.

"Oh, my God." Skye was beginning to feel queasy again, and this time she couldn't blame motion sickness for her nausea. "I'd better call my attorney."

Peterson nodded. "That might be a good idea. But if you do, we have to sit here until he arrives. In fact, once you get a lawyer involved, you could end up in jail, waiting to hear about bonds and things."

Could he really do that? Skye felt a shiver of panic run up her back. Of course he could. This was Stanley County, and Buck Peterson had been sheriff here for nearly thirty years, which meant he could do just about anything he damn well pleased, including searching her room without a warrant and throwing her in jail just for the hell of it. "But I haven't done anything!" She fought to calm down. "What's this evidence?"

"Well, I'm not sure I should tell you." He tried to sound coy, but the effect was lessened considerably because he looked like Hulk Hogan's father.

This was obviously a man who got off on power. Skye played along and begged. "Please?"

"I guess it wouldn't hurt, since you asked

so prettily." He smiled viciously. "It's not as if you won't hear it in court at your trial."

"Trial?" Skye echoed in a small, frightened voice. She could feel herself starting to lose it, and struggled for control. She had to be strong. She was innocent, and there was no way she was going to trial. He was just trying to scare her. Right now she had to find out what this so-called evidence was. After a deep breath, she asked, "What is it?"

"Your earring . . ." The sheriff watched her closely, then delivered the rest of his bombshell. ". . . was found at the crime scene."

"What earring? How do you know it's mine?" Skye babbled questions, then got hold of herself. "Besides, I discovered the body. I must have lost it then."

The sheriff's lip curled. "It was an emerald earring, which we discovered had been made especially for you as a Valentine's gift from your boyfriend."

Skye frowned. She wore those earrings only on special occasions, and she was certain she hadn't been wearing them when she climbed Mrs. Griggs's trellis. She'd been wearing gold hoops with tiny Route 66 signs on them since the yard sale began. But she couldn't let Buck Peterson know that. If she hadn't lost the earring the night she found the body, then it would point to her having been inside Mrs. Griggs's home another time. And she hadn't been.

She bluffed, trying to sort things out in her mind. "So I lost an earring the night I found Mrs. Griggs's body. That doesn't prove anything."

The sheriff sighed. "If that's the case, then how did it get underneath the body?"

Skye felt a flicker of apprehension. "What?"

"It was under Mrs. Griggs, between her and the bed."

"That can't be."

Peterson's polished-steel eyes shone with victory. "But it is."

"I didn't kill her." Skye felt panic swell in her chest and lodge in her throat.

"Then how did your earring get there?" the sheriff asked. "Tuesday night you stated you had never been in her house before then."

"That's true." Skye's thoughts raced. How did her earring get there? When was the last time she'd worn those earrings? She couldn't remember. Finally she asked, "How did you find out the earring was mine?"

"An anonymous tip. Then we checked with the local jeweler, who remembered the special order."

"Didn't you find that odd?" Skye seized on the inconsistency. "How did your tipster know you had the earrings? Most people don't even know Mrs. Griggs was murdered. Most people still think she died of old age."

Peterson looked momentarily confused, then brightened. "Maybe it's your accomplice — a falling-out among criminals. Happens all the time."

"And who would that be?" Skye asked.

"Your mother was with you that night, and she found Cookie Caldwell's body, too. Maybe it was her."

"So you think my mother and I killed Mrs. Griggs for some unknown reason, then my mother turned on me and called you to tell you my earring was at the crime scene?"

"Look, try to wiggle out of this any way you can, but the earring is yours." Buck crossed his arms, clearly unwilling to examine an explanation of which he had grown fond.

Skye straightened her spine and assumed a dignified pose. "Perhaps, but number one, I would hardly wear an expensive emerald earring to climb a trellis in a thunderstorm. Two, even if I did, how would anyone, including an accomplice, know I had lost it? And, three — the important question — why would I kill Mrs. Griggs? I have no motive."

"Not one we know of."

In exasperation, Skye blew a curl out of her eyes. "What was the time of death?"

The sheriff scowled, but clearly at least some of Skye's arguments had made him doubt his case because he got up and went out of the room. He came back a few moments later and said, "Between four and six p.m."

Skye took her first relaxed breath since he'd accused her of the crime. "I was with Trixie Frayne from four until ten before six. We were riding around the yard sale in an open golf cart, and we talked to several vendors and three or four of our students." She listed the names. "From six until we found the body I was with my parents. So unless I managed to get to Mrs. Griggs's house from downtown Scumble River, kill her, and get back to my parents' place in ten minutes, no way could I have murdered her."

The sheriff's expression was sour. "Give me those names again."

After Skye listed everyone she could remember having spoken to that late afternoon, Peterson said to the matron, "Keep an eye on her. Do not let her talk to anyone. If she has to go to the bathroom, watch her pee."

Skye's relief was so great she felt giddy, but after Peterson left, as she sat staring at an Abe Lincoln–shaped coffee stain on the table, she sobered up. How had her earring gotten under Mrs. Griggs? Who was the anonymous tipster? It had to be the murderer. Why was he or she trying to frame her?

The dispatcher's voice talking to the matron penetrated Skye's thoughts. "The sheriff says for you to bring her up to his office."

When Skye entered his domain, Peterson was slouched in his chair, looking peeved. "That will be all for now," he told the matron.

Skye fought to keep her voice neutral. "So, do my alibis check out?" She wasn't sure if he was in a bad mood because he had cleared her or because he had found more reason to think she was guilty.

"Yes. Lucky for you, you and Mrs. Frayne seem to be quite memorable."

"Can I go?" Skye asked, rubbing the goose bumps on her arms. She felt chilled, and she didn't think it was just from the air-conditioning.

"In a minute." Peterson leaned forward,

attempting an avuncular smile. "I spoke to Chief Boyd, and he said that you've probably been snooping and might have some relevant information, so since I may have been a little rough on you before, I'll give you a chance to come clean. I promise not to press charges for interfering in an ongoing investigation."

"And what do I get out of this exchange? I know you're not really going to arrest me for interfering, since I haven't done anything illegal."

"This is your chance to fill me in on anything you've discovered that you think I should know, *and* it's your chance to ask me one question."

She raised an eyebrow. "In other words, you've come up against a blank wall, and you want to see if I can give you a lead."

"Now, little lady, that's not very nice of you to say."

"I'll try being nicer, if you try being smarter."

He visibly struggled to retain his amiability, but there was a distinct tightening of his jaw. "Well, if you haven't found out anything . . ."

Skye hated having to cooperate with such an obnoxious man, especially when she knew she was right about his motives, but she reminded herself you can catch more flies with honey than with vinegar — although why anyone wanted flies, except to squash them, was beyond her. Nevertheless, she smiled and said, "Two questions."

He frowned, but nodded his agreement.

"Here's what I want to know. Did you find any usable fingerprints connected with Cookie's murder, and what was in the bag the lion found?"

"I'll give you a copy of the official list and tell you about the fingerprints *if* you have any useful information to give me."

"Okay. Let's see, what have I found out? Cookie's brother-in-law has already re-opened her stand and is selling off everything."

"But he doesn't get the money."

"No. But he's in charge of his nephew's trust, and the boy is mentally challenged, so Jarvis *could* siphon funds without much difficulty."

"Interesting." The sheriff grunted and made a note. "Anything else?"

"Were you aware that Montgomery Lapp, an antique picker staying in town for the festival, collects both old jewelry and swords?" Not waiting for a response, Skye went on. "Also, he knew Cookie, he somehow knew about details of her murder before you released the news to the press, and he knew that Mrs. Griggs had a houseful of valuable items that she was not allowing the pickers or dealers to see." Skye crossed her legs. "If you add that to the fact that someone broke into Mrs. Griggs's house and stole the pin that was used to murder Cookie, I think Lapp is an extremely likely suspect."

"How did you find out all that?"

"I hear a lot of stuff just by being around and available. Scumble River has no other mental health professional within miles, so people talk to me. They tell me things." Skye narrowed her eyes. "Which is why maybe Wally isn't such a fool to include me in his investigations after all."

"Civilians should never be allowed to participate in official police business." Peterson crossed his arms and scooted his chair back.

"Fine. Then you don't want to hear the other thing I found out?"

The sheriff heaved an exaggerated sigh. "Sure, go ahead. I might as well."

"Did you know that the TV crew that's filming the yard sale was supposed to do a segment at Mrs. Griggs's house the day after she died?"

"So?" Peterson looked confused. "What does that have to do with anything?"

"Mrs. Griggs told me that she wouldn't allow anyone in her house until she had the appraiser come, and he couldn't get there until the Monday after the yard sale."

"She must have changed her mind. Old ladies do that, you know."

Skye shook her head. "Not Mrs. Griggs. She was determined and very cautious after Cookie tried to rip her off earlier this summer."

"I'll check the TV thing out, but I don't see how it could have anything to do with her murder." The sheriff made a note in the file open on his desk. "Anything else?"

Skye debated whether she should share the other piece of information she knew. Should she mention that Justin might know something and that was why he had disappeared? Finally, she decided not to and prayed it was the right choice.

"So?" Peterson sat forward, his gaze sharp. "What else do you know?"

"Nothing I can think of."

"If you remember something, call me." The sheriff handed her a card. "This is my private line. I'll get a deputy to drive you home. You can wait downstairs."

She was obviously being dismissed. Did that mean he was about to welsh on his part of the bargain? "Uh, so, what about those fingerprints, and do I get the list of what was in the bag the lion found?"

He glared, but took a piece of paper from the folder and handed it to her. "Have the dispatcher make you a copy on your way out. And we found hundreds of fingerprints, but none we could isolate as being connected with the crime."

Skye lingered by the door. "Have you found many of Cookie's friends?"

"How many times do I have to tell you, I don't repeat myself?" The sheriff didn't look up from what he was writing. "Let's get this straight once and for all. You got your two questions, and that's all you're getting. We are not working together on this case." When she didn't say anything, he asked, "Got it?"

"Yes."

"Don't let the door hit you on the backside on your way out."

She was halfway down the hall when she heard him shout, "And I don't want to hear your name mentioned in connection with this case again."

Skye shrugged. Then he probably had better get earplugs. Now that she knew someone was trying to frame her, she was even more determined to solve the mystery.

Chapter 20
Strike it Rich

"Well, the good news is I finally talked to Bunny." Skye had indeed locked herself in the bathroom with her parents' phone, and now she was lounging in a tub full of Mr. Bubble. She hadn't questioned why her mother had saved the bottle of children's bubble bath for the past twenty-odd years — the last time she could remember using it, she had been twelve — she had just been grateful for the effervescence.

Simon halted her trip down memory lane by asking, "And the bad news?"

"Mmm, where should I start?" Skye trailed foam from her fingertips. "Bad, terrible, or awful?"

"Start with awful and work your way down."

"The worst news is that Mrs. Griggs was murdered." As soon as she said it, her throat seemed to close up, and the tears she had held back burst forth. Skye told Simon the details through her sobs.

Finally, both her tears and the story ended, and Simon offered words of comfort before asking, "Why didn't you call me when this happened?"

Skye frowned. Why hadn't she? Had it just been that everything afterward had happened so fast that the thought had never occurred to her? Or was it because she still didn't think of herself as part of a couple? Not knowing the answer, she hedged. "It was so late and I was exhausted, and there was nothing you could do."

He was silent for a moment before asking, "Are you all right?"

"I am now. But this morning I thought I would have to ask you for bail money." Skye related her experience with the sheriff, concluding with, "And I didn't think he was going to let me go, even after I proved I had an alibi."

"It would take Buck Peterson an hour and a half to watch *60 Minutes*." The derision in Simon's voice was obvious. "As your father would say, he's about as useful as a one-legged man in an ass-kicking contest."

Skye was startled. This was a side of Simon she didn't often see. "At least I seem to be off his suspect list."

"So, what's the terrible news?"

"Justin has run away."

"Shit!"

Skye felt a flicker of shock go up her spine. Simon almost never swore.

"When did this happen?"

Skye chewed her thumb. If he was upset about her not calling about Mrs. Griggs, he would go ballistic when he heard how long Justin had been missing. "Monday night."

"Damn it all to hell."

Skye winced; Simon was not taking her news well at all. She quickly filled him in on the particulars, finishing with, "But he left Frannie a message last night saying he's fine."

"So far."

"So far. He promised to come home soon and said he's in a safe place."

"If we can take the word of a sixteen-year-old."

"Right." Skye hesitated, not knowing what else to say.

Simon took a deep breath, sounding something like a vacuum cleaner sucking up a stray sock, and asked, "What's the bad news?"

Skye dreaded telling Simon this part. Mrs. Griggs's murder had saddened him, and Justin's disappearance had worried him, but this information would just plain infuriate him. She cleared her throat. Maybe she should wait until he got home to tell him.

"Are you still there?" Impatience bristled off each word. "Have we been cut off?"

"No, I'm here." Skye sat upright and braced herself. "The bad news is that Bunny's trying to sell her life story to the writer on the TV crew." Skye heard an audible gulp from Simon's end of the line, but she kept talking. "The writer said that her story is too racy for the Christian network he works for, but . . ." She paused, then rushed on. "But he told her he might be able to sell the idea to the Playboy Channel, if Bunny can come up with something attention-grabbing for an audition tape."

"Son of a —"

Skye cut him off. Might as well get all the bad news out at once. "Bunny has decided to have a party at the bowling alley tomorrow night, and she says she's going to figure out something dazzling for them to shoot during the festivities."

"What?" Simon's roar disturbed Bingo, who had been sleeping on the bath mat. The cat got up, glared at Skye, and stalked away to hide behind the toilet. "I should have closed the place down while I was gone. Just locked the door and taken the keys."

Skye was silent, not knowing how to comfort him.

Finally Simon asked, "When did you find out about this?"

Skye was relieved to be able to answer honestly, "Just yesterday."

There was a pause before Simon muttered, "I wonder if I could get a plane home tomorrow morning?"

Skye debated whether to offer her opinion and ended up saying, "What could you do if you were here? Bunny's a grown woman. Maybe you could stop her from using the bowling alley, but you couldn't stop her from making the tape."

"You're right." Simon wavered. "I've never been able to stop Bunny from doing anything."

"Look, I'll go to the party at the bowling alley and keep an eye on things. If they get too out of hand, I'll, I'll . . ." Skye hesitated. What *would* she do? "I'll steal the tape from the cameraman," she promised rashly, then added, "Of course, that means I won't talk to you tomorrow night, since I doubt I'll be home much before midnight."

"That's fine. I'll be out late, too. Spike got us tickets for a sold-out concert tomorrow night, then we're invited to the orchestra party afterward. But I'll phone you Saturday evening."

"I should be here for your call. The church is having an ice cream social, but that should wrap up pretty early. Don't worry. Everything will be fine." Skye crossed her fingers as she hung up the receiver. She was going to need all the luck she could get in order to keep Bunny in line.

Friday's daylight hours had been quiet. The truth about Mrs. Griggs's death was still not widely known, and the yard sale went smoothly — only minor traffic problems, a temporarily misplaced child, and a bad case of sunburn for Skye to deal with.

Friday evening was another issue altogether. It started off badly when Jed suggested to May at supper that they go to the party at the bowling alley, saying Bunny had given him two tickets. The fight that ensued was not a pretty sight, and Skye slunk off to her room, struggling not to get involved.

At seven she snuck out of the house. Her father was snoring in the recliner in front of the living room TV, while her mother had shut herself in the den, blaring that TV loud enough for Grandma Leofanti to hear — and she'd been dead for more than two years.

Since it was apparent that her parents weren't going to be using the tickets Bunny had given Jed, Skye helped herself to one of the pair sitting on the clothes dryer along with Jed's change, wallet, and pocketknife. She was surprised her mother hadn't torn them up and tossed them in the trash.

Skye parked in the bowling alley's crowded lot and walked around to the front, noticing as she did that most of the vehicles had out-of-state plates and many had small trailers hitched to them. Bunny's party had attracted the tourists who were staying in or near Scumble River for the yard sale.

Skye squinted as she pushed through the glass door and handed her ticket to the young woman guarding the entrance. The overhead lights had been dimmed, and some sort of strobe flashed red, green, yellow, and blue. The music was loud, but the overall noise level was even more deafening.

As Skye stood in the entrance area, trying to get used to the strange lights, earsplitting noise, and overwhelming smell of cigarette smoke, she heard her name being called.

Trixie was standing next to a table down by the rail that separated the bowling lanes from the rest of the establishment. She was waving her hands above her head and jumping up and down.

Skye waved back and headed in her friend's direction. As she made her way through the crowd, stopping every few feet to greet people and chat, she saw that the TV crew was present, busily filming the party.

Frowning, Skye quickly scanned the area. Everyone was fully clothed and seemed to be behaving themselves. People were mostly drinking, bowling, and talking. Nothing the Playboy Channel would find very exciting.

Good. Since things appeared to be under control, she could use this opportunity to talk to the TV crew about the mysterious appointment they'd had to tape Mrs. Griggs's house.

Skye hugged Trixie, then sat down and gestured to the remaining two empty chairs. "Are we saving these for anyone?" She was hoping the answer would be Owen, but she was disappointed.

"This is actually Bunny's table, so one is for her. The other is for the first cute guy I see."

Before Skye could pursue that remark, Trixie leaned forward and hissed, "Forget about the seating arrangements. What's this about you being arrested yesterday morning?"

"I wasn't arrested, just brought in to answer some questions. I wasn't handcuffed or anything," Skye denied, then asked, "How did you hear about it? Did the sheriff call you to verify my alibi?"

"No. The matron who sat in on your interrogation is the second cousin of my aunt's daughter-in-law."

"You're kidding." Skye paused to try and follow the branches of Trixie's family tree.

"The matron recognized your name and called her cousin, who called her mother-in-law, who called me."

"Wow. I think that's a record, even for this town."

"Quit stalling and tell me all about it. Don't leave anything out," Trixie ordered.

Skye had been through this with her parents, Dante, Simon, and Wally. The first four were furious at the sheriff and ready to recall him from office. Wally hadn't said anything negative against Buck Peterson, but his expression had been thunderous, and Skye would have bet her yard sale bonus that there was trouble brewing between the Scumble River Police and the Stanley County Sheriff's Department.

Regardless of everyone's reaction, after repeating her story four times Skye was well rehearsed, and she recounted her experience to Trixie without hesitation. She ended by saying, "At least the sheriff kept his word. He told me there were no usable fingerprints at Cookie's murder scene, and he gave me a list of what was in the bag the lion found."

"So, what was in it?"

Skye looked around, but no one seemed to be paying any attention to them — which was fairly amazing considering that Trixie was wearing a denim miniskirt and a pink lace tank top, both of which were barely bigger than doll clothes.

Skye beckoned her friend closer and lowered her voice. "A hand towel with bloodstains, a small cardboard box with cotton batting inside, and a woman's purple T-shirt, size extra small, also with bloodstains."

"Did the bloodstains match Cookie's blood?"

"I don't know. It was just a list of the contents." Skye took another scan of the room and asked, "You don't have any cousins twice removed who work at the county lab, do you?"

"Not that I know of." Trixie wrinkled her brow, thinking hard. "Nope."

They sat in silence for a while, staring at the bowlers and occasionally cheering someone who made a spectacular seven/ten pickup.

Finally Skye said, "I'm going to get a soda. Do you want anything?"

"Sure, get me a Bloody Mary."

Skye nodded and headed toward the bar. Was it her imagination or was Trixie drinking more than usual — the margaritas with May in Joliet, the mudslides and margaritas on the pontoon, and now a Bloody Mary? Maybe fighting with Owen was taking its toll on her.

As Skye pushed through the swinging door to the bar area, she admired the new sleek look. Simon had remodeled the bowling alley after he purchased it, enclosing the bar area to create a small dance floor and building a stage off to the side.

Tonight Godly Crüe was playing, and Skye wondered how Bunny had managed to book them. They should have been long gone from the area and back home in Alabama. She shrugged, then smiled. They didn't play the kind of music that the Playboy Channel would be interested in. So far, there didn't seem to be anything for the TV crew to film for their audition tape. Maybe things would be okay without her assistance.

While Skye stood in line at the bar, she spotted Bunny strolling from table to table chatting with the customers. Skye waved, and the older woman headed toward her.

Tonight Bunny had outdone herself. She wore a black vinyl tube top and matching low-riding bell-bottoms. A cherry red mesh top and ruby stiletto sandals completed her ensemble. Clearly it was time to cancel Bunny's subscription to the Frederick's of Hollywood catalog.

After Bunny had enveloped Skye in an Obsession-scented hug, Skye asked, "How did you get Godly Crüe to come back? Don't they live out of state?"

"They decided to stick around. They've been playing most nights up and down the yard sale. I snapped them up when I heard they were still in the area. People really like them."

"Great. Looks like everything is going pretty well." Skye sent up a little prayer before asking her next question. "Did you come up with something attention-grabbing for the audition tape for the Playboy Channel?"

"Yes. I've got a fantastic stunt planned." Bunny lowered her voice. "But Kirby told me we have to wait until Faith and her producer leave before we start filming."

Skye closed her eyes, trying to find the words that would deter Bunny from pursuing a career as a porn star, but before she could think of anything, the redhead caught sight of two men starting to argue in the corner and teetered off, saying over her shoulder, "I gotta take care of that. See ya later."

Skye turned back to the bar and placed her order. Hacker, the bartender, jerked his thumb at the band. "I heard you asking about those guys. Maybe the reason they been hanging around instead of going home has something to do with their lead singer's love life."

Skye raised her eyebrows. "Really?"

"Yeah. He's real popular with the ladies, especially the ones with a few years on them."

"You don't say? He seems so . . . so clean-cut."

"Everyone seems normal until you get to know them." Hacker continued to mix drinks as he talked. "Last Saturday night he was in here, and he started coming on to that broad that got killed."

"Cookie Caldwell?"

"That's the one." He poured a stream of clear liquor from a bottle into a glass without spilling a drop. "Then, when I was going home that night around midnight after I got off work, I saw him coming out of her apartment."

"You sure see a lot."

"Hey." Hacker grinned. "The early bird

may get the worm, but the second mouse gets the cheese."

"And who wants to eat worms, right?"

"Right. Anyway, a couple of nights ago he was talking to that TV star."

Skye raised her voice to be heard over the music. "Faith Easton? But she's not older than he is."

"He's in his late twenties, tops, and she'll never see thirty-five again." Hacker pointed to his temples and behind his ears. "She's had some nips and tucks."

"No. I can't believe she's over twenty-eight."

Hacker winked. "I'm good at my job, and one of the reasons I'm so good is that I can peg someone's age within a year."

"How old am I?"

He didn't even stop to consider. "Thirty-three, thirty-four."

This guy was insulting. Correct, but insulting. "Who else did he hit on?"

"Miss Bunny, of course." Hacker handed Skye her drinks and took the ten-dollar bill she gave him. "Not that he got anywhere. That lady can take care of herself. He won't get anything off of her."

"Except a job," Skye murmured to herself, then told Hacker to keep the change and went back to her table.

She kept Trixie company until Theresa Dugan, a teacher at the elementary school, and Abby Fleming, the school district nurse, joined them. After a few minutes of polite small talk, Skye excused herself to go chat with the TV crew before Faith and Nick left.

She found the TV group, minus its star, at a table in the back. After greeting them, she pulled out an empty chair and said, "I hope you don't mind me joining you for a bit."

"Sure, have a seat. The more the merrier." Nick smiled without warmth.

Skye sat, then said to the producer, "Having a good time?"

"Actually, we're working. Just taking a break while Faith changes clothes."

"Do you have to haul all her clothes and accessories around for the shoots?" Skye asked Jody, the star's personal assistant.

"Sure do. Thank goodness for my weight training." Jody flexed her arm, showing a small muscle.

"I'm sort of confused as to why the writer would be along." Skye turned her attention to Kirby Tucker.

He looked happy to be included and answered readily, "You really can't script this kind of show, and we never know what we'll end up taping. It depends on what hot tips we get or what we hear on the police scanner. A lot of times I'm writing lines only a few minutes before the shot."

"That explains why you guys just seem to show up everywhere." Skye was tempted to mention Kirby's plan for after the star and producer left but decided that if she did, Bunny and the writer would just make the tape later when Skye wouldn't be around to try and stop them. Instead she said to Nick, "I'm really curious how you persuaded Mrs. Griggs to let you film at her house."

"Mrs. Griggs? The name doesn't ring a bell." Nick suddenly became interested in the bowlers.

"Really?" Skye raised an eyebrow. "That's odd, because Kirby said you had an appointment to film at her house the day after she died."

"Oh, the old lady with the house full of stuff," Nick acknowledged. He picked up a paper from the pile in front of him and brought it to eye level. "I guess I didn't remember her name."

"Sure. Hard to remember everyone you meet in a situation like this," Skye agreed. Then she pounced. "So, how did you get her to let you shoot at her house?"

"I'm really not sure." Nick looked around

for help, but both Kirby and Jody were staring at him. "Faith arranged it, I think. Didn't she, guys?"

The other two shrugged.

"Why is it such a big deal?"

"Because Mrs. Griggs told me after Cookie tried to cheat her that she wouldn't let anyone inside her house until the appraiser came."

"Maybe the appraiser had already been there," Nick offered.

"Nope. He couldn't make it until Monday."

Nick swung around, facing the bowling lanes and putting his back to Skye. "Well, Faith is pretty persuasive."

"Maybe, but I heard Mrs. Griggs turn her down earlier in the week."

Nick spoke without looking back at her. "People change their minds."

"True. Guess I need to talk to Faith." Skye got up and moved in front of Nick, forcing him to look at her. "Where did you say she was?"

Jody jumped up. "I'll take you. I need to go check and make sure everything is okay anyway."

She led Skye toward the basement steps. "Bunny let us use one of the rooms down here." Skye followed the young woman down the stairs. When they reached the bottom, Jody turned and admitted, "I don't think we had an appointment to film at Mrs. Griggs's place. I think we were going to pull a Michael Moore and just show up and surprise her."

Before Skye could ask any questions, Jody opened the door and pushed Skye in. For a second Skye thought she had been shanghaied, but then she saw Faith sitting at a table, peering into a mirror.

The TV star spotted Skye and swung around. "What are you doing here?"

"I had a question, and your crew told me where to find you." Since Jody had not followed her into the dressing room, Skye figured the assistant didn't want to be pointed out as the snitch.

"Well, it's quite unsuitable." Faith turned back to the mirror. "It's of paramount importance that I have some time to get in touch with my muse before the next shot."

Skye moved closer. "Just answer this one question and I'll go."

"Very well."

"How did you get Mrs. Griggs to agree to let you film a segment of your show in her house?"

"Mrs. Griggs?" Faith leaned closer to the mirror and erased a smudge under her eye.

"Oh, the old lady outside of town. I asked and she said yes. Mystery solved."

"Except I heard her say no to you."

"She changed her mind." Faith swiveled around. "Say, do you know who her next of kin is? I still fancy a look around that house."

"No." Skye remembered Mrs. Griggs's saying she had no relatives, but she wasn't going to tell Faith that. She didn't believe for a minute that Mrs. Griggs had changed her mind, but there didn't seem to be any way to shake the TV star's story. Skye turned to leave, but then she came back. "One other thing. I understand you were talking to Will Murphy."

Faith looked puzzled.

"The singer from the band playing upstairs?"

"Yes. So?"

"Are you friends?" Skye wasn't sure what to ask.

"Dear, a lot of people try to chat up a TV star. That doesn't make us friends."

"Oh. Do you remember what he wanted?"

This time Faith looked put out. "Yes. All he wanted to talk about was antiques and collectibles, especially Civil War swords." She swung back to the mirror. "Now, if you're through, I'd be ever so grateful if you'd bugger off."

★ ★ ★

Faith and Nick left the bowling alley at nine, and Skye rejoined Trixie, Abby, and Theresa at their table as she waited anxiously to see what Bunny had come up with. Nearly half an hour passed, and the only thing that happened was that the bowling lanes emptied one by one as people finished their games and were not allowed to start new ones.

Trixie was telling a funny story when the PA system crackled to life.

There was a drumroll and then Bunny's voice ordered, "Anyone under eighteen must now leave the building."

Skye tensed. This had to be it. What had Bunny come up with?

After a few minutes, while the few underage teens grudgingly exited the alley, Bunny strutted out onto the lanes. She had changed clothes and now wore only three triangles of crimson Spandex. Two were tied together between her breasts with a satin bow and the other was held in place by two ribbons that circled her hips.

Skye groaned. Simon was going to kill his mother.

Bunny smiled widely and spoke into the cordless microphone she held to her glistening red lips. "We have a special treat for you all tonight. Bikini bowling! Most slots have already been taken, but if anyone wishes to join us I have several bikinis in the back room for you to change into." Bunny waited, but no one volunteered. Finally she said, "Okay, let's get started. Bikini bowlers, take your places!"

Kirby was standing by Skye's table, and she heard him mutter to his cameraman, "Get ready to shoot."

What could she do to stop them? Skye thought furiously, but no idea came to her, short of pulling the fire alarm. She covered her eyes, peeking through her fingers. Nine women marched onto the lanes. They all wore teeny-tiny bikinis, had great figures, and none was under fifty years old. Where had Bunny found so many older ladies with such fantastic bodies who were willing to bowl clad in nothing but a bikini?

Before Skye could figure out that mystery, her thoughts were penetrated by Kirby snickering to the cameraman, "Would you look at that? Geeze. Have you ever seen so many wrinkles? It looks as if a litter of shar-peis put on bikinis. Forget Playboy. What was I thinking?"

Skye missed the cameraman's reply, but she clearly heard Kirby's next statement. "No. Keep taping. Bunny said she has signed releases from all the old broads, and maybe we can sell the film to *America's Funniest Home Videos*. Nah, scratch that. We'll have to settle for the *Planet's Funniest Animals* show."

Skye gasped, whispered frantically to Trixie, and ran toward the Bikini Bowlers. She grabbed Bunny by the arm and dragged the redhead off the lanes and toward the storeroom. Bunny tried to struggle free, but Skye had pounds and adrenaline in her favor.

Once they were inside with the door closed, Skye hesitated, hating to hurt the older woman's feelings. When Bunny broke loose from her grasp and ran toward the door, Skye made a decision and repeated what Kirby had said, ending with, "Then he said he couldn't even sell it to *America's Funniest Home Videos*. He'd have to settle for the *Planet's Funniest Animals* show."

Bunny stood absolutely still, the color drained from her face and her breathing shallow. Skye was about to get her a chair when two spots of red appeared on her cheeks and her shoulders slumped. "When am I going to learn not to trust men? They're all the same. They lie, cheat, and steal your dreams."

Patting Bunny's shoulder, Skye wasn't

sure if anything she could say would make the older woman feel better. Suddenly Bunny straightened and clenched her fist. "I've got to stop him. He's out there taping my friends. They'll be humiliated." She rushed through the doorway.

Skye followed and as she rounded the corner, was just in time to see Bunny's flying tackle slam into Kirby's midsection. He toppled into the cameraman, who had been trying to get his equipment away from Trixie, Abby, and Theresa, who had formed a protective wall around his gear. Skye watched as the whole group went down like pins under the ball of an expert bowler.

As Skye rushed to untangle her fallen friends, she smiled in satisfaction. Kirby wouldn't be using any of tonight's events to further his career, and Simon wouldn't need to kill his mother.

Chapter 21
Price Is Right

Skye knocked on Will Murphy's cabin door at the Up A Lazy River Motor Court. She had debated with herself about coming here so late, but with only two days of the yard sale left, Godly Crüe would probably head back home come morning.

Although Bikini Bowling had been canceled, the party had gone on. Once Kirby's scheme had been explained to Bunny's friends, who were all ex-dancers from Chicago, they had changed back to their street clothes and joined the fun.

Skye had hung around until the band left at midnight, and then she followed the musicians back to their motel. She had seen the lead singer go into one cabin and the three women go into the one next door. Which is why, despite the fact that he was ignoring her knocking, she knew Murphy was there and hadn't been in his

329

cabin long enough to go to bed.

She pounded a little louder. This time the door was flung open.

"Babe, you're early. I thought you were going to give me fifteen minutes to get ready." Murphy stood there with a towel around his waist and holding a wineglass in each hand.

Skye felt the color start to rise in her cheeks, but kept her voice cool, as if greeting nearly naked men in motels in the middle of the night was a common practice of hers. "Sorry to bother you so late, but I wanted to catch you before you left town. Do you have a moment?"

"Uh, well, not really." He transferred both wineglasses to one hand and hitched up his towel.

"But didn't you say you weren't expecting your guest for fifteen minutes?" Skye took a step forward and, as she hoped, the singer automatically moved back.

"Well, yes, but, uh . . . couldn't we do this in the morning?" Murphy looked distinctly uncomfortable.

"You know, I'm so busy with the yard sale during the day, and I'm already here. It'll only take a couple of seconds." She fluttered her eyelashes and sidled farther into the room. "Please?"

"Okay." He sighed. "I'll be right back."

He disappeared into the bathroom, and Skye sat in a chair by the window, wondering what to say.

When he returned he had on jeans and a T-shirt and had ditched the wineglasses. "So, what's the emergency?" He sat on the edge of the bed, facing Skye.

"Just a couple of questions." Skye leaned forward. "I was surprised to see you tonight. I thought your group was heading home after last Sunday's concert."

"We were such a hit, a lot of the other little towns decided to hire us." He smiled charmingly. "Can't say no to a paying gig."

"I suppose not. With all the accommodations booked up so far in advance, how have you been able to find places to stay?"

"We've been put up in private homes, but Sister Bunny's friend Charlie, the guy who owns this place, had a couple of cancellations due to that murder."

"Oh, how convenient." Skye saw no reason to tell Murphy that Charlie was her godfather. "Are you staying through the weekend, then?"

"No. The cabins are reserved for Saturday night." Murphy was looking at her funny. "This is what you wanted to know?"

"As the yard sale coordinator, it's my job

331

to find out how things are going so we can plan better for next year." Skye was improvising like mad. She started to get up, then sat back down. "Oh, there is one more thing."

"Yes?" He snuck a peek at his watch.

"I understand you'd become quite friendly with Cookie Caldwell before she died."

"No. I mean, I met her once, but we weren't friends." He faltered. "Why do you say that?"

"Someone told me they saw you coming out of her apartment late one night."

"No. I was never in her apartment."

Skye widened her eyes, pretending artlessness. "Gee, the person who told me was really, really sure, because he said the night he saw you was the night she was killed."

Murphy slumped. "You gotta believe me, I didn't have anything to do with that." He put his head in his hands. "Honest. I didn't know her well enough to kill her."

"Then why were you at her apartment?"

"I was never at her apartment. I was only in her store." Murphy chewed on his thumbnail, then said, "I'll tell you what happened, but you got to keep me out of it."

"I'll try, but you know I can't promise

that." Skye knew she should probably just lie, but she couldn't.

"My mama's going to kill me."

Skye blinked. That was the last thing she had expected to hear come out of his mouth. "Mothers sometimes surprise you. Just when I think my mom couldn't possibly understand about something bad I've done, she does."

"Maybe you're right," Murphy said, but he looked unconvinced. "Here's the whole story." He got up and started to pace, the cramped cabin limiting his circuit. "It costs a lot of money to start a career in the music business."

Skye nodded.

"We're really close to a record deal." The look in his eye suggested he could see the winning lottery ticket just beyond his fingertips. "We can't stop now."

Skye nodded again, thinking she had just gone through this with her brother's band a few months ago.

"My granddad died a year ago and left me his collection of war memorabilia." Murphy halted his steps and faced Skye. "I promised my mama I'd keep it for my son, but . . ."

"But you need the money."

"Right. So, when you hired us for this yard sale I thought it was a sign from God.

I'd sell just one piece, the most valuable thing in the collection."

"A Civil War sword?" Skye guessed.

"How did you know?"

She smiled mysteriously, seeing no reason to give up her source.

"Anyway, I met Sister Cookie at the bowling alley bar Saturday night, and we got to talking. She told me she had a store in town that dealt in collectibles and antiques. I mentioned the sword, and she wanted to see it right away."

"Why not wait until morning?"

"She said if she was going to buy it, she wanted it that night," Murphy answered. "I had it locked in the trunk of my car, so I followed her to her store and took it inside."

"Did she make you an offer?"

"Yes."

"But not what you expected?"

"No." Murphy sounded angry. "What she said she'd pay was a lot less than what I had been told it was worth. She claimed that it wasn't as old as I thought or in as good condition as I said. But that was bullpucky! I knew how old it was. It'd been in my family since my great-great-great-grandfather carried it off to war. And there wasn't anything wrong with its condition, either."

"Did you sell it to her?"

"No. I figured I could do better."

"Have you?" Skye asked.

"I've got two offers right now, and they're bidding each other up."

"Who are they?"

A stubborn look settled on his face. "I'm not saying until I get my money."

Skye pondered whether she could force the information from him and decided she couldn't. "I understand. But what I don't understand is why my informant said he saw you coming out of Cookie's apartment, not her store." She scratched her head. "I know Cookie's apartment is on the top floor of her store, but they have separate entrances."

"I can explain that. Sister Cookie said she was expecting someone and didn't want them to see me, so she had me go out a different way than the one we came in. I had to go up one set of stairs and down another, and I ended up coming out a door in the back." Murphy looked at his watch. "Is that all?"

Skye got up. "Yes. Thanks for talking to me." After she had stepped outside, she turned and asked, "Since you have to check out of the motor court, are you leaving for home tomorrow?"

"Yes. As soon as I sell my sword."

★ ★ ★

Once the singer had closed the door, Skye ducked behind a truck and squatted down, making sure she was out of sight. She wanted to see who Will Murphy was expecting. Seconds later, a Honda Civic pulled into the space in front of the cabin. Jody Iverson got out of the car and went inside. Skye wondered how Faith's personal assistant and the singer had gotten together, and if there was any significance to their pairing.

Skye waited a few minutes to make sure Will and Jody were settled for the night, then started the hike to her car. Because the aqua Bel Air was such a distinctive vehicle, she had left it at the far end of the lot, near the footbridge to the park.

The air hung heavy and still, the heat and humidity of the day lingering. Skye wiped sweat from her upper lip with a tissue from her pocket. Something felt wrong. She looked behind her but didn't see anything.

Halogen lights illuminated the area near the cabins and office, but as she walked toward the outer edge of the asphalt, murkiness took over. She started to move faster. Were those footsteps behind her?

Skye swiveled around. Still nothing but shadows. Obviously the stress of the murders and Justin's disappearance were getting to her. She forced herself to continue into the darkest section of the lot.

Fumbling in her purse to find her keys before she reached her car, Skye screamed as suddenly something heavy and tentlike came down over her, sheathing her in darkness as she was shoved to the ground. Blows rained on her through the rough fabric.

At first Skye tried to fight her way free of the encasing cloth, but soon she curled into a fetal position, with her arms protecting her head, to try and minimize the damage from the beating.

After what seemed like an eternity, the blows stopped, and a muffled voice said, "Mind your own business. Next time I'll kill you."

Less than a second later, Skye heard the sound of running footsteps. She struggled to her feet. Ignoring her aching body, she tore at the material covering her. When she finally got it off, her attacker was gone.

She heard the squeal of tires and glimpsed a car speeding down Maryland Street. She looked around wildly for her keys but couldn't find them, although her purse, its contents spilled all over the asphalt, was where she had dropped it.

It took her a few seconds to remember

that her father had hidden another set of car keys in a magnetic box attached to the inside of the Bel Air's wheel well. Once she located them, she hurriedly swept her belongings back into her purse, then threw it and herself into the car.

By the time Skye drove onto Maryland, she realized that her assailant's car was long gone and there was nothing to follow. She pulled over to the side of the road to figure out what to do. After her awful experience with the sheriff, the last thing she wanted was to go to the police, but Wally wasn't Buck Peterson, and the police had to be told. There might be some clue from her assault that would lead them to the murderer.

Now that the adrenaline was wearing off, the pain from the beating was intensifying. Skye was pretty sure she had no broken bones, but her arms, back, and thighs, which had absorbed the worst of the blows, were throbbing, and she could barely move them to drive the car.

As she hobbled into the police station, she counted it as a blessing that her mother was not the dispatcher on duty. Unfortunately, May's good friend Thea Jones, who usually worked days, was behind the counter.

Thea took one look at Skye, screamed,

and ran into the reception area. "What happened? Are you all right? Should I call an ambulance? Sit down."

Skye tried to answer but found that she was too tired to battle Thea's waterfall of words.

Thea led Skye into the coffee/interrogation room and gently pushed her into a chair. She stood in front of her and wrung her hands, muttering, "What should I do?"

Skye summoned enough energy to say, "I'm okay. It looks worse than it is, but you'd better phone the chief. He'll want to know about this." Thea dashed off, and Skye called after her, "Don't tell my mom."

She must have zoned out, because suddenly Wally was looming over her, a look of mingled concern and fury on his face. "Who did this to you?"

"I don't know." Skye explained how the attack had taken place, then waited for him to lecture her about visiting suspects in the middle of the night.

Instead, he squatted in front of her and held both her hands. They were scraped, and the nails were torn from her fight with the tarp. He gently rubbed at the dried blood on her knuckles. "I promise, whoever did this to you is going to jail for a long, long time."

"I think it's the murderer." Skye battled to keep her tone steady and not start crying.

"Me, too."

"Maybe there's some clue at the scene."

"I already radioed Quirk. He's on his way to look things over."

Skye's voice cracked. "I suppose you'll have to call the sheriff."

Abruptly, Wally lifted her to her feet and into his arms. "Don't worry. You won't have to talk to him again. He's had his chance. This is my jurisdiction."

"Can you take over the murder investigation?"

"No, but if I should discover the killer while finding out who attacked you — oh, well, shit happens." He gently rocked her back and forth, tenderly smoothing her hair. "Now, let's get you to a doctor."

"No. I'm okay. Really. A doctor can't do anything for bruises." Skye knew she should be breaking free from his embrace, but it felt so good to be held, she convinced herself he was hugging her like a brother. "The cloth that I was wrapped in was padded and protected me from the worst of the blows."

He leaned his forehead against hers. His breath was warm and moist against her face, and her heart raced, sending warning flashes to her brain.

"But he hurt you, and that's enough." His last words were smothered against her lips.

Skye was stunned by her reaction to Wally's kiss. It sent a shock wave through her entire body, and she instinctively responded.

Wally deepened the kiss, crushing her against him and running his hands up and down her soft curves.

Skye's emotions spun out of control. She threaded her fingers through his hair and caressed his broad back.

Suddenly a voice penetrated their passionate fog. "I thought Thea said Skye *had been* attacked, not *was being* attacked."

Skye leapt back. Wally reluctantly let her out of his arms, trying to hold on to her hand, but she pulled it away. She looked into her mother's outraged eyes and felt her face flush with humiliation and anger. She was supposed to be in a monogamous relationship with Simon, so what the heck was she doing kissing Wally? More important, why was she enjoying it?

Chapter 22
You Bet Your Life

May drove Skye home, Jed following in the Bel Air. After Skye showered, her mother rubbed ointment and antibiotic cream into her various bruises and scrapes, clucking about doctors, X-rays, and hospitals throughout the process. Skye steadfastly refused formal medical treatment, knowing that a long wait in the emergency room would result in little more than the first-aid measures her mother was already providing. Both women avoided the subject of Wally and the kiss.

When May finally left Skye alone, sleep wouldn't come. Her mind played tag among guilt, fear, and anger. How could she have responded to Wally that way? What if the murderer came after her again? And how could she figure out who was behind the killings?

Finally Skye resolved not to deal with the issue of Wally until the murder was solved,

Justin was back safe and sound, and she'd had a chance to talk to Simon in person.

Having tucked guilt away, she was left with fear and anger. No way was she living her life afraid. If the murderer thought Skye would run and hide, he or she had severely underestimated her. Fear was also pushed away to be dealt with later.

Which left anger. Skye tested it out. Yes, anger was the emotion she needed to keep. She was tired of being the victim, of being framed for Mrs. Griggs's murder, being attacked, being beaten. It was time to kick some butt.

Skye eased out of bed, wincing with every movement. From her tote bag she retrieved a yellow legal pad and pen. She couldn't turn on the lamp or her mother would spot the light shining under the door and come to see what was wrong. Instead, she flicked on the closet's light switch and sat in the doorway using the dim glow to examine the list she had made after discovering Mrs. Griggs's body.

1. Who were Cookie's friends? Did she have a boyfriend?

2. How did the murderer get Mrs. Griggs's pin?

3. How did the murderer get the sword from Cookie's store?

4. What does anyone gain from either woman's death?

5. ?

Skye chewed the end of her pen. She had only partially figured out number one and hadn't made a dent in the rest. How could she find the answers to two, three, and four? And what was the question for number five?

As she stared at the paper, a plan began to form. It wasn't exactly legal, but after tonight she felt as if she'd been pushed beyond playing by the rules.

By ten o'clock Saturday morning the temperature was already in the nineties. Skye had begun to worry about heatstroke and dehydration among the yard sale customers. She checked with Abby, the school nurse she had hired to staff the first-aid tent, and was assured that there was an abundant supply of salt tablets, bottled water, and cold packs.

Skye had just hung up the phone after listening to the weather forecast — no break in the heat — when Dante yelled for her. She reluctantly limped into his office, hoping he wouldn't notice the bruises that decorated her arms and legs like prison tattoos.

"I hear you were attacked last night."

Dante sat behind his desk, swigging from a can of Pepsi.

So much for keeping anything around here secret. "Mom?"

"May called me early this morning. I hadn't even had my coffee yet."

Skye raised an eyebrow but didn't answer.

"I was thinking. You must be on the right track if the killer is nervous enough to assault you."

"Could be." Was he saying he was pleased she had made herself a target?

"So, who is it?"

"Darned if I know." Skye wasn't feeling particularly communicative this morning, but she noticed her uncle's face turning red and added, "I talked to a lot of people yesterday. It could be any one of them. I must have asked a question that made the guilty party worried, but I have no idea what the question was or who I asked it of."

"Give me a rundown of your day."

Skye obliged, ending with, "Then I talked to the singer and watched Faith's assistant go into his room, so they're the only ones in the clear, unless they're in on it together."

"At least Wally is taking over. Maybe now we'll get some results." Dante threw away the empty soda can and wiped his hands on his pants' legs. "Buck Peterson couldn't find his ass with both hands. With him, the wheel is spinning but the hamster is dead."

Skye froze. How much did her uncle know about the Wally situation? How much had May told him? She asked cautiously, "What do you mean about Wally taking over?"

"I mean, Wally was up here first thing this morning and told me that since you were assaulted within the city limits, he'd be investigating that case, and if he 'happened' to come across the murderer, that was how the cookie crumbled."

"Oh, yeah, that's good." Skye scrutinized Dante, who didn't seem to be hiding anything — like knowing that May had caught Skye and Wally kissing last night. Not that Dante had any right to judge Skye, but she didn't think that would stop him from doing so. "It looks like the yard sale is under control — only one day to go. You'd better have my check, including the bonus, written out and ready to hand to me on Sunday afternoon."

"Yeah, yeah. It'll be ready, *if* nothing happens to ruin the sale between now and then."

"Fine. I'm going to get back to finding the murderer this afternoon. Like you told me to. Okay?"

"Sure. Just keep me up to date." Dante

waved her off, but then stopped her. "Wait. You'd better take this."

Skye accepted the rectangular object her uncle handed her. It looked a little like a large electric razor, but had two silver prongs sticking out on one end and something like a trigger on the handle. "What is it?"

"It's a stun gun," Dante explained. "It shoots two hundred thousand volts and is guaranteed to disable an attacker for several minutes, giving you time to run away."

"Uh, thanks, Uncle Dante." Skye kissed her uncle's cheek and went back to her office.

She dug out her fanny pack, strapped it on, and put the weapon inside. At first she hadn't been thrilled with Dante's gift, but the more she thought about it, the more she figured it might come in handy after all.

Skye contemplated what she was about to do — search Cookie's apartment. Initially she had planned to do it at night, after the yard sale had closed down for the day, but as she considered it, she realized that it would be safer to look around when there were a lot of people on the streets.

Still, she didn't want to advertise her presence, so she tucked a pair of latex gloves and a flashlight in with the stun gun, then she dug a small key ring from the bottom of her purse and put it in her pocket.

If she was lucky, Cookie had never gotten around to having the locks changed on her store after firing Skye. And if she was really lucky, Cookie had continued to keep the key to her apartment in the drawer of the cash register.

During the short trip from the city hall to Cookie's store, Skye told herself it wasn't really breaking and entering if she had a key. Right?

She parked the golf cart on the corner and made a big deal of greeting people and looking over the sales booths. She spoke to Jody, who was manning Cookie's table, and noted that she was mobbed with customers, so she shouldn't notice much going on behind her inside the actual store.

This next part was dangerous. Hoping no one would notice, Skye crept around to the rear of the building and waited. No one followed her.

She slipped on the latex gloves and inserted the key into the back-door lock, praying that it would still work. It clicked open on the first try, and Skye darted inside, closing and relocking the door behind her, then stood still, straining to hear if anyone else was in the building.

After the noise of the yard sale, it was eerily quiet inside — these old structures had great soundproofing. Skye unconsciously held her breath as she mounted the staircase to the second floor. If she were to turn left, there would be the door to Cookie's apartment. Instead she kept right, walked along a small landing and down another set of steps that led directly into the storage room of the shop.

The darkness spooked her, and she quickly fumbled for her flashlight. As she groped through her fanny pack, something brushed her cheek, and she screamed. Locating the Mag Lite, she thumbed the switch, revealing a stuffed owl with its wings spread, ready to swoop down on its prey.

Skye closed her eyes for a second, waiting for her pounding heart to return to its normal beat, before entering the shop. The blinds were tightly drawn on the front window and door, making the interior dim and giving it a surreal feeling.

With the collectibles arranged in tableaux, Skye felt like she was coming into a house that had been abruptly deserted by its occupants in the middle of their everyday lives. It had been only a few days since Cookie's death, but already dust covered most of the surfaces and an occasional spiderweb decorated a delicate teacup or porcelain figurine.

Skye shivered, although the shop was hot and stuffy. This desolate room brought the reality of Cookie's murder home to her like nothing else had. All of a sudden, she wanted to be out of there, and she quickly moved to the old-fashioned cash register and pushed the NO SALE button.

When the bell rang it seemed abnormally loud, and Skye jumped back, her pulse racing. Taking a steadying breath, she grabbed the key and eased the drawer shut, steeling herself this time for the bell's shrill jingle.

Her main objective was Cookie's apartment, but she took a few minutes to look quickly through the woman's office. As she suspected, the sheriff's department had taken everything from the file cabinet and desk. Skye could only hope they hadn't been quite as thorough with her personal items.

The key from the cash register unlocked the apartment door, and Skye was inside within seconds. She had never been to Cookie's apartment but wasn't surprised to see it was decorated in the same manner as her office — Victorian lady's parlor.

It appeared as if the deputies had been

fairly neat in their search. Drawers were pulled out, but their contents weren't strewn around the room. Skye chewed her lip. It would be so much easier if she knew what she was looking for.

What would indicate who Cookie's friends and lovers were? No doubt the sheriff's department had taken her calendar and address book. What else would have that information?

The foyer contained nothing but an empty coat tree. In the tiny living room were a sofa, two chairs, and a coffee table, as well as an étagère with shelves full of a variety of figurines and glassware, but no pictures. This was clearly not a room Cookie spent much time in.

Nevertheless, Skye felt along the cushions of the chairs and couch and looked underneath the furniture. She found only two dimes, three pennies, and a pack of matches advertising some cigar bar in the city. She left the change but placed the matchbook in her fanny pack.

The kitchen was even tinier, having only a hot plate, a dorm-size fridge, and a microwave. Skye scanned the cupboards and drawers, opened the refrigerator and microwave, and examined the walls. Nothing.

All of a sudden she felt foolish. Who did

she think she was? Whatever the deputies hadn't found, surely Nick would have discovered after he learned he was the executor of Cookie's estate. He'd obviously been there — there was no rotting food, and the trash cans were empty. This had been a stupid idea. She should just leave.

Skye started for the door but paused. On the other hand, it seemed a little silly to leave without taking a quick peek in the bedroom and bath. After all, that was where most women kept their really personal items.

The bedroom was larger than Skye expected. It was painted a rich lapis blue with ivory satin curtains covering the windows that overlooked the street.

A queen-size white wrought-iron bed, swathed in a tent of lace, stood in the center of the room, looking like something from an Arabian Nights tale. The mattress was slightly askew on the frame, and the spread, linens, and heaps of decorative pillows were scattered on the cream-colored carpet.

A marble-topped table beside the bed held a crystal carafe, a lamp, and a pair of reading glasses, none of which had been disturbed. But the contents of both the dresser and the armoire had been emptied onto the floor. Either the deputies hadn't been as careful in here or someone, maybe Nick, had conducted a second search. Had they found what they were looking for?

Skye poked through the strewn clothes, but other than learning that Cookie had a penchant for silk teddies in jewel colors, she discovered nothing of interest.

The bathroom had been similarly ransacked. Skye looked over the array of makeup and perfume strewn across the marble countertop. Cookie'd had expensive taste. There were products from Lancôme, Chanel, and Elizabeth Arden, as well as many others Skye didn't recognize, but from their packaging she assumed they were pricey.

Curious, Skye picked up a bottle of foundation from the assortment and noted the shade — alabaster. Mmm, that color was all wrong for Cookie's warm skin tone. Skye picked through the rest of the cosmetics until she found another bottle of foundation. This one was honey beige, a much better choice for Cookie.

Skye made a face at herself in the mirror. She was wasting time. What woman hadn't bought the wrong makeup at one time or another? Still, at thirty or more dollars a pop, that was a costly mistake. And didn't expensive brands like these offer staff that helped you choose the right shade? Maybe Cookie hadn't listened to them.

As Skye walked back through the bedroom, she swept the room with one last glance, desperate to find something useful. She frowned. That pillow, the one sticking out from under the pile — why had it caught her attention?

Swiftly she crossed the room and picked up the pillow. It looked a little different from the others, which were all made of satin and lace. This one was plain tan and in a tweedy material. Now she remembered. A few months ago, she had seen a similar pillow for sale in a mail-order catalog. The catalog had offered everyday household items like books, shaving cream cans, and cereal boxes that had been hollowed out to secretly hold valuables.

Skye flipped the pillow over and unzipped it. Her heart sank; the opening revealed nothing but foam rubber. This was clearly not the pillow safe she had seen in the catalog.

She was about to throw it down when she heard a faint rattle. She pushed at it and felt something hard. Looking more closely, she saw a seam, and lifted out the square of foam. There, in the center of the pillow, was a box. She bit her lip as she lifted the lid. Nestled inside was a slim packet of letters tied with a blue satin ribbon.

This had to be what she was hunting for. Suddenly she felt uneasy and looked at her watch. Shoot! She'd been at Cookie's for more than an hour. She didn't know why, but it felt like too long. It was time to go.

Skye scooped up the letters and jammed them into her fanny pack. Was there anything else? No. Her instincts were telling her to get out.

She hurried through the apartment, ran down the stairs, and fumbled with the lock on the exit. Her hand was shaking, and she couldn't get the key into the slot.

Finally, using both hands, she was able to open the door. She edged out and relocked it, then leaned against the side of the building trying to regain her breath. Her head felt light, and the aches and pains she had been ignoring in her bruised arms and legs burst into her consciousness. They were stiffening up; she had to get moving or she might not be able to.

Skye sucked in one more lungful of air and pushed herself away from the building. Turning, she started to head out of the alleyway when she heard footsteps behind her. She broke into a run while unzipping her fanny pack. Just as her fingers found the stun gun, a hand clamped on her shoulder, and a male voice said, "Find anything useful?"

Chapter 23
Saturday Night Live

Skye screamed and whirled around, clutching the stun gun, prepared to go down fighting.

Wally jumped back and held up both hands, palms out. "Whoa. It's only me."

Skye lowered the weapon. "Oh, my God, you scared me to death."

"Sorry." Wally grinned. "I didn't think a burglar would be so nervous."

"I'm not." Skye crossed her fingers. "I mean I'm not a burglar. I didn't steal anything." Certainly letters she intended to copy and then mail back to the estate didn't count as stealing.

Wally raised an eyebrow.

"And I wasn't breaking in, either. I had a key."

"Good. I won't have to arrest you, then." Wally's smile widened.

"Right." Skye stared at him. Why wasn't

he yelling at her? Why was he in such a good mood? Did it have something to do with their kiss? Did she really want to know?

Wally took her arm. "Come on. I've got someone back at the station you might want to talk to."

"Who?"

"It's a surprise."

Wally's good mood was making her nervous. Surely he understood that their kiss had been a heat-of-the-moment kind of thing. "A nice surprise?"

"You tell me." They had rounded the corner and come up to the cruiser. Wally opened the door to the passenger side, and Skye got in.

He maintained his jovial disposition as they drove to the police station but refused to give a hint as to whom she would find there.

Wally parked in the garage, and they entered the building through the door that led directly into the coffee/interrogation room. Sitting at the table, a Coke clutched in one hand, potato chips in the other, and a computer magazine open in front of him, was Justin.

Relief swept through Skye, and she stepped forward to hug him, but the hostile glare he blasted in her direction stopped her in midstride. She glanced at Wally, confused. Why was Justin so angry at her?

Wally shrugged and pulled out a chair for her. "Have a seat. You want a pop before we get started?"

She nodded. Her mouth felt as dry as a day-old donut. Wally put a dollar into the machine in the corner and pressed the Diet Coke button. He got himself a Mountain Dew, brought both cans to the table, and then sat down.

Skye opened her soda and took a gulp, then said to Justin, "I'm really glad to see you safe and sound. We were all very worried about you."

He stared at his magazine, refusing to acknowledge her presence.

"Why did you disappear like that?" she asked.

He pretended not to hear her.

She looked at Wally for help. Justin was the master of long silences. It had taken an entire school year to get him talking when he was first referred to her for counseling as an eighth grader, and she had a feeling they couldn't wait that long this time.

Wally took a swig of his soda, then said, "I found Justin sneaking out of the bowling alley this morning. He told me that Bunny had been letting him stay there while he got his head together."

Ah, that explained the copy of *PC Magazine* on Bunny's coffee table. Skye was happy that one mystery was solved. She'd been half afraid that Simon's mom was starting an adult-only Web site. "But why did he need to get his head together?"

"That's all I know so far. I had to leave when Quirk radioed me to say you were breaking into Cookie Caldwell's."

"I told you before, I did not break in. I have a key." Skye wanted to make her innocence, at least on that point, perfectly clear.

Wally smirked at her and shook his head, then turned to the teen. "Now Justin's going to tell us the rest of the story, from the beginning."

Justin stared at the chief but didn't speak.

Wally stared back. "If you don't talk to us, I'll be forced to arrest Mrs. Reid for harboring a runaway minor."

Skye struggled to keep her expression neutral. She knew Wally was bluffing. Was harboring a runaway minor even a crime?

"That's not fair." Clearly Justin was torn between his anger at Skye and his sense of loyalty to Bunny, who had taken him in when he had nowhere else to go. He crushed a potato chip with his soda can, gazed at the ceiling, and heaved a put-upon sigh. "It all started last Saturday night."

"The night Cookie was murdered?" Wally clarified.

"Yes. I'd been trying to come up with a story about the yard sale for the school newspaper, but I didn't want to do the same old dumb kind of thing the local papers were doing. I was looking for an unusual angle."

Wally and Skye both nodded their understanding of Justin's quest for original journalism.

"Anyway, I decided to do a story about the effect of the sale on a local business owner, and since Ms. Caldwell's store was right across the street from the Lemonade ShakeUp stand where I'd be spending a lot of time, I picked her."

"Did you tell her she was your subject?" Skye asked.

Justin shot her a venomous look and stopped talking.

"Go on," Wally prodded.

"Not too much happened during the day on Saturday, but I thought maybe I'd see something more interesting at night. So after supper I went back to the ShakeUp booth and watched Miss Caldwell's place."

"What did you see?" Wally asked.

"Ms. Caldwell worked between her booth

and her store until about eight-thirty, then went upstairs for a half hour, then drove away. Lucky for me, she only went a few blocks down the street to the bowling alley, so I was able to follow her on my bike. I'll be so happy when I get my driver's license next week," Justin added as an aside, then continued. "Anyway, she sat at the bar there for a couple of hours. I watched her from the inside door, since I'm not old enough to go in the bar area.

"Around eleven, she came back to the store with that singer she'd been talking to at the bowling alley. I thought they were going to, uh, you know, hook up, but he took a sword out of his car trunk and brought it into the shop. He left about twenty minutes later through the back door, and a few minutes after that a lady showed up. I'd seen her around before, but since we don't have cable I didn't know her."

Wally let that last cryptic remark go and instead asked, "When did she leave?"

"I don't know. Not before I had to go home. My curfew is midnight." Justin frowned. "And then the next day I heard Ms. Caldwell had been murdered."

"Why didn't you come to me and tell me what you saw the night before?" Wally demanded.

"I did, but the dispatcher told me that the sheriff's department was handling that case and had me talk to one of the deputies."

"And?" Skye asked.

"And like all adults, he blew me off." Justin's voice cracked with anger. "Oh, he took down the description of the woman and all, but you could tell he thought I was just some crazy kid." He glared at Skye. "Lots of adults seem to think that way."

Puzzled, Skye looked back at him. What was he getting at?

Wally's eyes were dark with compassion. "Is that why you decided to run away?"

"No. I wasn't sure what I should do next, so I decided to talk to Frannie about it. She was out of town on Sunday, so I went to her house Monday morning. Instead of listening to what I had to say, she went all female on me because I had sat with some girl she didn't like at the concert in the park."

Skye raised an eyebrow. The innocent act didn't work. Justin knew very well the extent of the antipathy between Frannie and Bitsy, and he had done a lot more than just sit with the other girl. "Is that when you ran away?"

"No." Justin's tone was furious. "I went to talk to you, but you weren't at your cottage."

"I rented it out to the TV people for the

duration of the yard sale. I'm staying with my parents. Didn't the folks there tell you?"

"Yeah, eventually. But at first when some lady answered the door, I introduced myself and asked for you. It took me a second, but I realized the woman I was talking to was the one I had seen at Ms. Caldwell's."

Skye gasped. That's what he had meant by not recognizing Cookie's visitor because his family didn't have cable TV. Although even if he could get the channel Faith's program was on, Skye doubted Justin would have watched it. How many teenage boys tuned in to shows about garage sales and collectibles?

"From the expression on my face, she must have realized something was up, but at the time I didn't know she knew, because she invited me inside and was real nice. Then when I asked if she was a friend of Ms. Caldwell's, she got mean. She said why would a TV star like her be friends with a small-town shopkeeper? And that obviously I was too young to see how ludicrous that would be. And that's when I did something stupid." Justin squirmed in his seat, pulled at his T-shirt, and swallowed several times before saying, "I told her I had seen her going into Ms. Caldwell's store Saturday night."

Skye groaned, and Justin flashed her an outraged glower. "That's when she said, 'Justin Boward. Oh, now I remember why your name seems so familiar. You're the one Skye told me about. She said both your parents were barmy and she was afraid you'd grow up to be crazy, too. Do you really think anyone will believe what the town wacko has to say?' " Justin glared at Skye. "*That's* when I decided to run away. I hid in the garage behind the bowling alley, but Miss Bunny found me the next day, and when I told her someone had betrayed me and I had to think about it, she let me stay with her."

"I didn't. Really." Skye was appalled that Faith would lie to Justin like that, and that he would accept what she said as the truth. "Why would you believe her?"

"Because." The teen sneered. "How else would she know stuff that I only told you?"

"I don't know." Skye put her head in her hands. "Let me think." Breaking confidentiality was one of the worst sins a psychologist could commit. Skye had never told even her closest friends anything a client had said during counseling, and she sure hadn't told Faith Easton, a person she wouldn't trust to take a cake out of the oven. How had Faith known Justin's secrets?

Wally scooted closer and gave her a sympathetic one-armed hug. "Any ideas?"

Before she could answer, Justin shot a disapproving look at Wally's hand on Skye's shoulder and said pointedly to Skye, "Aren't you and Mr. Reid still going out?"

Skye's cheeks flushed. "Of course." Clearly Justin was seeing perfidy in the most innocent of gestures. Nevertheless, she moved away from Wally.

"Can't prove it by what I'm seeing," Justin said, his gaze rebuking her.

Skye ignored his comment and continued to try and figure out how Faith had gained confidential information. It finally came to her. "The file cabinet. She must have broken into my file cabinet." Skye explained about the school refurbishing and why she was keeping the records at home rather than at her office.

Justin pursed his lips, plainly not entirely convinced of Skye's innocence.

Wally grabbed his notepad and started writing. When he stopped a few minutes later, he said, "It's all coming together. Look at this." He showed them a list he had made. "First, let's assume that Faith and Cookie were friends, despite Faith's denial to Justin, and that she's the one who has been calling in the tips to the sheriff's department about Skye."

"That's the fifth question," Skye blurted out, then had to explain her "referral" list to Wally and Justin, concluding with, "That's what's been bothering me. The fifth question is, how did the killer obtain the information to try and frame me?"

Wally nodded and continued, "Faith and Cookie's friendship would explain how she knew about Cookie hitting Skye when she fired her and how she knew Cookie had been crying in Skye's presence the afternoon before she was murdered, especially if she was the person who made Cookie cry."

Skye agreed. "It really is the only answer, because no one in town seems to have been a close friend of Cookie's, at least not someone she would've confided in."

"Yep." Wally concurred. "It also explains the earring found under Mrs. Griggs." He turned to Skye. "I bet you left those earrings at your cottage, right?"

"Yes, I did. And I just now remembered what I did with them. I knew I wouldn't be wearing any good jewelry for the duration of the yard sale, so I put my whole jewelry box in with the confidential files, since that cabinet was the only thing in my cottage that locked." Skye looked at Justin. "That proves

Faith broke into it, because otherwise how could that earring have gotten underneath Mrs. Griggs's body?"

Justin stared at Skye, his expression showing both his desire to believe and his fear of further treachery. Finally, he nodded slowly. "That makes sense. And if she planted the earring, she's probably the one who killed Mrs. Griggs and Cookie. But why?"

"I think Mrs. Griggs must have known something about Cookie's murder, which is why Faith killed her. But *why* did she kill Cookie?" Skye tapped her fingers on the table.

Wally put his hand over hers to stop the drumming. "Okay, what do we know about Cookie and Faith?"

"They both were/are obsessive collectors, shrewd businesswomen, and not overly worried about ethical behavior," Skye offered.

"So, how would two people like that maintain their friendship? Wouldn't they be competing with each other?" Justin asked, staring at Wally's hand until the chief removed it from Skye's.

"The only way it would work would be if they didn't go after the same collectibles," Skye suggested. "And since Cookie was in the business, she probably steered Faith toward the items her friend was looking for, maybe even bought them for her and helped her set up the 'finds' for Faith's TV program. If there was something that Mrs. Griggs had that Faith was particularly keen on — say, old jewelry — that would explain not only Cookie's fixation with Mrs. Griggs but also Faith's."

Wally made a note, then said, "In that case, Cookie would have a lot of control over Faith. Both personally as a collector and professionally as the star of her TV show. Faith wouldn't want the world to know she didn't find all those treasures on her own."

"Hey, that reminds me." Skye chewed her lip. "Cookie had a box she kept on a shelf near the counter that she would put things in all week, and then on Monday it would be empty. She told me that the items in that carton were not for sale."

"And who would you see over the weekend but a friend?" Justin finished her thought.

"You know, Cookie grabbed the sword she whacked me with from that box, and it was the sword used to kill Mrs. Griggs. So if Cookie was selling the stuff in that carton to Faith, that puts the weapon into her hands."

"Excellent," Wally said. "If she was such

an astute businesswoman, surely Cookie kept records of her sales, even sales to her friends."

"But I told the sheriff that the sword had been at Cookie's store. Wouldn't he have checked her records?" Skye asked.

"You probably noticed that Buck isn't the sharpest cheddar in the deli case."

"Yeah, I kind of picked up on that when he tried to arrest me."

"I'll have one of the deputies check it out for me." Wally got up and went to the wall phone.

Skye leaned over to Justin and lowered her voice. "Are we okay now? Do you believe that I'd never tell anyone what you told me in confidence?"

"Yeah. Sure. No big deal." Justin stared at his hands. "Uh, do you think Frannie is still mad at me?"

Skye debated whether to say anything or not, then decided it was time. "Yes, she's probably still upset, but only because she cares for you."

"You mean she, uh, likes me?" He peeked up at Skye through his hair. "Like a boyfriend?"

"I think so, but maybe you should ask her yourself. That is, if you like her as a girlfriend."

Justin lined up his pop can, chip bag, and magazine. "I do, but she never gives me any signals she likes me like that. You know, touches me, flirts with me like Bitsy does. Are you sure she likes me?"

"I'm not a hundred percent sure, but I'm pretty sure. You need to talk to her."

"But what if she says no?"

"Then you try to stay friends, and maybe she'll change her mind."

Before Justin could respond, Wally returned. "You were right. Cookie sold Faith a sword the night before she was killed. I wonder why she didn't sell it to her a couple of months ago, right after she used it to hit you?"

Skye thought about his question. "Maybe Cookie and Faith had a fight and didn't see each other until the yard sale started."

"Could be." Wally consulted his notes. "One more thing. The blood on the towel and T-shirt in the bag the lion found was Cookie's."

"That reminds me." Skye's eyes widened. "Faith loves purple. When she moved in, they took down all my towels and replaced them with purple ones. And both the towel and the T-shirt in the bag the lion found were shades of purple."

"Faith is looking more and more like our

killer." Wally sat back down. "Too bad so far all we have is circumstantial evidence."

"Are you going to tell Sheriff Peterson everything we've figured out?" Skye asked.

"I'll give him a copy of my report, but I doubt he'll do anything with it."

"Are you going to do something?" Skye asked. "Surely she left her fingerprints at one of the crime scenes or at Cookie's shop or apartment."

"Maybe, but all she has to say is she visited those places as an invited guest. There's no way to prove otherwise. There were no prints on the sword or the pin." Wally shrugged. "I'll keep trying to find evidence against her, but it doesn't look good."

"Then I guess she'll have to confess." Skye lifted her chin, a stubborn look on her face. "No way is she getting away scot-free."

Chapter 24
Murder, She Wrote

"What did you have in mind?" Wally leaned against the wall and crossed his arms.

"It's pretty obvious she's trying to frame me. I don't know if it's personal or I'm just handy, but we need to figure out a way for her to think that she can really set me up. And we need to do it quickly, because she's leaving Scumble River tomorrow."

"How are we going to do that?" Justin asked.

Wally answered, "You're not. I'm taking you home to your parents, and you're staying there until Faith is either in custody or out of town."

Justin started to whine, but Skye cut him off. "We know she's dangerous, and she already knows you saw her with Cookie, so we have to let her continue to believe you're AWOL. You cannot be seen around town. Besides, you've worried your parents enough by disappearing like you did."

"Can I call and have Frannie come over?"

"Why don't you wait until Monday?" Wally held open the door to the garage and motioned for the teen to go through. "The fewer people who know you've returned, the better."

Justin nodded unhappily and walked out. "Bye, Ms. D."

"Bye, Justin."

"This should only take a few minutes. Don't go anywhere," Wally told Skye.

She nodded and waved until the door closed behind Wally, then immediately unzipped her fanny pack and pulled out the letters she had taken from Cookie's secret stash. She hadn't wanted to explain how she got them in front of Justin. He had a highly developed sense of right and wrong that didn't leave room for many flaws in the adults he respected, but she was dying to see if they were important.

Skye spread the letters out over the table. There were a baker's dozen, all the same pale lilac stationery, smelling faintly of lavender.

None had a return address, but Skye knew before opening them that they were from Faith. Now that she had remembered the TV star's fondness for purple, the scent and color of the paper were enough of a hint.

Skye put them in order by cancellation date. The first one was from just after Cookie had moved to Scumble River. The last one was sent a few days before the yard sale started. In it Faith apologized and asked to talk to Cookie during the sale. Skye's guess had been correct as to why the sword took so long to get into Faith's hands. Cookie and Faith had had a fight and didn't see each from the middle of June until the yard sale.

By the time she finished reading the small stack of letters Skye felt like slapping herself. She had been wrong, wrong, wrong. How could she have been so clueless? Faith and Cookie weren't friends — they were lovers!

Cookie had been miserable living in Scumble River, and Faith had played on Cookie's desire to please her, to keep Cookie tucked away in the small town and out of the way. It was clear from what she wrote that Faith was afraid that after the very public death of Cookie's husband, word of her relationship with Cookie would get out and her TV career would be ruined.

Skye wondered if that would have happened. After all, Ellen DeGeneres's and Rosie O'Donnell's sexual preferences hadn't hurt their careers. Still, they were Hollywood personalities, and maybe that was the difference. Faith's audience was more Midwest middle class, people not generally known for their liberal points of view.

Skye met Wally at the door when he returned and immediately exclaimed, "Look what I found at Cookie's." She thrust the letters at him. "They were hidden in a pillow safe that the deputies must have missed when they searched her apartment." Skye avidly watched him examine the stack of letters. "Cookie and Faith were lovers! Faith was desperate to keep that relationship quiet. I'll bet Cookie was going to reveal their affair and that's why Faith killed her."

Wally nodded and continued to read.

As soon as he finished, Skye blurted out the plan she had come up with while he'd been gone, ending with, "Then I tell her I have the letters, and as soon as she admits to killing Cookie, you pop out from where you're hiding."

After a lengthy discussion, with Wally trying to talk Skye out of her scheme, he finally agreed to run the idea past the city attorney.

When Wally came back from making the call, Skye asked excitedly, "What's the verdict?"

"He said to make sure you get the key back from Faith before she admits anything. That way the cottage is yours again, and she doesn't have the expectation of privacy. He also said it would be best to have you wired." Wally's good mood had dissolved, and he looked worried.

"Do you have the equipment to do that?"

"No. I'll have to borrow it from the sheriff's department. Just cross your fingers that Buck is already gone for the weekend or he'll want to run things, and we don't need that bozo involved."

"True," Skye agreed. "I was thinking we should do it tomorrow. The yard sale ends at noon. I'm supposed to get my key back from Faith at three. We just need to make sure her staff has left before I go over. She needs to be alone when I talk to her. Any idea how to do that?"

"The truth is always good. Call her tomorrow morning and tell her you want to speak to her alone when you come for the key."

"Brilliant." Skye smiled at Wally. "What time should I be here to get wired for sound?"

"Better come at one. We want to have plenty of time to do this right." Wally walked her to the door, but before he opened it, he said, "The only reason I'm going along with your idea is because I know if I don't, you'll go ahead and do it without me. At least this way I can protect you."

"You're right."

"If this were a bigger city or a larger police department, you know I wouldn't be able to do something like this."

Skye nodded.

"Or something like this."

Skye felt her knees weaken as his mouth descended on hers. One part of her mind admonished her that they had to stop all this kissing, but another part asked *Why?*

"Here are the keys to the French doors in back. The silver one opens the lock on the knob, the gold one is for the dead bolt." Skye passed the ring to Wally, who sat in the passenger seat of her Bel Air.

She had steadfastly refused to discuss yesterday's kiss or her reaction to it. When she had finally broken it off and fled through the reception area, she had decided that the first priority was to capture Faith. After Faith was arrested, Skye planned to sit down and carefully examine her feelings for both

Wally and Simon. And as soon as Simon returned from his trip, she would talk to him about whatever she decided. Only then would she be ready to discuss the matter with Wally.

"Okay. As soon as I hear Faith answer the front door, I'll slip inside and hide in the bedroom," Wally said, confirming the plan. "Make sure you stay in the great room so I can hear what's going on, and don't get close enough to Faith that she can grab you."

"How far does the microphone I'm wearing pick up?"

"You're fine as long as you're in the same room," Wally said. "Quirk, a deputy, and one of the techs from the county are parked over at your nearest neighbor's, monitoring what's going on."

"Okay, I'm almost there, so you'd better get out." Skye watched as Wally left the car. "Did you remember the treats for Faith's dog?"

He nodded before heading toward the cottage. Skye gave him ten minutes, then drove on. As she pulled into the driveway she felt her stomach clench and was suddenly afraid. She was about to confront a woman who had murdered two people and would have no qualms about killing her, too.

Pushing her fear aside, Skye got out of the car and walked up the steps. She touched her fanny pack, which contained Dante's stun gun, and hoped that Wally was in place. As soon as she rang the bell, she heard yapping, then Faith's voice soothing the dog, and finally the door opened.

Faith, dressed in jeans and a purple T-shirt, held the Pomeranian in the crook of her arm. "Come in. I haven't got all day. What did you want to talk to me about?"

Skye forced herself not to look over the shorter woman's shoulder toward the French doors. "This won't take long." She entered the foyer, keeping eye contact with Faith. "Let's go sit in the great room."

The women took seats, Faith on the couch and Skye across from her on a director's chair. "So what's so important you had to talk to me in private?"

"Do you have my key?" Skye ignored Faith's question and followed the city attorney's direction.

"Here." From the right front pocket of her jeans Faith produced the key and handed it over to Skye. "Now, why did you want to talk to me?"

Skye reached into her fanny pack, grabbed the folded sheet she had placed on top, and gave it to Faith. "This is a photocopy of one of the letters I have that you wrote to Cookie."

Twin red circles appeared on Faith's pale cheeks. "Where did you get this? She promised me she burned my letters after reading them."

"She lied." Skye looked Faith in the eye and lied herself. "She gave them to me for safekeeping, in case anything ever happened to her." The city attorney had mentioned that it probably wouldn't be a good thing for Skye to admit on tape to having stolen them.

"I don't believe you. Cookie did what I told her to. She trusted me explicitly."

"Yet I have the letters."

"So?" The expression in Faith's violet eyes was dismissive.

"So, I want a million dollars."

Faith gave a short bark of laughter. "I don't have a million dollars. I live from paycheck to paycheck."

"I understand your collection of swords and Art Deco jewelry is outstanding. Sell them."

"I'd rather sell my child."

"Yes, I bet you would." Skye stared at the woman without blinking. "Okay, here's an alternative for you. You tell me the truth about what went down around here, I write a book — changing things just enough to protect the guilty — and you help me sell it to TV."

"I don't know anything about what's happened around here."

"Please, don't be coy. I've guessed most of it; I just need the missing links, like *why* you killed Cookie and Mrs. Griggs, *why* you were at my family's stand, and *why* you've been trying to frame me."

"I tell you, I don't know any of that. I didn't kill them." Faith's upper-crust British accent was disappearing and being replaced by the sound of London's East End.

"If that's how you want to play it, I guess I'll go to the police." Skye paused dramatically. "No, I'll go to the media." She got up. "Someone will pay for this story and those letters."

"You're batty."

"Am I?" Skye raised an eyebrow. "Then why has the *National Enquirer* already made me an offer?"

Faith shrugged, her expression indifferent.

"You're right," Skye continued as if Faith had answered. "I'm going to hold out for TV. I've got a call in to that new reality show, *Shark Attack*. You know, the one where they leap out at celebrities and reveal all their most humiliating secrets."

"No!" Faith jumped up. "Please." She grabbed Skye's arm. "Not *Shark Attack*. That show ends people's careers. I'll tell you what you want to know. I'll help you sell the book to TV."

"Okay, start with why you and Cookie were at my family's booth and why you killed her." Skye freed herself from Faith's grasp and moved nearer to the bedroom door.

Faith followed. "Cookie wanted to move back to Chicago and live together openly. We argued and didn't see each other for a couple of months. Then she found out I had gotten engaged to Nick and she went mad. She threatened to tell everyone that she and I had been lovers if I didn't go back to her." Faith clutched her dog so hard it yelped and leapt out of her arms. "My agent is negotiating with one of the big three networks to buy my show and put me on prime time. I couldn't take that kind of exposure."

"So you killed her?"

"I didn't mean to. I told her we could get back together, but we had to keep the relationship quiet. She talked me into driving out to your family's booth to see an Art Deco liquor cabinet she said I could pick up for next to nothing. That it would be a perfect 'Faith's Find.' "

"And?" Skye prompted.

"We were arguing by the time we got there." Faith started to pace, and Skye was forced to accompany her, afraid the mike wouldn't pick up her voice if she was facing away from it. "We were standing next to the open cabinet — she had unlocked the door with a straightened-out paper clip — when I told her our relationship would never work. She had to let me go. I reached into my pocket and tried to give her back the jewelry she had given me as a gift on Friday."

"Mrs. Griggs's pin."

"Yes. I didn't realize at the time that Cookie had broken into the old bat's house and stolen it. Trust her to get me into trouble even after she's dead." Faith scowled. "Anyway, the pin was gorgeous. I hated to part with it, but it was the only way I could think of to make her see I was serious. She refused to take it, and we wrestled over it until the box fell to the ground and the pin popped out. I picked up the pin and started to hand it to Cookie, but at that moment she threatened to expose me."

"So you killed her." Skye moved closer to make sure Cookie's confession was clear on the tape.

"I pushed the pin at her, trying to get her to take it, but it went into her throat. The tip was really sharp, almost like a real arrowhead. At first she went wild, grabbing at me and screaming she'd kill me. Then shock must have set in, and she fainted. I panicked, pushed her into the cabinet, and locked the door with the unbent paper clip she had used to open it." Faith stopped pacing and faced Skye. "I didn't mean to hurt her, and according to the officials it was her pulling the pin out that caused her to bleed to death."

Skye decided not to argue the point. "Then what did you do?"

"There wasn't much blood, just a little on my shirt and hands. I cleaned up with a towel I had in my car and used it to wipe my fingerprints off everything I could remember touching. Then I put it, my T-shirt, and the jewelry box into a plastic bag. I stuffed the whole thing into a sewer pipe and piled some dirt on it."

"What did you wear home?"

"That wasn't a problem. I always have extra clothes in the trunk."

"That explains Cookie," Skye said. "But why Mrs. Griggs?"

"She recognized the pin."

"What?"

"I'd been wearing the pin Cookie had given me Saturday during the yard sale, and you remember I tried to talk Mrs. Griggs into letting me see inside her house?"

"Yes."

"Well, later on, when it got out that the pin that killed Cookie had belonged to Mrs. Griggs, she called me and told me she remembered seeing me wearing it the afternoon of the day it was used to murder Cookie."

"Why didn't she go to the police?"

"How should I know? Maybe she wanted to blackmail me, too." Faith shot Skye a spiteful look before starting to pace again. "I convinced her to let me come to her house and explain."

"But instead you killed her."

"Not right then. She wouldn't listen to me. She closed the door in my face, saying she was going to take a nap and think about what to do. I watched until she went upstairs. Then I climbed the trellis, and once she dozed off, I killed her."

Skye frowned. That must have been when Mrs. Griggs had tried to call her. "You just happened to have the sword in your car."

"Cookie had sold it to me a few days earlier, and I never took it out of my trunk. When I was looking for something to use to do away with the old crone, I spotted it and tucked it into my belt. It was so big, I nearly couldn't walk; this time I was prepared. I had latex gloves to wear so I didn't have to worry about fingerprints." Faith shrugged. "Then when I circled the house, I noticed the trellis, and there you have it."

"One last thing. Why have you been trying to frame me?"

"It was convenient. I had access to your things, and I happened to have your earrings in my pocket that day — I had decided to take them because they were too pretty for you. Anyway, it seemed like a good idea to steer the police in some direction other than my own. It wasn't personal until you started nosing around. Then I thought it would stop you."

"You were the one who ambushed me at the motor court?" Skye asked, wanting to make sure she covered everything.

"Yes. I covered you with one of the padded tarps we use to protect the antique furniture we buy. I knew you wouldn't be badly hurt, but I thought a beating would stop your infernal poking around."

Skye considered. Was there anything else? No. That was it. "Okay, then I'll write the book and you'll help me sell it, right?"

"Right. Let me give you my private phone number." Faith walked into the foyer and picked up her purse.

Skye followed, congratulating herself, and thinking that if things went as planned when Faith stepped outside, Quirk and the deputy would be there to arrest her.

Instead Faith pulled a gun from her purse and aimed it at Skye. "Sorry. Can't leave any loose ends."

Shit! She had been stupid and gotten careless. Skye started to back toward the great room, where she could get Wally's attention, but before she took two steps Faith grabbed her arm and stuck the gun barrel in her back, forcing her through the kitchen and into the utility room.

Skye fumbled for the stun gun, but Faith moved away before she could free it from her fanny pack.

"I think you'll just fit into this hamper back here." Faith seemed almost to be talking to herself. "Since you're so heavy, Nick will just have to come back and help me load it into my car. I can tip it into the river as I drive out of town."

Skye looked around for a weapon she could use from a distance. There was a bottle of bleach on the washer. She moved in front of it while Faith was emptying out the hamper. Skye managed to take off the cap and get a grip around the neck before Faith finished.

As Faith looked up, Skye flung the bleach in the TV star's face. At the same instant, Faith raised the gun from her side and fired.

Both women screamed, and Wally burst into the tiny room, yelling, "Skye!"

Epilogue
Unsolved Mysteries

"You're a very lucky young woman." The doctor smiled and patted Skye on the head. "The bullet passed through the under part of your upper arm without hitting anything vital. Good thing you had some extra fleshy tissue there."

It was Monday morning, and Skye was in Laurel Hospital.

"Lucky," she murmured, thinking this was the only time that a doctor had been happy she had some spare padding on her body. Usually they were advising her to lose weight.

Skye remembered very little about the past twelve hours. At first she had thought that Faith's shot had missed her, since she didn't feel anything, but soon afterward the pain was so intense she'd thought she was about to have a heart attack.

Skye also vaguely recalled Wally cradling

her in his arms until the ambulance arrived and riding with her to the hospital. But after they shot her full of pain medication in the emergency room, everything was a blur.

The doctor was talking again, and Skye struggled to focus on what he was saying. "So, we want to observe you for the rest of the day, but if everything continues to go well, we'll release you late this afternoon."

"Great."

"Are you up to having visitors?"

Skye considered saying no, wanting some time alone to process what had happened, but she knew her parents would be frantic, so she nodded. "Sure."

"No more than three at a time."

"All right. Do you know if Faith Easton is okay? She was probably brought in right after I was."

"She's fine. The police officer with her rinsed the bleach off right away. The only damage was to her T-shirt and jeans." The doctor stopped at the door. "I believe the officer said they were taking her straight to the county jail."

A few seconds later, Skye's mother rushed into the room, sobbing, "My baby, my baby."

Her father and brother followed.

Jed awkwardly put one arm around May and used his free hand to squeeze Skye's leg. "You okay?"

"I'm fine. It's only a flesh wound."

May turned into her husband's arm and continued to cry. He patted her on the back and smoothed her hair.

Skye stared. To a casual observer a wife seeking comfort in her husband's arms wouldn't be anything out of the ordinary, but Skye couldn't remember the last time she had seen her mother and father embrace. For May and Jed, showing this much affection was almost as if they had started making love in the middle of the hospital room.

Vince took up a position on the other side of the bed and cleared his throat. "I told them Superwoman couldn't be stopped by a single bullet."

It took close to an hour to calm her mother down, but after talking to Skye, May seemed to feel a little better.

After a while, Skye asked her father and Vince to step out of the room, and when she was alone with May she said, "I take it you and Dad made up."

"Yes. When we got word you had been shot, we rushed to the hospital, and since we had a long time together with nowhere to run away to, we finally talked. I explained that I needed more of his attention, and he said that if anything else went wrong with Bunny's car he'd get someone else to work on it for her."

"Good."

"Best of all, he promised to fix the toilet in the big bathroom this afternoon." May's expression was dreamy.

Skye smiled. Fixing a toilet might not seem romantic for most people, but for her mom and dad it was as loving as roses, champagne, and candlelight.

May kissed Skye on the cheek. "I'd better let some of your other fans in to see you."

"Love you, Mom."

"Me, too, honey."

Skye's godfather was next. Then Trixie came in with Justin and Frannie. The teenagers were holding hands. Skye exchanged a look with Trixie, who gave a barely discernible shrug.

Trixie hugged Skye's good side. "Why didn't you call me? I could have gone with you."

"Do you really think she'd have confessed in front of both of us?"

"Well, no," Trixie admitted. "But I could have been your backup."

"I think the police were enough."

"Then why did they let you get shot?" Trixie demanded.

Skye thought about asking Trixie how she would have stopped Faith's bullet, but decided not to. Instead, she said to the teens, "It looks like you two have made up."

Justin turned red, but didn't drop Frannie's hand. "Yeah, we're cool."

Frannie beamed. "Dad and I are going to drive Justin over here to get his license on Thursday. His father can't drive anymore, and his mom doesn't like to leave the house."

Justin shifted from foot to foot, looking uncomfortable with Frannie's garrulousness. Finally he said, "So, uh, you're really alright, Ms. D?"

"I'm fine." Skye wondered how Justin's reticent nature and Frannie's lively personality would mesh as a couple. She hoped a little of each would rub off on the other, but in her experience that rarely happened.

"Uh, then, when you're all better, do you think I could interview you for the school paper?" Justin stepped closer to the bed. "I think you'd make a way cooler story than Ms. Caldwell."

"Thanks. I'm really flattered, but I kind of like keeping a low profile. You know what I mean?"

He frowned but nodded. "I get it. The stealth psychologist, right?"

"Right."

Trixie turned to the teens and said, "I need to talk to Ms. D alone for a minute. I'll meet you in the waiting room."

After they left, Trixie turned to Skye. "You'll never guess what Owen did this morning."

Skye was almost afraid to ask. "What?"

"He sold all the livestock."

"Wow!"

"And he brought me a dozen roses, a box of Godiva chocolates, and tickets for a weekend getaway to Lake Tahoe."

"Wow!" Skye felt like a parrot, but she didn't know what else to say.

"He said your being shot made him realize that we couldn't save everything for a rainy day, and that working all the time for the future isn't a good idea because you don't know how much future you'll have."

"That's terrific." Skye smiled. At least her injury had proven useful in mending the relationships of all the warring couples in Scumble River.

"I'd better go. Uncle Dante is outside, and there's a guy in a suit waiting to see you, too. Both of them are starting to get impatient. Do you need anything?"

"I forgot to ask Mom. Could you have her call me with Simon's friend's phone number? It's on a pad on the desk in the kitchen."

"Sure. Do you want me to call Simon?"

"No, I missed him Saturday night and left a message, and I'm guessing he left a message last night, so we need to actually talk."

"Okay. Then shall I send in your uncle or Mr. Suit?"

"Uncle Dante." Skye narrowed her eyes. "And he better have my checks."

Trixie grinned and hurried out the door.

A few seconds later Dante came in scowling. "Are you okay?"

"I will be after you pay me." Skye had learned she had to be as curt as he was when she dealt with her uncle. Otherwise he would walk all over her. "Did you bring my checks?"

"Here." He thrust them at her. "Won't do you any good, though. Those asses you rent from sold the cottage right out from under you."

"What?" Skye fell back against her pillows, feeling faint. "They promised to give me until September first."

"Did you get it in writing?"

She shook her head, a sinking feeling in

her stomach. "They said their word was their bond."

"Please." Dante snorted. "You didn't fall for that, did you?"

Skye cringed. She really was a trusting fool. "How did you find out?"

"When your mom told me you were hurt, I got in touch with the real estate agent to make sure you didn't miss your deadline, since I wasn't sure when it was."

"That was so sweet of you, Uncle Dante. Thank you." Skye was taken aback at his thoughtfulness.

"I didn't want anyone taking advantage of my niece." He shrugged off her thanks. "The agent said you never put in a formal offer or a deposit, and this morning, right before I called, the owners agreed to sell it to someone who bid twenty percent over the asking price."

"Shit!"

"Shit is right. You're too trusting to live." Dante shook his head in disgust.

"Is there anything I can do?"

"Yeah. Next time you want to buy real estate, let me help you." He headed for the door, then turned back and said grudgingly, "The yard sale was a big success. If you want the coordinator job next summer, it's yours."

Skye gasped. "Not if you doubled my salary and got Brad Pitt as my assistant."

"Don't be too hasty." Dante pushed through the door, saying as it closed, "We'll talk about it again later."

"No, we won't!" Skye shouted after him, then leaned back on her pillows and thought about how much she was looking forward to going back to school. The routine would be so soothing after the craziness of the summer. She drifted into a daydream of sitting in her office at the high school and writing a report, everything calm and under control.

Her reverie was interrupted when the man Trixie had mentioned entered. "Good morning, Ms. Denison. You're a difficult person to locate."

"And you are?" The guy looked like a lawyer, and Skye wondered if Faith was suing her for burning her with the bleach.

"I'm Pruett Canfield, Alma Griggs's attorney."

"Oh." Skye straightened, and a pain stabbed through her arm.

"I'm here to inform you that Mrs. Griggs changed her will a few days before she died and made you her sole beneficiary," Canfield explained. "I just got back into town yesterday and learned she had been murdered, which is why you weren't notified earlier."

Skye was dumbfounded. "She left everything to me? Why?"

"She was sure you were her deceased daughter reincarnated." The attorney looked ill at ease giving that explanation.

"I told her that wasn't true."

"So Mrs. Griggs said, but she still believed it. She had no one else."

Skye wiped her eyes. She was not going to start crying. "I don't know what to say."

"The bulk of the estate is property — her house, its contents, and the land. There's a small life insurance policy that will scarcely cover her burial, but no other liquid assets." Mr. Canfield adjusted his tie and looked at his shoes. "And then there is the matter of the back taxes."

"So, I shouldn't quit my day job."

"No. In fact you might want to take a second one." The lawyer showed a flash of humor, then sobered. "Perhaps that's why she left her estate to you. It was a way for her to feel as if a part of her would live on. The house is in poor shape. If you don't pay the taxes and restore it, there's a good chance the state will tear it down and sell the land to get its money."

Skye was silent and Mr. Canfield finally

said, "When you're feeling better, please make an appointment. We need to go over matters more fully and sign some papers. Meanwhile, if you want to arrange for the funeral, I'll approve the cost."

"Thank you." Skye shook his hand. She slumped back onto her pillows as he left. What a bizarre day. First she lost her beloved cottage, then she inherited a huge, dilapidated house. What was she going to do? Could she ever live in a house in which a murder had been committed? She bit her lip. Yes, she could. Mrs. Griggs would certainly never haunt her. The old woman had trusted Skye, and Skye wasn't going to let that grand old house be torn down.

When Wally came into the room a little while later, Skye pretended to be asleep. Things had gotten out of hand. Wally had said a lot while waiting for the ambulance, but he hadn't expected her to answer. Now he would, and she had to talk to Simon before she gave Wally any answers. She was torn between the two men and she needed time to sort out her feelings.

Wally stayed for several minutes, touched her hair and kissed her softly on the lips, then left. Almost immediately the phone rang. It was May with Simon's friend's number.

After copying it down, Skye looked at the wall clock. It was noon here, so ten a.m. in California — a good time to call.

She dialed and waited. On the third ring a female voice answered.

Skye frowned. Did she have the wrong number?

She said, "Hello, is Simon Reid there?"

"I'm sorry, he's in the shower."

"How about Spike Yamaguchi?" Had Simon mentioned if his friend Spike was married?

"This is she."

Skye froze, then quietly hung up the phone and lay back, stunned. This certainly put a different twist on things. She would never have thought Simon capable of being unfaithful, but what other explanation could there be?

About the Author

Denise Swanson has worked as a school psychologist for more than twenty years. She lives in Illinois with her husband, Dave, who is a classical music composer, and their cool black cat, Boomerang. For more information, visit her Web site at www. deniseswanson.com.

The employees of Thorndike Press hope you have enjoyed this Large Print book. All our Thorndike and Wheeler Large Print titles are designed for easy reading, and all our books are made to last. Other Thorndike Press Large Print books are available at your library, through selected bookstores, or directly from us.

For information about titles, please call:

(800) 223-1244

or visit our Web site at:

www.gale.com/thorndike
www.gale.com/wheeler

To share your comments, please write:

Publisher
Thorndike Press
295 Kennedy Memorial Drive
Waterville, ME 04901